NEEDING A COUGAR
COUGAR CHALLENGE

REGINA CARLYSLE
JAYNE RYLON
FRAN LEE

ELLORA'S CAVE
ROMANTICA PUBLISHING

DRILLED
Regina Carlysle

Lori Donovan accepts the Cougar Challenge and pledges to snag a hot young stud, knowing it'll be tough once she moves back to her Texas hometown. She expects barren plains and rattlesnakes but finds hunky Jackson Blue drilling for oil on her property instead. A driller. Hmm. Lori has a few ideas about that and just about all of them involve her poor, needy, sex-starved body.

Jackson takes one look at the curvy, sexy, older woman and puts his expertise into action. After all, drilling is what he does best. Against the wall, on the floor or in the middle of her bed, he's the man right man for the job. It's a hot time in Texas when a tough, sexy drillin' man meets a sassy cougar, and playing it safe just isn't an option.

DRIVEN
Jayne Rylon

Lynn Madison transformed from repressed corporate drone to bold seductress overnight when her online friends at *Tempt the Cougar* encouraged her to take charge of her destiny. Their advice haunts her as she drools over the hottest Italian stallion on the planet while stranded in an airport.

Sebastian Fiori is a master of speed. A rally car driver, he's used to winning on and off the track. He sees no need to put on the brakes when a sexy sophisticate revs his engine. After spotting Lynn's decadent ménage novel, he decides to take her for the ride of a lifetime—with his navigator Mark.

Storm delays would be far more upsetting if Lynn's young stud wasn't offering a first-class ticket to indulge her fantasy. Neither of them expects their rendezvous to last beyond their transatlantic flight on his private jet. But sometimes there's no escaping the forces of nature.

NOTHING BUT SEX
Fran Lee

Lee Blackhorse is hardly Cougar material, no matter what her friends over at Tempt the Cougar say. A forty-two-year-old woman who lusts after her thirty-year-old weekend helper is just plain nuts. Or is she? Mike Running Elk is the sexiest thing ever to don tight jeans and a second-skin t-shirt. She's secretly yearned for the man for years.

Mike has no problem seeing himself in the role of Lee's lover. In fact, if he can just get the hot-as-hell woman to realize he's plenty old enough to ring her bells, he plans to do more than just clean her barn and mow her grass. He's waited for her long enough.

When Mike shows up at her door with an injured hand, he notices Lee can't pull her eyes off his naked, ripped chest. Mike can't believe she's as oblivious as she acts. The ice has been broken and he intends to heat things up even more...

An Ellora's Cave Romantica Publication

www.ellorascave com

Needing a Cougar

ISBN 9781419963537

Trade paperback publication 2011

NEEDING A COUGAR

ഔ

DRILLED

Regina Carlysie

ഔ

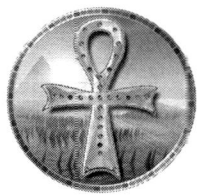

Dedication

ℬ

This one is for my fellow cougars, especially Desiree Holt, my "extra set of eyes". You ladies rock the house. I am in awe of your talent, passion for writing and sense of fun. I also dedicate this to my dad, a hard-working man who spent his life gambling on Texas crude.

Author Note

ℬ

You'll find the women of Cougar Challenge and the *Tempt the Cougar* blog at www.temptthecougar.blogspot.com.

Trademarks Acknowledgement

ℬ

The author acknowledges the trademarked status and trademark owners of the following wordmarks mentioned in this work of fiction:

Ben Wa: Ben Wa Novelty Corporation

Rabbit: Ann Summers Limited

Rascal Flatts: Rascal Flatts Entertainment Corporation

Spackle: Muralo Company

Superman: DC Comics Corporation

Chapter One

∞

A bet was a bet!

Damn it!

Whatever had possessed her to jump on the Cougar Challenge bandwagon and pledge to snare a hot, young stud? Knowing she only had the alcohol and a lack of common sense to blame, Loralee Donovan, plain old Lori to her friends, looked around her grandparents' old house and considered what her life would be like living out here in no man's land. Not a hot, eligible young stud muffin within a twenty-mile radius, she figured. She'd only been here a few days and already the thought of the work facing her made her forty-one-year-old bones ache like hell. Boxes were stacked everywhere waiting for her to begin unpacking and then she faced the daunting challenge of getting on with her life after the divorce. Just thinking about what Grant had done to her made her want to cuss. Jackass!

Sighing deeply, she trudged into the old-fashioned kitchen and poured herself a cup of coffee before heading into the dining room to boot up her laptop. Time to check in with the other cougars. They'd met a few short months ago at an erotic reader and writers convention and they'd instantly clicked, each vowing over drinks in the bar to stop wallowing in misery and reach out for the hot, younger man of her dreams. Seven of them had already taken the plunge and now it was her turn.

Shit!

Feeling none too confident, she signed into the cougar blog they shared to exchange news, confidences, and advice.

Hey, ya'll! How are my fellow cougars and champion margarita drinkers? Wanted to let you know that I finally made it back to Sandy Creek and I've settled into my grandparents' old place. Lordy! You should see it. The Permian basin in west Texas sure as hell wouldn't be featured in any travel brochures let me tell ya! Remember that movie "Giant" when young Rock brings young Liz to her new Texas home? The look of fear and wonder on her face? Talk about a flashback. The old Victorian sets smack-dab in the middle of acres of nothing. Dirt everywhere and winds that blow like a storm from hell every day and every night. Think desolate. But hey, what can I say, I'm home. Siiiigh. When I was a teenager, I couldn't wait to shake the dust of this place off and have a great adventure. Now a little over two decades and a nasty divorce later, here I am back where I started. Don't know whether to laugh or bawl like a baby. Starting over is never easy and now, on top of it all, I promised to snare and seduce some young stud. Why did ya'll let me drink so much and can I get OUT of THIS? LOL. I've already talked to Autumn and she says no way in hell am I allowed to back out at this point. Crap. Looks like I'm stuck. So once I get settled in, this cougar is going hunting. Wish me luck.

Lori hit the *publish* button, tempted to bang her forehead on the keyboard. What had she gotten herself into? Well, if nothing else, she was a woman of her word and a deal was a deal. If she was to fulfill her promise, take the challenge, she had to find a younger guy, screw him silly and rediscover that wicked, naughty woman she'd once been. Could she do it? Here? The very notion made her laugh and shake her head. No way. Sandy Creek was one of those lonely little towns populated by the geriatric crowd and young families who barely scratched out a living on these desolate plains. It was the epitome of small town Texas and she very much doubted there was a bevy of young hunky studs just waiting to jump her forty-one-year-old bones. Laughable.

Before she could turn off the computer an IM box popped up on her screen. Autumn. Perfect timing as always.

Autumn: Hey chick! Did you get moved in?

Lori: Barely. Lordy, this place needs work. I've been back a couple of days. Currently staring at a bunch of unpacked boxes. How are you?

Autumn: Great! Couldn't be happier. Can't wait for you to meet Mitch. HA. The man rings all my bells and then some. Think you can come for a visit in a few weeks?

Lori: Damn! Lucky you! I'd love to come for a weekend but I just don't know. There is so much to do here. Grandpa kind of let the place get run down after Grandma died. God, I miss him. Both of them. Anyway, when they left me the place, I was touched but I knew it was a real fixer-upper.

Autumn: Good luck with that. Okay, gotta ask. Are you ready to do it? The challenge?

Lori: Well, about that, hmm, yeah, I reckon so but I have a lot on my plate right now. First there's the place and then I have to get a handle on all the stuff Grandpa had going on before he died.

Autumn: What stuff?

Lori: Looks like I'm sitting on a whole boatload of crude. Grandpa leased the land to a petroleum company and pump jacks are all over the place. Damn things look like a bunch of skeletons stretching off into the horizon.

Autumn: Wow, lots of money in that black stuff.

Lori: Don't I know it. Need to check things out with all of this. I stand to earn a percentage of every barrel of oil

they bring in so I need to stay on top of things. Oops.
Phone. Gotta run. Talk to you later.

Rushing to the phone, she grabbed it up and breathlessly
said hello.

"Mrs. Donovan?"

"Yes."

"This is Jackson Blue of Blue Petroleum and Drilling. Did
I catch you at a bad time?"

Damn but the man had a voice like dark, melted
chocolate. Rich, slow and with a bit of an edge. Kind of like
good sex. She settled in on the couch and tucked the phone
against her face. "No, I'm still up. Um, I've been meaning to
get out to the site. I'm behind. Sorry."

His laughter was low and deep. Dear sweet heaven! The
sound moved through her center to settle in the pit of her
belly. Her pussy quivered just a little. Um. What the hell was
wrong with her? Was she so desperate for the touch of a man
that even a voice on the phone could turn her on? Pathetic.
Yes, she was pathetic. He sounded young but there was no
way to know for sure. "Some of the fellas said you'd taken
possession of the house and I just wanted to give you awhile to
settle in. I have some papers for you to sign to transfer the
royalties over. Think you or your husband could meet me
sometime tomorrow?"

Lori closed her eyes wishing he'd just keep talking
forever. "I'm not married. Divorced."

There was a pause over the line. "Ah, okay, that's fine,
Ms. Donovan."

"Lori, please."

"Sure, Lori. Tomorrow then? Want me to come by the
house?"

She thought about the mess, the boxes, and shook her head though she knew he couldn't see. Jeez! Dumb. "No, let me come out there. I'm dying to get a look at everything."

Oh yeah! She'd crawl through gravel to get a look at the man behind that sexy come-fuck-me voice.

Jackson Blue laughed again. "Not a hell of a lot to see but, yeah, come on by. We're drilling about half a mile south of the house. Can't miss us."

"I'll be there with bells on."

"Better make that boots. This is rattlesnake heaven out here."

"Damn! I didn't think about that." Lori laughed and shivered simultaneously. "Snakes. It's been a long time since I've lived out here. How could I have forgotten?"

There was another short pause. "I didn't know you used to live here."

"A long time ago, yes. My grandparents raised me but then I moved to Dallas after I married."

"Must feel pretty weird to be back," he said. "Coming from the Metroplex to the boonies is a flat-out culture shock."

Laughter bubbled up. "You couldn't be more right about that but honestly? A little solitude right now won't hurt me a bit."

Jackson's voice came low and soothing. "That can get pretty lonely though. You know, all that solitude."

She sighed, enjoying the conversation, enjoying him. "Guess I'll find out. Ah heck, maybe I'll hit Smoky Joe's one night and join the land of the living."

"Hey, that's not a bad little honky tonk. I've been there a time or two since we rolled into town."

"Best dance floor east of Midland."

"So they tell me. Maybe we could head out there for a drink one evening? There's not a lot in the way of entertainment around here and I get sick of hanging with the guys all the time." He chuckled. "Could use some civilized company."

"Who says I'm civilized?"

Lori wanted to bite her damn tongue off. Where in the hell had that flirty comment come from? She didn't know a damn thing about this guy. He was just a smokin' hot and dead sexy voice on the other end of the line.

Jackson only laughed. "A real wild woman, huh? This is sounding better and better. I can't wait to meet you, Lori. Tomorrow then?"

"Yeah, see you then." When they'd disconnected, she groaned as embarrassed heat climbed over her body. She'd really stepped in it this time.

* * * * *

Late the next morning, Lori climbed into the cab of Grandpa's old rattletrap truck and after a couple of false starts got the engine going. It was pretty close to noon now. She'd spent the wee early hours unloading and putting her personal stuff away. The time would come later to redecorate the old place but that wasn't happening today. Afterward, she'd showered and changed into a fresh pair of her comfiest jeans, a scooped-necked baby blue tee shirt and had tugged on a pair of ancient shit-kickers that she'd worn back in high school. They were tucked away in the closet of the room she'd used as a girl. Still fit. Hallelujah! Thinking of last night's conversation with Jackson Blue, she was damn happy to have them. Snakes! Yeesh. As an afterthought, she shoved a battered straw cowboy hat over her streaky blonde hair. The summer sun in these parts was deadly.

Lori pulled out of the drive and headed toward the back of the property where a dirt road led in the direction of the well drilling in progress. Already pump jacks worked steadily as far as the eye could see. Ugly damn things but boy howdy, did they ever bring in the cash. The old truck kicked up a rooster-tail of sandy colored dust behind her as she headed south taking in the land around her. In years gone by, Grandpa had grown acres of cotton but those days were long gone. Now the land was good for nothing but what lay beneath it in the form of crude oil. One day, when she'd been little, she'd wrinkled her nose, commenting on the bad smell of natural gas in the air. Grandpa had smiled, patted her head and said. "Don't you worry about that, sweetie pie. Just smells like money to me."

Thinking of those days always made her smile.

In the distance, she spotted the giant drilling rig outlined by a painfully blue but empty sky. To those who'd never seen a rig, it might resemble a small Eiffel Tower with a few alterations, but to her, drilling rigs and pumping units were just part of the landscape of the Permian Basin in west Texas. Every bit as rough and tough as the cowboys, oil men had forged this land with sweat, grit, determination and instincts worthy of any Vegas gambler. She drove closer and stopped the truck among roughly half a dozen dark blue pickup trucks that bore the silver logo of Blue's Petroleum and Drilling Company. There in a clearing stood the rig. Engines roared, filling the desolate silence. Pipe twisted and turned on a mechanical thingamajig that lowered the steel cylinders down, down, down into a hole that was hidden by the raised platform. Several men in grime-stained jeans, tees and hardhats guided the pipe as it inched its way into the ground.

One man stood just a bit taller than the rest. At least six foot four of long, lean muscle, he gripped the pipe with grease-stained hands that looked strong and competent. Unlike the other men, he didn't wear a hardhat, the big, gorgeous daredevil. He laughed at something one of the other men said and she caught his smiling profile. Her mouth went dry as west Texas dust. *Lordy, lordy, some mama somewhere sure grew a pretty man.*

Okay, how long *had* it been since she'd been laid? Mentally ticking off the years, months, weeks, days and hours since her dreadfully painful divorce, she gathered herself and stepped from the truck to hunt down Jackson Blue. A pristine straw cowboy hat caught her attention as she saw a man who stood propped against the door of one of the trucks talking on his cell phone. He looked to be close to sixty and she wondered if this was the owner of the drop-dead sexy voice. He spoke into the phone for a few more seconds then disconnected before turning toward her. He paused for a miniscule moment then smiled and tipped the brim of his hat. "Ma'am."

This wasn't Jackson Blue. Not the same deep drawl. She smiled and reached out a hand. "Hi," she said, stepping forward. "I'm Lori Donovan and you must be—"

"Tom Harper. I'm the foreman of this outfit. Good to meet you."

"Same here. Could you point Jackson out to me? We have an appointment."

"You bet." Together they looked toward the raised platform and Mr. Hot and Handsome turned to give them both a wave before he headed down the shallow steps leading to the ground. The man had a long, loose-hipped stride that only served to emphasize the fine way he filled out a pair of worn denim. His black cowboy boots were as scuffed and well used as her own except his carried a layer of red Texas dust. The dark blue tee shirt he wore molded a solidly muscular chest that was, in a word, perfection. Once again, Lori's mouth went dry as a flash of hot lust whipped through her body straight to her suddenly damp pussy.

Lord have mercy!

The man was sex on a stick and then he grinned at her, flashing a set of sparkling white teeth and she felt her knees go slightly weak. A dimple scored one bronzed cheek. Harsh sunlight caught his short, wavy black hair.

Wow! Just wow!

18

Hiding the sudden insecurities that swamped her, she smiled and held out a hand as he drew closer. He might be the guy who put the *g* in gorgeous but she knew full well that a man like him must have incredibly beautiful young women throwing themselves at him every day. Lori had no illusions about herself and those few she had previously clung to were dashed to bits when her ex left her for someone else.

Jackson reached into a back pocket for a bandana which he applied to his hands. Finally he looked up with an apologetic grin. "Sorry. My hands are too dirty to touch a lady," he said with a shrug. "Nice to meet you at last, Lori."

The shy, insecure cougar buried deep inside ducked her head and slunk into her cave. Mr. Hot and Handsome wouldn't be interested. She plastered on a bright smile, mentally cussing her lack of bravado and the sense of being *nothing* that Grant had left her with. "Same here, Jackson. Looks like you're already running pipe in the hole." Jeez, why did that common oilfield lingo sound so damn sexy? Heat climbed over her cheeks and she was suddenly relieved her face was shaded by the old straw cowboy hat.

Fortunately he didn't seem to notice. Turning his head, he squinted his eyes and glanced toward the engine. Fine lines radiated from the corners practically screaming the fact he made his living in the outdoors. Lori found herself wishing she'd been able to shake his hand. This man wouldn't have manicured nails or soft palms. His hands would be calloused, just a little rough. Raising his voice slightly to be heard over the roaring engines he glanced back at her. "Yeah, the geologist read the logues last week and we found a nice shallow pocket that looks good. It's there, all right. Now we just have to get the pipe in the hole and get her completed." Suddenly he smiled. "This probably sounds like Greek to you."

She shook her head. "Not really. Grandpa was a cotton farmer but I grew up around these parts and we all know oil is king here. I managed to pick up lots of things over the years."

Conversation was disrupted when a pickup pulled up and braked to a stop. A young guy, no more than twenty, climbed out of the cab and grabbed up a big box stuffed full of paper sacks.

Jackson smiled at her and then nodded toward the younger man. "Hey, looks like you're just in time for lunch. You hungry?"

Before she could blink much less answer, Jackson trotted over to the kid and grabbed a couple of sacks from the box. "Come on. We'll eat in my trailer."

It wasn't until they'd tromped past the roar of the rig's engine she spotted a neat little mobile home in the distance. "Is this where you're staying?"

"Yeah, I drag it around from site to site. It's a combo office and sleeping space for me. Not fancy, mind you, but serves a purpose."

"You'll hear no complaints from me."

Together they went up the three steps and she preceded him into the darkened mobile home. Immediately he brushed in behind her and she felt the strength of his sun-warmed body against her back. "Excuse me," he said his voice slightly husky. "Let me shed some light on things around here."

He moved into the living and kitchen area and set the paper sacks on a small dinette table before opening the old-fashioned mini-blinds that covered the windows. Light streamed in as Lori removed her hat and ran nervous fingers through her hair. Being in such a small space with this hunka hunka burning love did crazy things to her libido.

"Um, this is handy, huh?"

He smiled, went to the kitchen sink and turned on the water. "The trailer? Yeah, couldn't do without it. Mind if I clean up a bit?"

"No, of course not. Can I get some plates or something?"

"Paper plates are in the cabinet over there," he said as he dipped his hands under the water and began to soap up.

Lori went to fetch the plates and some napkins while keeping up a steady, covert study of his big hands spreading suds over his muscular forearms. His shoulders bunched beneath the worn cotton of his tee shirt and she had the insane urge to drop what she was doing and rush over to see if he felt as utterly yummy as he looked.

Down girl!

Before her mind could sink further into the gutter, they were seated together at the small table, digging into the deli sandwiches and chips. Jackson had fetched a couple of soft drinks for them.

"I didn't realize I was so hungry," she said after swallowing a bite. "My feet hit the ground running this morning and I completely forgot breakfast."

"What's going on at your place?"

Lori rolled her eyes. "What isn't going on? I swear. Unpacking. I've only been here a couple of days and I'm already overwhelmed."

"Nice house. I drive by it every time I head into town."

"It used to be a nice house, you mean. It's going to take a lot of work to get the place back into shape. After Grandma died, Grandpa didn't do much toward fancying things up. And redecorating? Forget about it. Typical guy."

Jackson accepted her teasing with a grin. "I admit it. Most of us lack that particular set of skills. Hey, look at this place. My mama raised me right but she didn't teach me a damn thing about that stuff."

"Ah, this is just a place to catch a nap and relax a bit, isn't it?"

"Yeah, I have a place in Amarillo. Pretty nice for a single guy but I don't get home all that often these days."

Oh boy. Well that certainly answered one big question for her. Jackson Blue was single. The wicked, naughty imp in her mind did a little two-step as she zeroed in on his deliciously delectable lips. Her mouth went dry. "That's too bad."

"Not really," he said as he shoved his empty sandwich wrapper into a sack and smiled. "Got nothing better to do than work these days."

"No girlfriend back home?"

His smile widened and that sexy dimple peeked out at her. "Not lately."

"Hm."

"Hey, listen, Lori, you're back in town after a while away and I'm fairly new around here. Why don't we hit Smoky Joe's tonight? Do some dancing?"

Lori's heart thumped hard in her chest. She focused on his face and, for the first time, noted the narrowing of his eyes as he studied the shape of her lips. Hunger simmered deep in his chocolate brown eyes. It had been a very long time since that kind of interest had been directed her way. Years. For a split second she questioned the arrested expression on his face, thinking she might be wrong but no, she was no longer naïve nor was she oblivious. The handsome, thirtyish, Jackson Blue was showing some interest in her other than as a passing acquaintance.

The hidden cougar crawled from her little cave and unsheathed her claws.

Remember the challenge. Don't be a dumbass. Go for it. Take it. Grab it. Enjoy it.

Phrases unrolled through her mind and she knew right then that if she was ever going to jump it had to be now. With this man. She wasn't a fool.

Lori leaned back in her chair and noted the instant movement of his gaze from her lips to her boobs. A tingle of awareness swept her from the top of her head to the tip of her toes and all points in between. Jackson's nostrils flared as his tongue swept his bottom lip. Her nipples tightened against the satin cups of her bra, impossible to miss beneath the cotton tee. An ache set up deep in her belly then arrowed straight to her needy pussy.

"I have a better idea," she whispered.

"Yeah? All ears here."

She leaned forward and brazenly took his hand across the width of the table. "Why don't you come by my place tonight? Sevenish? I'll cook. I might even be able to rustle up a beer or two."

"Damn, woman. You cook? Think I'm in love here."

Lori laughed at his teasing, gave his hand a squeeze and stood. His gaze swept her body with heightened interest and the atmosphere of the small space fairly sizzled with expectation. No, he wasn't obvious about the attraction but it was there, nevertheless.

"Do you like lasagna?"

"Hell, woman, I'd like anything you gave me."

"Hm." She mustered up her sauciest grin and moved to the door. "We'll just see about that, won't we?"

"Reckon we will."

Chapter Two

∞

Jackson watched Lori Donovan drive off and leaned back against the truck. Damn but she was pretty. Soft and touchable. A little bit older than himself but hell, he was more than ready to deal with a bona fide woman instead of a girl. He was a man not a green-assed kid and he knew what he wanted and he definitely was developing a *thing* for the blonde bombshell. Flighty females held no appeal and Lori seemed a woman who knew her own mind. He'd seen the interest hiding behind that sassy *fuck me* smile. Her body was made for sin, curvy and seductive, and his cock practically sat up and begged to sink deep into her pussy.

She intrigued him. He sensed an under layer of vulnerability hiding somewhere deep inside her and it made him wonder at its cause.

"What do you know about her, Tom?" he asked.

Tom tilted the brim of his cowboy hat back with his thumb. "Little bit. I moved here not long after she headed off to Dallas but people talk and this is a small town. She was raised right here by her grandparents and she married her high school sweetheart. They did the college thing and lived in Dallas. Her ex's parents still live here and I think they were pretty torn up about the divorce. Nice folks."

"Has she been divorced long?"

"Couple of years maybe. Heard the ex remarried before the ink was dry on the divorce papers."

Well now didn't that set off some alarm bells? Another woman?

Jackson kicked at a clump of dirt with the toe of one boot. That would certainly explain that tiny bit of insecurity he'd homed in on. She was definitely a woman with a past but that didn't bother him. Anyone worth knowing would be layered, complicated, and a puzzle worth deeper study. Tonight was going to be interesting but the way he was feeling now, nothing was going to stop him from getting to know her better. Much better.

* * * * *

By late afternoon, she was in a dead panic.

Walking a tightrope comprised of her very last nerve, she dragged in a deep breath and booted up her computer. Time for a cougar pep talk.

Cougar Alert!!! OMG! I really stepped in it this time, ladies. Met this guy, right? He's drilling on my property but I pretty much suspect he wants to drill me too. Part of me wants to just laugh maniacally and the other part wants to bawl. His name is Jackson Blue. Cool name, huh? Anyway, he's one long, tall drink of Texas tea, let me tell ya, with a body that melts my knees like a big blob of butter left out in the sun. Black hair, eyes the color of dark chocolate and he fills out a pair of worn denim better than any man I've ever seen.

And his voice!

Um. Hot buttered sex.

Sorry. Got off topic. *Fanning self*

He's coming over tonight and I'm scared shitless. Panic-city here, ladies, and there's not a margarita to be found. Okay. So I made a pan of lasagna, whipped up a salad, and picked up a loaf of French bread at the local bakery. Yeah, I'm gonna wine and dine him. Literally. Picked up a nice bottle of red, plus some beer since he looks like the beer type to me. Ah, damn. I'm blabbering. Somebody shoot me!

So what else do I do? Dim the lights? Please tell me to dim the lights and maybe he won't realize how much older than him I really am. Jeez. He's at least ten years younger and I'm certainly no longer an eighteen-year-old hardbody. I swear I'm a nervous wreck. What do I wear? Jeans or a skirt? Have some cute, sexy little sundresses. Maybe that would work.

Help! I'm losing it. I swear.

Lori sat back, stared at the computer screen and waited, her fingernails tapping nervously on the dining room table. It didn't take long to hear from several of her naughty cougar pals and fellow margarita lovers. She had to smile.

Rachel: First of all, TAKE A BREATH. Secondly, hot damn! You are on your way to becoming a full-fledged cougar, girlfriend. Go with your gut, your instincts, the flow, but GO, GO, GO!!!

Then tell us all about it.

Lynn: Who cares about the dress! Just make sure you leave off the undies.

Cam: Hey now! Hot buttered sex? Sounds like the perfect accompaniment to the meal you have planned. And I'd go for the dress—much easier for hands to run up legs or fingers to slip straps off shoulders or...well, you get the picture. Dim the light? I like that. Or candles. Lots of candles. But hey, if the man has drilling on his mind then to hell with lights and dining. Go straight for dessert. And BREATHE...remember, it's just like riding...you don't forget how and the rhythm comes back to you pretty quick. I want details tomorrow!!

Rissa: You're looking at this the wrong way. You're an experienced, sexy, desirable woman. He's lucky you're giving him the time of day much less cooking for him. Relax and be yourself, then follow up with lots of juicy details.

Elizabeth: There's only one kind of drilling to be done after dark, and he's planning to be there. How much do you want to bet he's wondering what's sexier on him, boxers or briefs? 'Course, commando would do the trick, too!

I know exactly what you're going through—we all do. But you'll be fine, I promise. I'd wear the sundress. Easier to keep what's underneath—or not underneath!—a surprise. I'm so excited for you!

Lori: Thanks! Leave it to you guys to want all the sizzling details. Snicker. Okay. Count on the lowdown straight from the cougar's mouth. Tomorrow, okay? Yes, breathing here. In. Out. In. Out. My, that sounds sexual doesn't it? Wow, maybe I AM ready for this. You think?

Lori rushed into the bedroom then forced herself to do some of that deep breathing. Yeah, that was it. In. Out. In. Out. God, she loved her friends. Smiling a little, she ran a bath full of frothy bubbles and soaked for a good half hour. Once she was as limp as a well-cooked noodle, she slathered scented lotion into her skin, smiling a little. Yeah, she still had good, good skin thanks to some spectacular genes. Maybe Jackson would be so overwhelmed with how soft she was, he would fail to notice some of the other less than perfect things.

She restrained herself from outright snorting but it was a close thing.

She wasn't an idiot. She could've been wrong about all those *fuck me* vibes. It was entirely possible that he was lonely and just wanted a friend for the short time he was stuck out here in the boonies.

Still she couldn't stop the flock of butterflies that set up housekeeping in her tummy. Closing her eyes, she concentrated on her primp-fest, dried her shoulder length blonde hair and lightly spackled her face with a touch of makeup paying special attention to the lashes that rimmed her light-blue eyes. Guys like blue, right? Sure they did.

By the time she'd slipped into a silky black dress and padded barefoot into the kitchen, the earlier sense of being relaxed completely evaporated. The sun had begun to set. He'd be here soon. Giving in to temptation, she opened the bottle of red wine and foregoing the whole "breathing" thing poured a glass. Anything to soothe the jitters that dipped and dived her body.

What the hell was she thinking?

Oh yeah. The challenge. A hot, torrid, fuck-me-inside-out affair with a smokin' younger guy. Insanity. Dragging in a deep breath, she headed into the living room of the old Victorian throwback and flopped on the couch. She took a sip of false courage and propped her bare feet on the coffee table, wiggling toesies painted in Risky Red. When she'd first read the gung ho posts from her nutty cougar friends, she'd been encouraged but now she just felt tired. When Grant had left her for another, much younger woman, after twenty years of marriage, she'd been too shell-shocked to date. Devastated, lonely, incredibly hurt, she'd locked herself in a room with premium chocolate and a bottle of very fine bourbon. No, it had accomplished nothing but expand the size of her butt so she'd abandoned that little pity party quickly enough. That had been two years ago and in that time she could count on one hand the number of guys she'd dated. And intimacy? Forget about it. After hearing Grant tell her in no uncertain terms that she just didn't do it for him anymore, her confidence had been smashed liked so many atoms.

The big question remained. Did she have the guts, the sheer bravado, to reach out for what she wanted? Was she ready to live again? The answer was simple.

"Hell, yes," she whispered to herself just as she heard the sound of tires crunching on gravel and the roar of a truck engine. She gasped, closed her eyes for a second to blink away the sudden tears that had swept the surface of her eyes. Memories were painful and she just wasn't going to revisit them tonight.

It was time for this little cougar to finally have some fun.

Standing, she swept her hands over the cute, casual and sexy little number she wore. Lori glanced down at her feet. No shoes. What the hell! Smiling, she went to the front door listening to the heavy fall of boots on the front steps and opened the door.

"My, my" she said. "How very punctual!"

Jackson grinned and her bones melted just a bit. He looked like a sexy dream in jeans and a dark-blue, pearl-snapped, western-style shirt. In one big fist, he clutched a handful of multi colored daisies wrapped in green waxy paper and in the other hand he held his cowboy hat. He loomed over her in the doorway that dimple peeking from one cheek, and held up the flowers. "It was a close thing, let me tell ya. The only florist in town closed at six on the dot and that left me with the Grocery Mart flower shop. Not very classy of me." He shrugged. "What can I say? These are called Crazy Daisies. I swear I've never seen blue and purple daisies before. They looked cool though and reminded me of you. You seem like a pretty colorful woman to me."

She laughed and took the flowers, unbelievably touched. Stepping back, she watched him fill up her space as he moved into the living room. She'd fully expected him to start looking around at things but no, he kept his eyes leveled on her.

Unexpected.

"What a nice compliment. I don't think I've been called colorful in a very long time. If ever." Lori stroked a petal of a bright orange daisy and wanted to curse her unruly tongue. If babbling was a disease, she was suffering from it.

Suddenly, Jackson took the flowers from her hand and set them along with his hat on the coffee table. And before she could blink, he had her pressed against the front door. The heavy muscles of his chest settled against her breasts and her nipples instantly responded. His breath fell warm on her lips as he spoke against them. "I've been thinkin' about this all day, darlin'," he whispered before brushing them with tantalizing slowness against her mouth. A soft sigh escaped and he drank it down as he took the kiss deeper. His tongue swept, tasted, parried and retreated and Lori felt her body practically dissolve against the sturdy door. Jackson's body shifted as he angled the kiss and Lori's nipples pearled tighter, growing hard enough to pulse with a tiny ache.

Touch them. Touch me.

A low moan caught in her throat seconds before Jackson drew back slightly and stared into her eyes.

He wasn't unaffected. His words when he spoke, sounded rusty. "Too fast?"

"No," she whispered. "No, not too—"

"Good. Didn't think I could hold off until after dinner." He went for another kiss, a deeper one, a hungrier one, and the sensation it inspired had Lori's toes curling against the hardwood floors. The press of his chest against her breasts sent her teetering on the edge of just giving up and jumping his hot bones right then and there. Instead, she returned his kiss with all the pent-up passion she'd been storing up over the past long, empty years. In a tender gesture that threatened to undo her, Jackson reached up to cup her face. He broke the hungry tasting with gentle nips. His lips curled slightly. "Something smells damn good."

"Lasagna."

He laughed. "No, you. You smell good enough to eat."

Responding to his teasing, she grinned. "I'll remind you of that later, Big Guy." She gripped fistfuls of his shirt and kissed him playfully before moving away from him. Feeling happy and sexy and more than a little hungry herself, she grabbed his hand and tugged. "Come on. Let's get you fixed up. I have a longneck in the fridge with your name on it. And I should get these pretty flowers into some water."

"Sounds good." He followed her into the kitchen, took a quick look around and then took the bottle and tipped it to his lips. Finally he looked at her. "Where's yours?"

"In the living room."

"Then let's go get it and find some tunes."

A bit later, while slow country music played, they sat together and she had the pleasure of watching him devour two helpings of lasagna along with a couple of beers. He only picked at his salad but she figured he was a carnivore at heart. Candles flickered from three chunky candlesticks she'd placed on the large walnut dining room table. Shadows sifted over the sharp planes and angles of his face, softening them and making her wish she were brave enough to crawl right over the tabletop to him. Since there was just the two of them, she'd placed their settings close together at one end of the table to foster an air of intimacy but, truth be told, they could've achieved that without the physical closeness. The air around them practically smoldered. Lori had no doubt they were both remembering that hotter than hell kiss they'd shared the minute he'd walked in the door tonight.

"So have you always lived in Amarillo?" she asked after she took a sip of wine.

He smiled. "Yep. Dad travelled a lot with Blue Moon so most of time it was just mom and us kids. I have four sisters. "

"Four? Wow. They had you surrounded."

"Yup." Jackson gave her a naughty wink. "So when I tell you I love women, you'd better believe it's the honest-to-God truth. I was the baby so they spoiled me rotten."

Lori shook her head. "I love it. I can only imagine. So how did you get hooked into the whole drilling thing?"

"When I was a teenager, Dad took me with him in the summers. I earned a little money and he liked showing me the ropes."

"Did you feel pressured to join the family business?"

"Not really. I like the work and after college it was a natural progression for me. Think I've always had crude running in my veins though so it wasn't a problem."

Lori laughed. "I don't know. I think I sense some red blood in there somewhere." He laughed and she continued, wanting to know more about him. "I suspect it's pretty cool striking oil."

"Like winning the lottery. There's an excitement to this business. Kind of like what a high stakes gambler might feel when he scores big in Vegas, I reckon."

"Ahh, a gamblin' man."

"You know it. Dad retired a few years ago and I took over." He shrugged and leaned back to look at her through the glow of candlelight. "The work suits me. Kind of like *you* suit me, Miz Donovan. Tell me about you."

Lori was amazed at how easily she fell into conversation with him. Aside from his rugged good looks, Jackson was polite, funny, and interesting. She wanted to learn more about him but she understood the give and take involved in getting to know someone. And boy did she ever want to know Jackson Blue.

Giving in, she neatly folded her napkin and set it on the table. "Not much to tell really. I grew up in Sandy Creek right in this very house. I married my high school sweetheart and we moved away after high school. Neither of us could to wait to get the hell out of here."

"I doubt this town has much to offer young people."

She sighed. "The bitter truth of small town Texas and that's a fact."

"So you were married for a long time?"

Lori shot him a look. "Do you really want to hear about my pitiful marriage and the divorce that followed? Most guys wouldn't want to know that stuff."

"Maybe I'm not *most guys.*" He reached across the expanse of the table and took her hand. His was firm and warm causing Lori's heartbeat to pick up in pace. Slowly, as if memorizing everything about her, he traced each of her fingers, touching each bit of skin with butterfly touches that made her flesh tingle. "I find you fascinating. Something lurks beneath those sweet baby blues and I'm curious. Tell me your secrets, Lori."

A nervous laugh escaped. "All of them?" She blew out a breath. "I doubt they are much different from those of lots of women my age. I was married for a long time to the only man I ever loved and it took him about twenty years to figure out that wasn't enough for him. That's all. Pretty damn clichéd, if you ask me. I don't talk about it much."

"He's a jackass."

She grinned, hoping to dispel the seriousness from his face. She was looking for an affair not forever from this gorgeous younger man. "I happen to agree."

Jackson laughed as she hoped he would then he surprised her by lifting her hand to his lips. His kisses were lingering, sweet, heating her blood and making her wish she could keep and hold some of that tenderness. Hard to imagine gentleness living deep within his big, rugged body but it did. His gaze turned hot when he focused in on her. "How about some dessert? I'm hungry for something sweet."

Lori stood to head into the kitchen but before she could take a step, Jackson was there pulling her into his arms, giving her a slow, sexy smile. "Yeah, I'm talkin' about you, darlin'," he whispered before moving in for a hot, hot tasting. A low sound broke from her lips as Jackson reached around to loop his arms underneath her butt. When he lifted her against him, she sent her arms and legs around him, holding on for all she was worth as he carried her from the dining room.

"Bedroom," he whispered urgently.

Lori laughed breathlessly. "Off the living room. Can't miss it." But her laughter died a quick death as each long stride caused her pussy to connect seductively with the hard erection hidden behind the fly of his jeans. The instant teasing friction dampened her panties and urged her to press closer to the pleasure he offered. She writhed against him.

"Fuck."

The crude whispered word smacked of desperation. Excited beyond anything, she gasped when she felt the press of a wall against her back. "Jackson!"

"Hang on."

Jackson pounced and kissed her again, filling his hands with her breasts, thumbing the nipples until they were diamond hard and aching. Pleasure, hot and wild, whipped through her body to center in her core. Her pussy responded and the miniscule thong she wore went instantly wet. Jackson ate at her lips like a man starved for the touch of a woman and she couldn't help responding to the ferocious seduction. He huffed a frustrated breath then reached out to unhook the snap that held up the halter neck of her silky little dress. Bits of black fabric draped downward momentarily covering his hands but he brushed it hastily aside. Jackson drew back his eyes narrowed, and stared with rapt attention at her bared breasts.

"You make me hungry, woman. Damn you're pretty."

Jackson bent his dark head and latched onto a pulsing, tightly drawn nipple, sucking lightly at first. Warmth, then raging heat whipped from the point of contact straight to her center. Her pussy felt empty, needy and in response she moved it against his hard cock. Lori tightened her legs, digging her heels into his backside in an effort to pull him closer.

No prodding was necessary.

Jackson took full advantage of her open position, moving closer to press his length where she needed it most and every nerve ending she possessed sat up and sang. The rough press of denim against her mound caused her breath to hitch. His cock filled his jeans to perfection, every hard inch moving with agonizing slowness against her weeping slit. Wild sensation blasted through her body like a rocket as she clung to him. Eager fingers found his hair and then the firmly toned muscles of his long back as she stroked in tandem to the brush of his erection against her vulnerable flesh. She wanted to touch him everywhere. Needs, long denied, unfurled in her body, and her fingers practically itched. If she'd been a true cougar she might have tugged the pearl snaps on his shirt until they played a slow, sexy song but things were raw, new, and more than over-the-top for a woman who hadn't been touched by a man in so long.

"You taste as good as you look," he breathed against the softness of her breast. "I wanted you the minute I saw you standing there beside that beat-up old truck." Jackson sent his hands beneath the skirt of her dress and fingers flexed on the globes of her ass. He buried his face against her throat sucking lightly as he dipped his fingers beneath the elastic of her thong. His fingers went on a quick, sexy quest, finally sinking two of them into her eager cunt.

"Jackson, I—"

"Shh."

"Oh God."

She wanted to speak but the slow fingerfucking stole her words. A real conversation killer for sure because who wanted to talk when all she really needed was to fuck. Hard and fast.

Drilled!

Yeah, she wanted him to drill her body into the damn wall, not stopping until she was screaming with pleasure.

Chapter Three

Jackson looked down into her eyes, saw the hunger there but also the uncertainly. He knew he was moving awfully damn fast but lust just flat out overwhelmed his good judgment. He sent his fingers deeper into her body and then slowly withdrew them.

"Damn, Lori," he breathed. "I love the way your pussy feels. Give it up to me."

"Jack…Jackson, yes."

Slipping his thumb over the distended knot of her clit, he rubbed gently, teasing until Lori made a frantic little sound that had his cock pulsing. His mouth went dry and breath stilled in his lungs. Over and over, he swept the tender flesh until her body writhed against the wall. She was so close but he didn't want their first time to be a quick hand job in the living room. He had nothing against a good hand job but, no. Not now.

Jackson removed his fingers from her weeping slit and tried to ignore her sharp cry of loss at his touch. Kissing her quickly, he settled his arms under her ass and carried her straight into the bedroom. Night had fallen and a sliver of moonlight cast the room in shadows but he easily found the big four-poster and tumbled her gently to the mattress. Reaching out, he flipped on a lamp that rested on her nightstand.

"What?" Lori propped herself up on her elbows, a look of worry on her face.

He went still and looked at her. "I want to see you."

Emotions flickered across her face but then she nodded and gave him a determined look. Passion caused her cheeks to blush in a pretty, sweet way that had feelings of savage possession pumping through his chest. Her breasts, pink tipped and deliciously puckered heaved a little. She was turned on too. No doubt about it.

Maybe, just maybe, she was as lonely as he.

Jackson gave the front of his shirt a tug and the pearl snaps gave way with a subtle sound. Lori sighed suddenly, lay back on the bed and grinned at him. "Hey! I wanted to do that."

Barking a laugh, he focused or the rise of color to her face. "Next time, honey. I promise. Got a few more of these shirts back at the trailer."

"Ah, that's good. I see a hot little sliver of skin there, Jackson. Show me more."

He watched the tip of her tongue sweep across her bottom lip as he drew the shirt from his body and tossed it aside. Her eyes veered down, then up, pausing for an incremental moment on his belly, which tightened in response. Those pretty blue eyes darkened. God, she was hot.

Wasting little time, he tugged at his boots and socks then went to her. Jackson leaned over her deliciously sprawled, very succulent body and nipped her swollen bottom lip.

"Hey wait a minute," she whispered. "You can't leave a lady hanging. Take off the rest."

"Ladies first."

He pressed his lips to her throat dragging the scent of her subtle perfume into his lungs then tasted the soft, tender skin stretching across her collarbone. Jackson's lips surrounded one deliciously hard nipple and sucked gently before moving to the other.

Undressing a woman had never been so incredible.

Lori sent her fingers into his hair. "Gotta tell you something."

"Um-hm." He released her nipple, gave it a quick lick then looked up. "Tell away but make it fast. I'm working here."

She laughed softly. "Maybe you don't want to hear this but I've only been with my husband."

Through a red haze of lust, he managed to focus on her. He went still. "Ever?"

"Uh, yeah. Ever."

"And you've been divorced a couple of years?"

She was embarrassed by the question. He knew because her emotions practically reached out and grabbed him. He smiled gently. The asshole ex had hurt her. Maybe it was long past time she learned that *all* men weren't like that. "Then quit talkin' and let me get down to business here. We've got some time to make up for and it's damn certain you don't need a rush job. Let's do this slow and easy. How's that sound?"

Jackson saw any hint of uncertainty fade from her eyes as she smiled. He reached behind her to find the zipper of her dress and slid it down. Taking his time, he drew the sexy bit of silky material from her body until she lay there blinking up at him wearing only a tiny scrap of black lace over her delicious pussy. Reaching for her legs, he drew his hands up the insides of her thighs from knee to groin, noting the softness of her skin beneath hands that were too callused to touch a lady.

"I don't want to be rough but I have to admit, I'm feeling a little savage right now."

"All part of the experience, isn't it?" she said. Her voice was low and a little gruff. "Take my panties off, Jackson."

He grinned at her. "Yes, ma'am."

Slipping his fingers beneath the top of her little thong, he dragged it over her hips and down her legs before dropping it to the floor. For all her bravado, he heard her suck in a breath when he stood back to look at her. She was truly a beautiful woman. Her face was a delicate oval. Her nose was small and straight, her lips wide and mobile, but it was her eyes that held him spellbound. They were expressive and honest with an underlying hint of mystery that made him want to dig deeper to get to know her. And her body? Killer! All lush curves and soft flesh that he made him want to wrap her up in his arms and never let go.

"Ready for me, darlin'?"

"Yeah. Hurry Jackson. I like slow, but damn."

Getting inside this woman prodded him into action. He plucked a condom from his back pocket and stuck it between his clenched teeth. Her gaze locked on him, hot and needy, as he unzipped his jeans and kicked them aside.

God, his cock ached. Fisting his hand around the base, he dragged it up and then down. A drop of fluid appeared on the head, a full-blown reminder of how badly he needed to come. Knowing she watched so avidly caused his belly to tighten, coiling like a spring and he'd finally had enough. He opened the condom wrapper with his teeth and slid on protection before settling one knee on the mattress between her thighs.

Jackson didn't need to touch her pussy to see if she was wet and ready for him. In the meager light of the lamp, he could see her pink flesh glistening with moisture. Unable to resist, he drew his fingers over her, opening her labia, playing with the slick layers. He plucked the swollen knot of her clit and knew before this night was over, he would taste her there.

Calling on his self-restraint, he gently lifted her legs until her heels were pressed flat on the bed. He gripped her knees and moved to splay her open wider. Taking his cock in his fist, he drew the head of his erection through hot layers of flesh and watched her eyes flutter closed. Settled firmly between her thighs, he dipped his cock into the entrance of her pussy and felt her internal muscles clamp down hard.

"Ah fuck."

Losing control, needing to bury himself in her clasping warmth, he sank deep into her channel. Sweat beaded his forehead as fiery heat wrapped him up and his balls drew up tighter than a miser's fist. In. Out. In. Out. Slowly he fucked her until taking his time was no longer an option. Jackson latched hungrily onto a tight, thrusting nipple and sucked it hard as her soft moan curled up into the heavy air around them. Her hips thrust upward, taking him in, taking him deep and Jackson increased his pace as he plowed his cock through her tight pussy. Lori squeezed hard at every withdrawal, coaxing him back into her sultry heat. Jackson released her nipple and gritted his teeth as lust danced frantic fingers over his spine. Rearing back, he gripped her soft ass as he pounded deep and hard. The head of his cock rubbed that sensitive spot behind her pubic bone and a fresh flood of cream coated him as she cried out.

"Jackson!"

"Hell, yeah."

Striking like a cobra, he increased the pressure until Lori stiffened. A tiny shriek, a repetitive clenching of her body on his erection, and she flew apart, flinging her arms out to grab hold of the bedspread. Finally, finally Jackson let go. One pump, then two and he blasted his cum into the end of the condom. A low growl caught and held in his chest. His skin prickled as sensation carried him over the sharp edge of pleasure. Catching his breath was tough but finally he moved to lie over Lori's trembling body. He gathered her against his heaving chest, loving the feel of her, smiling when she wrapped him in her arms.

Moments later they lay together under the covers of her big bed. He'd flipped off the lamp on the nightstand and the room was bathed in shadow as he tucked her head on his shoulder and sent his hand on a skimming journey of the long length of her back. Lori sighed against his chest and reached up to trail the tip of her finger over his nipple. He settled his face against the top of her blonde head and breathed her in.

"Can I ask you something?"

Jackson leaned back to look at her. "Shoot."

Lori shifted a little to insert one leg between his thighs. "You've been working here, what? Months?"

"Yeah, about three months now."

"Why is it some local woman, some *young* local woman, hasn't nabbed you already? In case you haven't figured it out you are total eye candy."

Frowning, he traced the outline of her cheek. "Do I sense some insecurity here, honey? Surely you know you are a beautiful woman?"

"Maybe I do have some insecurities and I just didn't realize it. Maybe it's lurking me somewhere. For whatever reason, we just had sex and I'm not about to complain."

"Good. That's a relief. Lots of us guys have performance anxiety."

She laughed as he hoped she would. Her hand traced a path over the muscles of his chest then wandered lower. His sleepy cock twitched with renewed interest and he knew she felt it when her eyes twinkled wickedly. "You've got to know you were amazing. I think I could become a happy addict to sex with you."

"You think you're the only one who wants more? You're the first woman living in these parts I've had the slightest interest in since I got here."

"Do you expect me to believe that big, huge, whopper?"

Something about her made him want to smile. He kissed her lips, softly at first but then took the kiss deeper before finally answering. "I do. I've met a few of the local women but, to tell you the truth, none of them appealed to me. Maybe I've just been waiting for you. Someone warm, funny and with enough curves to make a man's cock hard just from looking. Don't you realize how hot you are?"

"Hot? Me?" Lori laughed. "You might want to have a talk with my ex about that assessment." Then she shook her head. "Never mind. I'm sorry I said that. Pillow talk about a woman's past isn't too cool, is it? As a matter of fact, it's rather pitiful."

Jackson saw the flash of vulnerability in her eyes along with embarrassment. Taking hold of her shoulder, he flattened her to the mattress and loomed over her. "Don't apologize to me. For what it's worth, your ex-husband is a fool but I sure as hell am *not* and I don't want to discuss him. Especially not when I'm in bed with you."

He took her mouth with unexpected fierceness and wondered where the emotion came from but then everything that spoke of his physical attraction took over. Plunging his tongue deep, he settled his chest against the delicious softness of her breasts. He move his thigh until it pressed the delicate flesh of her moist pussy. A single slight movement made her gasp but he took the kiss deeper sweeping his tongue through the sweetness of her mouth, needing to devour. Jackson shifted to settle between her thighs and his cock rubbed the damp flesh of her pussy. Without the condom as a barrier, her delicious heat practically burned him. Needing more, he pushed against her, dragging the thick stalk of his erection through tempting layers that grew wetter by the moment.

Talk about addictive.

Her scent wrapped around him like a song and he drew it into his lungs as he broke the wild kiss and trailed his lips over the curve of her cheek, her throat. He sucked one nipple and finally the other as Lori began to squirm. Her panting breaths, hot and full of desire, ruffled his hair. He scraped the edge of his teeth across the surface of one pink puckered nipple. Lori moaned. Her fingers went into his hair, digging in, holding on.

"Another question," she whispered, gasping. "How many condoms did you bring?"

"Couple."

"That's all?"

Jackson laughed. "I'll come better prepared next time, darlin', but I promise, I don't need a bit of latex for what I have planned next."

"Ooh. Show me." Her voice was a mere sexy breath of sound. What a turn on.

Sliding his body down her torso, he filled his hands with her sweet ass and trailed his lips over her belly. It was the kind of belly he loved, soft and rounded, completely feminine. He'd never been a guy who enjoyed stick-skinny women and to him, she was heaven, perfect. Sinking his teeth gently into her warm flesh, he swept the spot with his tongue, sucked it and then moved lower. He trailed his thumbs over the tender notch between her legs and groin loving the feel of her velvet soft but ultimately hot skin.

Settling his mouth there, he drew his tongue over it. He spread her labia with his fingers and focused his attention on her pussy. Lori went completely still. Then her breath broke when he licked a path from her opening to the swollen knot of her clit and back again. Stiffening his tongue, he probed her vagina, loving the way her inner muscles tightened.

She whimpered softly. "Jack. Yes."

Jackson replaced his tongue with his fingers and went to work on her clit, gently sucking the morsel until she was writhing and arching to meet him. Keeping her on the edge, wanting to take things slow, he withdrew, heard her whispered sound of frustration. He went to his knees and looked down at her.

"You're killin' me here," she whispered.

"Shh. Be patient. Let me play." Her eyes went wide moments before he flipped her to her belly then brought her to her hands and knees. "Don't you know I have big plans for you, sweetheart?"

Gently, he kneed her legs apart and gripping her hips, drew his tongue over the length of her pussy then higher to circle the bud of her anus. "I want to fuck you here," he said. He bent to nip one rounded ass cheek. "You ever done that?

"No."

"You wanna try sometime?"

"Oh yes," she breathed.

"Since I get the feeling we're just beginning a red-hot affair, let me promise you that we'll get to it. Eventually."

"Oh boy. A red-hot affair, huh?"

He chuckled, nipped her again and then released her. Lying on his back, he slid under her so he could look up at her pretty, drenched pussy. "Gonna eat you now, darlin'. Come here."

Gripping her butt, he brought her down until her pussy hovered over his lips. He felt her go still at the first stroke on his tongue and then he took the tasting deeper. When she relaxed against his mouth, Jackson went to work. Eating her like a starving man, he clutched her ass and felt her squirm against mouth. He dipped his tongue deep in a parody of hot fucking then trailed it higher to suck and pull at her swollen clit. Soft, sexy sounds broke from her lips. A shudder swept her body. Jackson drew gently at her clit again holding her at the very edge and then finally she fell over it with a tiny shriek. Her limbs trembled in the aftermath so he swept his hands over the length of her thighs, loving the way the tender flesh of her pussy pulsed against his tongue.

"You're so damn sweet," he breathed against her flesh. "But I'm not done. Hope you're ready for more."

"Shit! I can't do it," she gasped.

Jackson laughed and slid from beneath her. How he could laugh when his cock was ready to blow was beyond him. Bending behind her, he kissed one globe. "Don't move."

"You're killin' me here."

Eying her bare backside and her gleaming pussy, he wasted no time grabbing his jeans from the floor and ripping open his last remaining condom. Hell, he'd blown it big time with that. Two condoms would never be enough with Lori. She was so smokin' hot and so damn responsive. Yeah, he'd bring the whole damn box next time.

Next time.

Oh yeah. Without a doubt there would be a next time because the woman rang all his bells and then some. He'd crawl through gravel on his hands and knees for more of her.

Sliding on the condom, focused on the beautiful picture she presented, he came up behind her and gripped his cock. Jackson gritted his teeth and stifled a groan as he trailed the heavy head of his erection through hot, sweet, flesh. "Can't go slow, honey," he managed. "Not Superman here. Not by a long shot and you've got me all torqued up."

"Dyin' here, Jackson. Give it to me. I'm ready."

He slid deep into her heat. "Thank God!"

She whimpered at his slow withdrawal, gripping his cock with strong internal muscles and Jackson thought the top of his head was going to spin plumb off. "Not going to last. Fuck!"

"Come on."

"Yeah," he said on a gasping breath before plunging deep again. He wanted to linger, wanted to take it slow, but it was impossible. Thrusting, pumping, pounding deep, Jackson felt his balls tighten against his body as wicked fingers raced with lightning speed up his spine and over his scalp. Lori cried out as another orgasm crashed over her and then he just lost it. He dug his fingers into the globes of her ass and let go with a low groan.

They were both gasping by the time he dragged them into place at the head of Lori's big bed. Jackson bent to place a kiss on the tip of her nose. "Be right back."

"Okay. Hurry."

By the time he'd finished some business in the bathroom and come back, he noticed she was grinning wickedly at him.

"Um. So *that* was wild monkey sex." She drew the covers back and he joined her in the bed, drawing her against him.

"Sure as hell was."

"Ooh. I think I like it."

Jackson settled his face in her hair and smiled. She was so damn cute. Still, he couldn't help wondering about the utter joy she seemed to feel for what was, to most people, fairly commonplace. Sounded to him like her ex had been a selfish dud in the sack. He'd bet on it. "Then we'll have to do it again. You know, practice."

"Again?" He laughed at the shocked expression she wore when she leaned back to look at him.

"Probably not tonight, sweet thing. You wore me out."

Lori smiled dreamily then leaned close to rub her nose in the hair on his chest. "I did, huh? Mmm. I think I like the sound of that."

Then she yawned sleepily and his heart turned over. He'd known a lot of women. Fucked a lot of them too but there was something about all that kittenish warmth wrapped inside such a sexy package that did him in. He sensed in Lori Donovan a woman who was innately honest and completely real. He liked that about her. He liked it a whole lot.

Jackson hugged her close as she relaxed against his body. "Can I stay with you tonight?"

"Yes, Jackson," she murmured sleepily. "Stay as long as you want, honey."

Chapter Four

ହେ

Lori opened her eyes to a room full of morning sunlight and smiling sleepily, she stroked a hand over the now cold pillow next to her. She traced the slight indentation and recalled the moment, hours earlier when Jackson had pressed a kiss to her forehead and tucked the sheets more tightly around her.

Pushing back the covers, she sat up on the bed and surveyed the scene of her raunchy seduction. Her thong lay on the floor next to her rumpled dress. Her bedroom was now the site of her cougarfication. Yep. She'd been courgarized. Or had she cougarized Jackson? Laughing a little at the crazy train of her thoughts, she stood and groaned loudly. Lordy, lordy. Was she ever out of shape! Normally she managed long brisk walks or popped an exercise DVD into a machine for her workouts but this was a different kind of ache and a totally different kind of regimen for her.

A sex regimen.

Hell yes! She could get used to that.

Stumbling bare-assed naked into the bathroom, she took care of important business and then leaned against the vanity to stare at herself in the mirror that hung above the sink. Widening her eyes, she studied the reflection of the well-screwed woman in the mirror. Her lips were swollen and red. Lori traced a fingertip over them and then noticed a few reddened spots on her neck from Jackson's five o clock shadow.

Ooh. Look!

There was another mark on her left breast.

47

Nothing like a little red badge of courage. She'd done it. She'd broken, finally, the two-year drought that had left her feeling less than a full-blown woman.

Finally!

Feeling victorious and spunky and sassy and, oh so satisfied, she headed back into her bedroom and dug in a drawer for an oversized tee shirt and a pair of panties. Pulling them on, she wandered into the living room, realizing belatedly that she had been so overcome with horniness, she'd completely forgotten about trivial things like dirty dishes. Suddenly she stopped and gazed around.

Wow!

Every dish and every plate had been removed from the table and the surface sparkled with cleanliness. The candles she'd lit had obviously been extinguished at some point.

How could she have been so foolish?

Oh yeah, she'd been bowled over by lust and the hot loving of a sexy, sexy man.

Yeah. That was it.

Thank heavens Jackson had obviously gotten up at some point and kept her from having to call the fire department. What a guy!

Lori looked around in amazement before heading into the kitchen drawn by the scent of freshly brewed coffee. Next to the almost full coffee pot sat a stoneware mug and a note with one of those cute little crazy daisies lying on top of it. Another cup had been washed, rinsed and plopped upside down on a dishtowel next to the sink.

Her heart melted.

Jackson had cleaned up everything, fixed coffee and made himself at home. She loved it. Sighing, she picked up the hot pink daisy, gave it a little twirl, and then eyed Jackson's broad scrawl across a single sheet of white paper.

Lunch? Today? I'll pick you up around noon. Don't plan on waiting until tonight. J

Hmm. Impatient. She kind of liked that about him.

Mr. Hot Buttered Sex was quite a bit more than a yummy guy and it didn't take a rocket scientist to figure that out. Warmth uncurled in her belly and then, damn if it didn't move even lower. Memories of the way he'd made her body scream for mercy tore through her with a force strong enough to steal her breath. Visions of how his muscles bunched as he moved over her or reached to draw her against his hard body colored her mind and opened it to the infinite possibilities she could explore with this man.

Lori took her coffee cup to the living room, where she curled up on the couch. Staring mindlessly at a morning news show, she recalled the early years of her marriage. She'd felt that excitement in those days. She'd reveled in intimacy then but it hadn't lasted. As work pressures built and life happened they'd lost that spark. Lori had tried, she really had but nothing, not even months of marriage counseling had fixed what was broken between her and Grant.

He hadn't been interested in repairing things or trying to recapture the love of their youth. And maybe it was his lack of interest that had killed her so. When Grant had shaken his head and walked out the door straight into the arms of a much younger woman, something inside her had died.

But suddenly, today, at this exact moment, she wanted that wholeness that came from being with a man. The right man. It might not be Jackson, hell it probably wasn't. At least she now knew there was a spark inside her that wanted to take life by the reins and control her destiny, find happiness again. This morning she had hope when she hadn't had it the day before.

In a bit, she fetched another cup of coffee and grabbed her laptop. Once she'd settled in, she opened the Cougar blog and began to type. After all their great advice, the least she could do was share a little bit.

Hey Ladies! Last night was the most incredible experience. For the first time ever, I had wild monkey sex! Umm. Am I officially a monkey now? Snicker. Sorry, I'm a little giddy. Jackson's lovin' last night just flat blew the top of my head off. This morning, after I woke up and found it, I also discovered the sweetest note! He insisted on lunch today, not that I'm complaining. God! I can't tell you how great it feels to be done with this two-year sexual drought. After those years of Grant making me feel totally inadequate, it was an incredible feeling to just let go. I mean, really, this is just an affair but I swear, it's just what I needed to get my confidence back. Hm. Wondering if a nooner is in the cards today? OMG. I'm such a horny slut! I can't believe I'm thinking this way but he is the hottest man ever and doesn't seem to notice the ten-year age gap at all. Amazing. Hey! I made up a new word. Wanna hear? Cougarized. I cougarized Jackson Blue. Or wait, maybe he cougarized ME. Lord knows he 'ized' something and I just want more. I'll keep you posted.

Lori sipped her coffee and watched the local weather. Another hot one. Just like yesterday. Temps in this part of Texas in dead of summer never varied much. She shook her head. Things always went from hot to hotter. Then she smiled when a couple of messages popped up on the blog.

Edie: it sounds like you had a really great time! Attagirl!

Monica: I read that as "cougarized Jackson BLUE". And I thought, damn woman, slow down. You don't want to screw him black and blue. *G* Or maybe you do. Whatever floats your boat. But it sounds like he's up for whatever you want to dish out. Or take. Either way.

Rissa: Cougarized, I love it! And a naughty nooner...whoo-damn. You are the ultimate cougar. Have fun and roar loud.

Lori chuckled as she logged off and then set her laptop on the coffee table. Anticipation curled through her belly. Only a few more hours and she'd see Jackson again. Already wondering what she would wear, feeling an excitement she hadn't experienced in too many years to count, she was considering a nice long bath when her cell phone rang. Frowning a little, she looked at the display screen. Grant. Wow, talk about turning a smile upside down. Her good mood plummeting faster than the speed of light, she answered.

"Hi, Lori. How are you?"

"I'm fine, Grant. Guess you heard I moved back to Sandy Creek? Did your mom and dad tell you?" Richard and Patsy Donovan still lived here and no doubt word was all over town that she'd returned. She hadn't gone into town much, dreading questions that would surely come about the death of her long-term marriage. Sandy Creek was a small town, after all, and nothing stayed secret for long.

He paused a moment. "Yeah, they did. Mom is wondering why you haven't been by to see her."

Lori sighed. This was none of Grant's business but she didn't want to fight with him. She'd had enough of that during the last five years of their marriage. "You know I love your folks, Grant, and I don't need a lecture from you. I've been busy unpacking. I've barely settled in. There just hasn't been time."

"Yeah, I understand that. I'm still trying to figure out why you moved back to that hole-in-the-wall place. You could've stayed here. You had a job and a life you loved. You had friends here."

"*Couple* friends, you mean." Lori shifted and closed her eyes briefly. He just didn't get it. "They all took sides or drifted away after the divorce. My job was okay but not my dream."

"What *are* your dreams these days?"

Anger whipped at her and her hand tightened around the phone. "My dreams? You are just now recognizing the fact that I had them? What the hell, Grant? I wanted kids and I wanted to run my own business. None of that ever happened. Either the time wasn't right for kids or there wasn't the money for me to start up a business."

"I'm sorry."

"Jeez. Why are we having this discussion now? You should be concentrating on your new life. How is Victoria, by the way?" Not so long ago, she might have used a snarky tone when referring to the woman who'd replaced her in Grant's life but there really was no animosity left. She was moving on with her life and feeling happier than she had in a very long time.

"She's fine." Lori heard an answering coldness in his voice but didn't have the patience with him required to dig deeper. "What about you? Are you seeing someone?" Then he laughed. "Probably not in Sandy Creek. Pretty isolated place."

He sounded so downright pleased about that, her temper finally snapped. "As a matter of fact, I am." Then she forced herself to calm. Blowing out a breath, she thought of last night and her upcoming lunch date with Jackson. "Look, this is none of your business. I've moved on with things just as you have. Did you call to ask about my love life?"

Another pause hung over the airwaves. "No. Look, calling was a mistake. I just wanted to see how you were."

After a few more awkward moments they disconnected leaving Lori feeling confused and angry. They'd been divorced for two years yet just hearing his voice brought back memories of pain and loss and inadequacy. She and Grant had grown up together and grown older together. Losing him had been like losing a limb and his final abandonment had nearly killed her. Now, here she was, starting over again, finding a man, and rediscovering herself, and he had to call and bring it all back.

"No," she said with finality. "I'm done with this." Standing, she glared at the little cell phone as if it would argue with her. She wasn't going to let Grant mess with her emotions for one more minute. She was done with him. She'd moved on and for the first time in years she felt great about her life. Some people were just energy suckers and her ex was one of them. This wasn't something she needed and she sure as hell wasn't going to waste another moment of this sunny, beautiful day on Grant.

Resolve burning in her bones, she made her way into the bathroom to get ready for her date.

* * * * *

The crowd at The Coffee Cup, a local lunch spot, was beginning to thin by the time she and Jackson finished eating. He'd picked her up promptly at noon and now, here they were, talking about everything and nothing over the remnants of their lunch. As the waitress cleared away the dishes and refilled their tea glasses, Jackson reached across the expanse of the table and took her hand. Several sets of eyes focused on them but Lori ignored the uncomfortable feeling of being scrutinized. His thumb brushed across her knuckles and his gaze locked for a nanosecond on her lips. He smiled.

"Glad you came to lunch today. You don't know how old it gets hanging out at the rig constantly. This is a nice break."

"For me too. Wish I could be selfish and ask you to spend the day with me but I guess that's not in the cards, huh?"

He grinned and shook his head. "I wish." Lifting her hand, he leaned close and pressed his lips to her fingers. His dark eyes connected with hers, full of smoldering emotion. Jackson spoke quietly in the low, husky drawl that sent instant heat to her pussy. "I keep thinking about last night, darlin'.

There's nothing I'd like better than to spend the whole day in bed with you. You are a dangerous woman. Don't know why I thought I could have a simple lunch with you and not remember last night." He sighed. "I probably won't be able to get away tonight. We'll be setting the pumping unit on the new well today and tomorrow we'll head down the road a ways to build the new location. I figure we'll be working long into the night getting ready for that."

"Think this is gonna be a good one?"

Jackson's thumb stroked again sending a whip of warm pleasure dancing over her skin. Small talk was becoming increasingly difficult. "Yeah, you are going to be a very wealthy woman by the time we've finished. What are you going to do with all that money?"

Lori laughed and rolled her eyes. "I think mink coats are definitely *out* considering where I live and I don't have a taste for fancy cars so I reckon I'll just have to fix up the old house, for starters. Funny, Grant and I were always so stressed out about money. Not a good way to live."

"No, I guess not," he said. "Lots of couples split up over money. Is that what happened to you?"

She shook her head. "No. We both did okay. I worked in retail and he's an accountant. We were planted firmly in the upper middle class but that didn't cause the break up. As a matter of fact—"

A kid who looked to be about sixteen came up to the table. "Sorry to interrupt but I have a big box of sandwiches and stuff ready for you, sir. Do you want me carry them out for you?"

Jackson released her hand and nodding, reached for his wallet. He handed the kid a couple of bills for a tip and pointed through the window. "Yeah, if you don't mind. That black double-cab is mine. Just set the box in the bed, will you?"

"Sure."

The boy took the money and grinned before heading off. Lori watched the kid hold the door open for an older couple and her eyes went wide. Grant's parents saw her instantly and came over. Richard was a heavyset man with thinning gray hair and Patsy, equally plump with a pretty face that reminded her so much of her ex. Instantly, Lori got up and gave them both hugs. They had been part of her life for so many years and despite the divorce, she loved them. Patsy's blue eyes, behind the lenses of her glasses, carried a tinge of worry. "How are you, honey? Why haven't you been by?"

Jackson stood then and Lori stopped Patsy's questions with a quick introduction. The older couple both frowned slightly and looked from Lori to Jackson and back again, certainly wondering why they might be together. She'd been a part of their family for twenty years and she knew it had to be hard for them to see her with someone else, despite Grant's remarriage.

"Richard and Patsy are my former in-laws," she explained briefly.

"I see. Well, nice to meet you folks." Jackson tugged her to his side and bent his head to hers making his affection for her obvious. "Honey, I'll pay the bill while you catch up." He nodded to the Donovans and walked the short distance to the cash register.

Lori sat back down in the booth and smiled. She was *not* going to act like an uncomfortable teenager. "I'm sorry I haven't been by to see you. Grandma and Grandpa's old place was a mess and I've been dealing with settling in. There just hasn't been time. I did talk to Grant this morning. He sounds good."

"That's understandable, honey," Richard said. "You just come on out for dinner soon. I'll bet Patsy could whip up something good for supper."

Patsy wasn't paying a bit of attention to her husband, seemingly focused on what Lori had just said. "You said Grant called? Guess he told you about Vickie?"

Lori frowned and shook her head. "Um. No."

"They are expecting."

"A baby?" Lori widened her eyes as unexpected hurt blasted through her. She and Grant had talked for years about starting a family but he'd never been receptive to the idea. It took her a few seconds to realize Jackson was standing nearby listening to the exchange. She got a grip and smiled. Grant was their only child. They had to be thrilled. She smiled and stood to give Patsy a hug. "That's wonderful." Looking between the two of them, she saw their worry about how she would take this news. Mustering her most cheerful expression, she settled her hand on Richard's shoulder. "You'll be great grandparents. I'm so happy for you."

Jackson cleared his throat and came up beside her. "You ready to go, honey?"

When he opened the door of the truck and she'd settled into her seat, he leaned in. "I need to run an errand next door. Do you need anything?"

Lori looked over at Cooper's Drug Store and shook her head. While Jackson went inside she mulled over the information she'd learned. Was this why Grant had called her this morning? Was it possible he was feeling a tad guilty about his treatment of her over these many years of saying no to things that were important to her? Probably not. One thing she knew for sure about Grant was his tendency to be *me first*. She didn't wish Grant and his new wife ill. She really didn't. She just wanted to move on.

In about five minutes, Jackson came out of the store carrying a small white sack, which he set between them in the truck. It wasn't until they were miles out of town that he looked over at her, an intense expression on his face. "I got you something."

"Me?"

"Yeah, open the sack."

Lori peered inside, saw a giant box of condoms, and laughed. She looked at Jackson's and rolled her eyes. "What a guy! Nice gift."

"I thought so."

"Considerate."

"Yeah, you laugh now but you'll be thanking me next time I take you to bed for marathon sex and we have plenty of supplies." He wagged his brows at her and in that moment, she thought Jackson Blue was the sexiest man alive. He was charming, funny and to-die-for good-looking.

Grant?

Grant who?

By the time they pulled up at her place, she was as glad as hell she lived out in the boonies. There wasn't a soul around and she wanted nothing more than to jump sweet Jackson's very hot bones. The second he turned off the ignition, she unhooked her seatbelt and slid across the bench seat to press herself to his side. Settling her lips next to his ear, she nipped his earlobe. "Thanks for lunch. Thanks for the gift."

"You're very welcome."

Lori wanted to touch him, needed it like air, so she pressed her breast to his arm and slid her hand over the front of his tee shirt until it lingered at the waist of his jeans.

"You said I wouldn't be seeing you for a day or two."

"Yeah." He groaned, closing his eyes, when she slipped her hand beneath his tee shirt to settle her palm on his belly. "You're playing with fire, Lori."

"Just want to give you something to think about while you're working. Do you have a problem with that?"

"Hell no. Keep it up."

When had this aggressive woman been born? Oh yeah. Last night. Feeling confident in herself and loving the touch of his belly, warm beneath her fingers, she moved her hand low to settle over his fly.

"You're hard."

Jackson groaned, arching into her hand as he unsnapped his own seat belt. "Been hard for the last hour. Just looking at you gets me hot. Figure you must be reading my mind."

Lori kissed his cheek, his strong jaw and then settled her lips at the heavy pulse in his throat. "After the little gift you bought at the drug store, I sorta put two and two together."

"God, I love a smart woman. Yeah, that's it. Unzip me, Lori."

The rasp of the zipper sounded loud in the confines of the truck cab. Lori reached into his jeans and slid his cock from its cocoon of worn denim. From the moment, he'd stood naked beside her bed, she'd wanted to taste him. He was thick, long and deliciously hard, the head dark with color. A single drop of fluid settled there, teasing her so Lori fisted her hand around the heavy stalk then sent in down until her fingers could stroke his tightly drawn balls.

Jackson sucked in a breath, the sound encouraging her exploration as she began to work his hard flesh. Finally giving in to temptation, she bent to drag her tongue over the head of his erection, gathering up the single drop of fluid, pulling him into her mouth to suck lightly.

"Ah, yeah, honey. I love your tongue on me. Suck my cock." He gathered her hair, hanging on as if for dear life. Taking him deep, she heard his indrawn breath. Satisfaction curled low in her belly as his grip on her hair tightened. She sucked him hard, then lightly, moving her lips over his cock. Power mingled with lust as Jackson arched into her mouth. "Lori, honey, you've gotta stop. Shit. I'm gonna—"

"Yes. Come on." She whispered the words, encouraging him but Jackson wasn't listening. He moved into her mouth once more then used his grip on her hair to jerk himself free.

Lori looked up, momentarily confused. His dark eyes were heavy-lidded. His teeth were gritted and a muscle worked furiously in his jaw. "Not like this," he said. "I need to be in your pussy. I need to feel you come too."

Then suddenly Jackson was upon her, undoing the button and zipper on her shorts, sliding her out of them, plunging his hands into the front of her drenched panties. His fingers on her flesh had her gasping. He worked her like a master, a low frantic growl coming from his lips.

"Can't wait," she whispered. "I need to come. Now."

Lori shimmied out of her panties and toed off her sandals. Desperation to take Jackson's hard, thick cock blasted through her body like a jackhammer. She wanted hard and fast and now. She heard the crinkling of paper as Jackson dug through the white paper sack and before she could say *fuck me now, fuck me hard,* he grabbed her around the waist and settled her over his cock.

She came down on him with a sigh of relief but it was short lived.

Nerve endings she'd never known she had sat up and howled. Jackson dug his fingers into her ass cheeks as his mouth moved over her silk and lace covered breast. His teeth found one tightly drawn nipple and scraped with delicate precision until she cried out, writhing on his cock like a wild woman. Up and down she moved as Jackson rose up to meet her, burying his penis deep, touching parts of her that were unbearably sensitized.

Crying out, she squeezed his cock, milking him, taking him. Jackson reached between them, pinching her throbbing clit lightly as he bit harder at her nipple. Lori stiffened, screamed, as pleasure pulsated through her body and then Jackson was there with her, holding her as he followed her over the edge.

Chapter Five

౯౧

The oil business was an ever-changing kind of deal, Jackson mused as he stood back amid the roar of the drilling rig and watched his hands get about the business of drilling another big hole in the ground. Maybe that's why he loved the work so much. It was never boring. From the looks of the geologists' map, they were dead on to hit another big pool of crude. Several weeks ago they'd completed the other well, set the tanks that would receive the oil along with the jumping units that would stir the black stuff and pump it out of the ground. The newest well was currently bringing in close to one hundred barrels a day but that would steady out after awhile to probably nearer fifty barrels a day. Not bad and at today's prices on the market would bring a nice chunk of change to everyone who'd invested.

Lori had already started spending some of her royalties. She'd taken out a loan at Sandy Creek's only bank and started renovating the old Victorian she'd inherited. Already the stately house had gotten a fresh coat of paint, both inside and out and she'd bought new furniture. Smiling, he remembered the night he'd shown up to give her the good news about the well's production. Her laughter had led them straight to the bedroom. She was the most joyous person he'd ever met. Sweet, sassy, and funny. So easy to talk to and unlike anyone he'd ever met. She'd been through a rough couple of years but that was all changing for her. Lori was grabbing life, claiming it, and Jackson only hoped he played a part in her voyage of self-discovery.

Digging a bandana from his back pocket, he wiped the sweat from his forehead and squinted out across the barren landscape. It wasn't a bit pretty to look at but he could get used to it.

But by far the best thing about this place was Lori.

Over the past few weeks, he'd grabbed nights here and there but now he knew it would never be enough. The woman just *did* things to him that no other female had ever managed before. The age difference didn't matter to him. They might have mentioned the age gap a few times in casual conversation in a teasing sort of way but it wasn't an issue. Certainly not for him and Lori was confident enough that it seemed not to bother her either.

Good thing because he damn well wasn't going to let a few years' age difference stand in his way.

Why was dating a woman ten years older any different from him dating a much *younger* woman? Didn't seem right to his way of thinking and with her, he found there were no games. Things were real and Jackson liked *real* a whole lot. He loved the responsive way her body moved against him, the way she listened to him, not with pretense of caring but with honest understanding.

Off in the distance, he saw a rooster tail of red dust kick up behind a familiar old truck. Smiling, he watched it approach. Jackson stepped down from the elevated platform and jogged down the four steps just as Lori got out of the truck. Pleasure whipped through his system and before he could think, he had her wrapped up in his arms, his lips hungrily devouring hers.

Her response to his kiss almost brought him to his knees but then hoots and hollers from the crew had him drawing back, grinning. Fortunately Lori was smiling, too, even as she gasped for breath.

"Hey," he said, bending low to give her another quick kiss. "This is a surprise."

"Ooh. I think I like surprising you if this is your response. I thought I'd be nice and pick up some lunch today. I know you guys are really busy with the drilling."

"Ah, now that's sweet."

Lori chuckled. "As long as you keep remembering that I can be naughty too."

"How could I forget?"

Once the crew got their lunches, Jackson lowered the tailgate of Lori's pickup and they sat together with chips, turkey sandwiches, and a couple of soft drinks. "So what's going on at your place?"

"Things are quiet around my place at the moment. The furniture store delivered some more stuff this morning." She flashed him a naughty grin. "Got a new bed. A bigger one. Wanna help me break it in?"

"I wouldn't miss it. How about tomorrow night? I have a present."

Lori laughed. "Another one? Honey, I think we're all set with condoms."

"Hey, credit me with being more original than that." Jackson pulled a face and wagged his eyebrows at her. "I placed an order from this sexy online company and I have some new toys for my girl."

"Surely I won't have to play with them all by myself?"

"Hell no! Honey, these are toys for two."

"Sounds like—"

His cell phone buzzed so he stepped down from his perch and fished it out of his pocket. "Hold that thought." He answered the phone and smiled at the sound of his mother, Pamela's voice.

"Hey, Mom. How are you? How's Dad?"

"Jackson, how are *you*, honey? I haven't heard from you in so long I figured I should call. We're both doing well but missing you."

"Miss you too. I'm up to my neck in crude around here so I've been a little tied up."

"Did I catch you at a bad time?"

He hurried to reassure her. "No, Mom, not at all. As a matter of fact, I'm having lunch with a pretty woman at the moment. She's almost as sweet and every bit as pretty as you, too." Jackson watched the sexy glint in Lori's blue eyes soften into a dreamy expression. He gave her a wink and reached out to take her hand.

"I'm glad you've met someone, honey. Since she's there with you, I won't press for details but you'd better believe I'm calling you back for all the deets."

"I'll look forward to it. What's going on around there?"

"Your sister, Ashley called. Phil has some time off and they are bringing the kids and coming to Amarillo for a few days. I was hoping to have a little mini reunion next weekend since they don't come in from Cali all that often. We'll have lots of food, barbecue in the backyard, kids swimming in the pool and tearing the hell out of my house. What do you think? Can you come? Bring your girl. What's her name?"

"Whoa. Mom you're speed-talking again. I swear my head is spinning." He laughed. "Her name is Lori Donovan. Let me ask her."

Jackson looked at Lori. "Want to come to Amarillo next weekend? Meet the family? Pig out?"

Surprise bloomed on her face, coloring her cheeks and he wondered at it but then she nodded. "Sounds good."

He spoke into the phone again. "She said she'd love to come. Can we bring something?"

Pamela Blue laughed. "Heck no, Jackson. Just bring an appetite."

When he disconnected, he saw Lori stick her empty drink can into a sack along with other trash. A tiny frown line appeared between her eyes. "Did I put you on the spot?"

She looked up at him and smiled, shaking her head. "No, not at all. Just a little concerned about what they might think about the gap in our ages. That's all."

Jackson moved in and planted his hands on either side of her thighs. "Honey, I'm a grown man. I'm thirty-one years old. I'll go out with whom I please. My folks know that."

"I just don't want them to get the wrong idea."

"About what? What the hell are you talking about?"

Lori rolled her eyes. "I don't know. I'm not expressing myself very well." She settled her hands on his shoulders. "I don't want them to start speculating or suggest this is something more than it is."

Something cold and hard moved through his body and it felt a hell of a lot like anger. "What the fuck do you think we have here, darlin'? Are you trying to convince me and maybe even yourself that this is nothing more than a meaningless affair? Is this just a bunch of hot humping between the sheets and then we say, 'hey this was great' and then head off our own separate ways?"

"You don't have to say it that way."

"Level with me. You've never played games with me before so you'd damn well better tell me what you mean. How do you feel about me, Lori?" Her eyes instantly filled with tears. He gentled his voice. "Aw, damn it, woman, don't cry. I can't stand it. You're making me feel like an ass."

She blinked rapidly then gave him a weak smile. "I'm sorry, Jackson. I didn't want to read any more into our relationship than something casual. I just—"

"Shh." He reached out and cupped her cheek as he leaned closer. "Don't overanalyze everything. I know you've been hurt and you're skittish. We have fun right?"

"Uh-huh."

"Then let's make sure that continues. I care about you. You are a great woman with a huge heart and I'm not going anywhere. Let us leave it at that for now."

Jackson helped Lori down from the tailgate of the truck, slammed it shut, then walked her to the door of her truck. Once she was settled inside, she looked up at him. Her expression was soft and just a little confused but he didn't want to be dishonest with her. It wasn't his style. Cupping the side of her neck, he leaned in and kissed her long and hard. Once she was breathless, he drew back and stared into her eyes. "Just one more thing, honey, and it has to be said. This isn't just an affair for me. You have the right to know that."

* * * * *

Lori returned home, shaken to her core. She immediately booted up her laptop and fired off an instant message to her friend, Autumn.

Lori: Hey, Autumn. Are you there?

Autumn: I'm here. You okay?

Lori: I don't know. God, I wish we lived closer. I'd love to chat face-to-face but it's just not possible. I need help.

Autumn: What's wrong, honey?

Lori: It's Jackson. He just told me that what we have is more than an affair.

Autumn: Aw, sweetie, why is this a problem? This is a good thing, right?

Lori: I'm scared, Autumn. Just plain out-of-my-pants scared.

Autumn: About what? Tell me.

Lori: I don't know. I just don't know. When I'm with him, I can't keep my hands off him. He's sexy as hell and funny. He's intelligent. He's everything a woman would want. And when I'm not with him, he is on my mind constantly.

Autumn: I don't get it. What's holding you back? Sounds to me like you're crazy about him.

Lori: siiiiigh. I AM. I'm falling hard and fast. Jackson is perfect for me.

Autumn: Still not getting it. Go for it, honey. You deserve it.

Lori: Maybe I just don't trust my judgment, Autumn. I knew Grant forever. We grew up together and were married for twenty years and I couldn't make it work.

Autumn: You??? It takes two to make a marriage successful and from what you told me, Grant quit trying. Not you.

Lori: I guess I'm just scared.

Autumn: Are you worried about the age difference between you and Jackson? If you are, hang on to your hat because I'm coming out to west Texas to smack some sense into you.

Lori: lol. Nah, not necessary. Honestly? Our age difference seldom comes up. It hasn't been an issue for us. Jackson is a grown man and really grounded. And the way he touches me? Nope. It hasn't been a big deal.

Autumn: Like I said, go for it!

Lori: Listen to this…he invited me to meet his family in Amarillo.

Autumn: Holy shit! That sounds serious.

Lori: I'm trying not to think about it as a big deal but I can't help it. Age hasn't been an issue between Jack and me but his family might think differently.

Autumn: They'll be nuts not to love you. In the end, this is about you and Jackson and what you want.

Lori: You're right, Autumn. Why are you always right? sigh. I can do this. I'm going to grab what I want and, hell yes, I want Jackson. Life is about taking chances and maybe I'm ready.

Autumn: Of course I'm always right. Seriously, you've already taken the first step. The rest should be a piece of cake. Happiness is rare and you have a chance here. Grab it and hold on tight.

Later that night, Lori sat snuggled against Jackson on the brand new outdoor couch on her backyard patio. Autumn's words ran through her mind, sinking in and holding on. She was right. Life was short and if a woman was lucky enough to get a second chance at love, she would be a fool to let fear stop her. Tonight, Jackson had shown up with a couple of thick t-bone steaks he'd cooked on her new barbecue grill and the scent of charcoal hung heavily in the air. Stars were sprinkled across the dark blue sky and in the distance a coyote howled.

A perfect night.

Lori pointed to the center of the fairly ordinary backyard. "And right there is where I'm putting the pool."

"Mm. And some nice decking, maybe? I know a guy who does great work. That would look nice, honey."

"I'm trying not to get carried away here but, dang it, Jackson, I'm staying. I might as well improve the property. My grandparents would want that. This is my home. When I was a kid, I dreamed of having a pool. Silly, I know."

Jackson's arm was draped over her shoulder and he sent his hand on a lazy path over her bare arm. "Not silly at all. What else do you want to do with this oodles and gobs of cash?"

She ran her hand down his hard thigh to settle comfortably on his knee. "I don't know. I've been thinking about starting my own business."

"Tricky deal with the economy these days."

"Don't I know it. I have a business degree and I figure I should put it to use. I might open some kind of gift shop. Pretty small scale with some unique items in addition to a few antiques."

Jackson laughed. "Ah, girly foo foo stuff."

Laughing too, she made a fist and playfully popped his rock-hard belly. "And what's wrong with girly foo foo stuff?"

"Not a damn thing." Jackson caught her puny fist and kissed her fingers. "I love women. Don't forget I have four sisters and a mother."

"Bet it was nice having such a big, loving family."

"It was. Still is. We're a rowdy crew but we care about each other. Ash and her family live in San Diego. Marilyn and her husband are in Boulder. The other two sisters married and stayed in Amarillo. The folks love that."

Lori went quiet as worry teased the edges of her thoughts. "It was nice of your mom to invite me to the family shindig." She tried to keep her tone light despite how nervous she was.

Jackson reached out, placed his finger under her chin until he stared intently into her eyes. "Stop it, Loralee."

"Stop what?"

"Don't play innocent with me. Even if I didn't know you so well, I'd pick up on all those nervous vibes you're giving off. My family will love you."

Like you love me, Jackson?

She wanted to ask it. It was on the tip of her tongue. Yeah, she might be more forward than ever before but she wasn't crazy. Love was a gift and a smart woman didn't beg for it. She accepted when it was offered and he wasn't offering, at least not yet.

"And I'll love them, too," she said. "What will they think about our age difference? Really? I don't want to cause you any trouble with them."

He smiled and kissed her softly. A tender whip of heat electrified her flesh, making her shiver. "Know what they'll say?"

"What?" she whispered.

"They'll say, 'Damn, Jackson how did a big lug like you get so lucky and meet such an amazing woman?'"

Emotion hit her along with a huge blast of love. Her heart tightened then threatened to pound from her chest. "They will huh?"

"They will. Kiss me, sweet thing, and stop your worrying."

She didn't have to be asked twice. Lori sank into Jackson when he wrapped her up in his arms and kissed her hungrily. He buried his tongue deep, sweeping the sides of her cheeks, her teeth and her tongue. Whimpering at the pleasure that flashed through her system, she felt her nipples pearl tight to press against the lace of her bra. And then Jackson's fingers were there, oh yes, right there, sweeping lightly and then with increasing pressure. Her panties were soaked through, her pussy responding to his touch. "Take me to bed," she murmured. "Please, Jackson."

He settled his mouth at the curve of her neck, teasing the sensitive spot with his lips. Lori shivered. "Yeah, we have a new bed to break in."

"We do. Come on."

They'd been sitting outside since dusk but now it was dark, so together they turned on assorted lamps to light their way. Jackson paused in the living room to shuck his boots and Lori, kicked off her flip-flops. When he straightened, he held out his hand. "Let's go."

Lori headed for the nightstand and turned on a small lamp and then heard Jackson's chuckle. "That's some bed. I noticed you'd traded up for a king sized."

"You're a big man, Jackson. What other kind of bed would I get?"

Jackson's dark eyes glinted with hunger, his expression intense. "You did good."

Lori had fallen in love with the big four-poster at first sight. Whitewashed wood glistened, displaying intricate carvings and the new spread she'd bought was perfect. Varying shades of blue shot with silver threads gave the room an elegance that Lori loved. Fussy without being overwhelmingly feminine. Yes, the bed was impressive but her eyes locked on a big red gift bag in the middle of it. A fancy logo on the side said *Naughty Naughty*. No, he hadn't been joking about the toys because she'd heard of this company and knew what they sold.

"Oh boy, what did you do, honey?"

Jackson's laugh was low, rich, and so sexy her bare toes curled on the carpet. "I sneaked it in here while you were busy in the kitchen."

She glanced at him, saw his big, muscular body backlit by the meager light and her pussy responded to the sexuality he exuded. All that raw power blasting in her direction was a complete turn-on. Here was a man who wanted her, thought her sexy and desirable. Hurtful words spoken in years past by Grant, a man who was supposed to love her, whispered tauntingly through her mind and she suddenly knew, with overwhelming clarity that she wasn't in any way deficient. She saw herself through Jackson's dark eyes and realized she had a perfect opportunity to do the kinds of things she'd always wanted. Now was the time. This was the place.

She and Jackson might not have forever but, damn it, they had now.

Lori arched her brow and tilted her head. "Show me what you've got."

Jackson went quiet then walked to the bed and dumped the colorful contents across her brand new bedspread. "A nice selection. Lady's choice."

Walking to his side, she reached out, a smile pulling at her lips as simultaneous heat rolled through her body in a giant wave. Picking up a slender vibrator, she noted the little notches that would press her clit and touched them with a finger. "A rabbit."

"Do you have one?"

"No. You can use it on me tonight." She looked through the other toys finding nipple clamps, Ben Wa balls, a silver bullet, and some cherry flavored gel. Lori picked up a box of condoms and grinned at Jackson. "Hm. We already have a year's supply of condoms."

"Hey! These are ribbed. You'll like 'em."

"Bet I will, cowboy. How about we try them out but first I'd like you to take off your clothes."

"Bossy. I like it. Why don't you just tell me what you want and I'll deliver."

"Sure you can? Deliver? I can be awfully demanding."

Jackson was obviously turned on by her aggressive behavior. He moved in on her sending one arm around her waist and hauled her flush against his hard belly. He leaned close enough that she could feel his hot breath against her lips. Lori shivered. "I happen to like demanding. Give it to me. I promise I can take it."

Chapter Six

ꙮ

Jackson had no problem, none, with Lori taking the lead. To him there was nothing sexier than a woman who knew what she wanted and went for it. She reached for the hem of his tee shirt and he obliged her by bending a little so she could more easily remove it. When she tossed it aside and focused her hungry gaze on his chest, Jackson felt his cock go rigid against the fly of his jeans. She buried her nose against his chest and drew her hands gently over his muscles. Jackson sucked in a breath

"You feel so good, Jackson. I love the way your skin feels against my fingers." Lori sent her hands on a teasing quest over his ribs, his belly, then traced a small circle around his belly button.

"You're teasing me, darlin'," he managed. Bending his head a little, he inhaled the subtle scent of her hair, then gritted his teeth when she reached for the snap and zipper on his jeans. Her hand sank into the front of his briefs to stroke him. "Pull it out. Yeah, like that."

"God, Jack." She breathed the words as she gripped his heavy length. Her hands went down then up slowly examining every inch. Finally, she snagged a bit of denim with her fingers and pushed his jeans down his hips.

Jackson shoved them down the rest of the way and kicked them aside. Finally he stood there stark naked as Lori looked her fill. His cock rose higher, harder.

"Undress me too."

"My pleasure." He moved in and lifted the skimpy bit of silky fabric over her head and tossed it aside. Then he reached for the button and zipper on her casual khaki shorts all the while keeping his eyes locked on her pretty breasts pressing against the soft pink lace of her bra. It was low cut and sexy, flesh mounding over the tops. His mouth went dry.

When he pushed the shorts from her hips and they slid down her long beautiful legs, she kicked them away and stood facing him wearing nothing but the pale pink bra and a little scrap of satiny pink panties. A tiny smile curved her lips.

"Like what you see?"

"Hell darlin', I *love* what I see."

When her smile widened, he moved in, gathered her hair in one fist and pulled gently to expose the long expanse of her neck. Burying his lips against that tender flesh, he sucked at it, nipped gently, before pressing kisses to her shoulders and the tempting mounds of her breasts overflowing the top of her bra. Jackson scraped his teeth over diamond-hard nipples and Lori gasped in response. "Take it off, Jack. I want your mouth on me."

Bossy.

He liked it.

Obliging her, he reached around to the bra fastening and within seconds, her breasts were bare and his for the taking. Her puckered nipples were pure temptation and he pulled one and then the other into his mouth to suck. He glanced up to see her eyes closed as she absorbed each sensation. "Hang on."

Jackson lifted her into his arms and settled her amid the naughty toys in the middle of the big bed. He gathered some up and pushed them out of the way and then, bending over her, he kissed her hard. "Ready to break this bed in good and proper?"

"Oh yeah. Bring it on."

Laughing, he looked through the stash of things until he found a pair of nipple clamps. Silky black feathers hung from them and Jackson thought they would look beautiful against her fair skin. He held them up for Lori's inspection and watched her eyes go wide. Then she flashed a sexy grin. "Put them on me."

"Yes, ma'am." Testing the pads of the clamps for softness, he sucked one nipple lightly, feeling it pucker against his tongue and then he settled the clamp into place. Lori sucked in a breath. Jackson blew on the feather and watched it dance against her breast. "How does that feel? Comfortable? I don't want it to hurt."

"It doesn't." At least not in a bad way. *Can I get any wetter?*

"Good." He went to work on the other nipple and when he was finished, licked and played until Lori was squirming against the mattress.

"More. I need more, Jackson."

"And you're gonna get it, too, but not before I lick every sweet inch of your skin. Have I told you how great you taste, darlin'?"

"Tell me again."

"You are sweet and you have the finest skin. I have a weakness for blondes. Did you know that?"

"Blondes named Lori, I hope."

He laughed. "Ah, honey, you are the only over-the-top sexy blonde on my radar these days. The only woman *period.*"

Spreading open-mouthed kisses over her sternum and down her ribs, he trailed his fingers over her belly, the curve of her waist. Finally Jackson moved between her thighs. Kneeling there, he reached beneath her to grip the globes her of ass. Kneading her, he bent low to snag the top of her panties between his teeth.

"Jackson!"

Hunger blasted through his body as he caught her scent in his nostrils and heard the sexy sound of Lori's voice. Tugging, he pulled at the tiny scrap of satin until he exposed her pussy. Jackson slid his fingers beneath the elastic in the back and soon the panties were history, tossed to the floor with the other discarded clothing. He reached out for a slender tube.

"What's that?"

"Cherry stuff. Suddenly I'm hungry for desert." He removed the cap and squeezed out a dollop of reddish tinted fluid, which he carefully spread over every bit of her drenched pussy. Spreading her labia, he painted her pink flesh with the liquid. "This is a clit stimulator. Ever use this before?"

"No. Umm, that feels warm."

Paying particular attention to the swollen knot, he gently spread it all around, pinching lightly until Lori moved her hips upward. She began to pant. "Lick me. Eat me, Jackson."

"You are so demanding, honey. I like that."

"Now, Jack!"

Bending low, he stiffened his tongue and sent it suddenly and deeply into her vagina. Inner walls clamped down hard as she cried out as if in relief. Fucking her with his tongue, gripping her ass with his hands, he inhaled the scent of cherry and woman and heat until he knew she needed more. The whimpering little sounds she made tore him apart and he wouldn't stop until he'd given her everything he could.

He swept his tongue over the melting flesh of her pussy, tasting the cherry, fucking her with his mouth until he finally drew on her clit, sucking gently. Lori's cry was sharp and edgy. He kept her there, hanging on by her toenails, until finally he grabbed up the rabbit vibrator. A soft whir of sound surrounded them. Jackson sat back on his haunches and smeared lube on the pale pink toy before sliding it deep into her pussy.

Lori's eyes went wide, connecting with his for a brief intense moment, before she finally closed them again.

Her clit was hard and swollen so it was easy to slip the ears around either side allowing her to absorb the vibrations where she needed it. "Talk to me," he demanded.

"Can't. I can't. Jackson!"

He stroked her vibrating clit with his tongue. Lori panted out short staccato breaths. Her hands fisted in the bedspread and then reached up to frantically grab his shoulders as if seeking any kind of solid thing in the storm. He increased the speed of the toy and Lori cried out as she flew apart beneath him.

Flipping off the vibrator, he removed it and tossed it aside. Unable to resist, he gently applied this mouth to her pussy, calming her for a moment before gradually bringing her up again. She writhed against his mouth and then made a frantic little sound as he sat up again.

"Please."

"I'm not going anywhere, darlin'." He reached for a condom, so desperate for relief his hands shook as he tore into the box. Ripping open the wrapping with his teeth, he slid the heavily ribbed condom over his aching cock. And then Lori was there, sitting up, stroking him with frantic fingers. She cupped his balls, playing gently with them until Jackson wanted to howl. They were hard and tightly drawn against his body.

"Fuck, Lori."

She nipped his chest as she played and suddenly even that wasn't enough. Gripping her shoulders, he pushed her down so that he could come over her. Belly to belly, thighs rubbing together provocatively, he settled his mouth over her nipples confined in the clamps. He sucked, licked and pulled on them while Lori squirmed. Heat rolled through his belly when he took his cock in hand to drag through the soft, warm layers of her cunt. Momentarily dipping the head into her opening, he quickly withdrew to circle it over her clit.

Damn! Lori wasn't the only one breathing hard. Air billowed in and out of his lungs as if he'd run a race. Sweat beaded his forehead. Knowing he must get inside her or die, he plunged deep. He sucked in a sharp breath and went still as vaginal walls compressed to squeeze him tight.

His focus zeroed in on the soft black feathers lying against Lori's pale breasts. He moved upward a tiny increment then went to work on her breasts, sending his tongue over her nipples, first one then the other. "Going to take these off, honey."

"Okay. Yes."

Unclipping the first one, he quickly drew it deep into his mouth to gently suck, offering relief and then he released the other nipple, too. Lori made a soft, low sound and he began to plunge deep into her body. Still it wasn't enough. Not hard enough. Not deep enough.

Jackson lifted her ankles into the bend of his elbows and increased the pressure of each stroke until pleasure raced over his flesh. Lori's head moved back and forth and then her neck arched. The temptation was irresistible so he opened his mouth there briefly before moving lower to suck her nipple.

With brutal force, he fucked her, feeling the hard press against his balls, the tightening of her pussy, the pulsing of it against his cock. And then it hit. Pleasure swept him like a wildfire, burning, pulsing. When Lori's orgasm sped through her body, her shriek of pleasure sounding like music to his ears, he finally let go.

* * * * *

Smoky Joe's was packed with partiers tonight, as she and Jackson sat at their table taking a breather from all the dancing they'd done. It was a fairly big honky tonk and a nice place to have some fun considering the small size of Sandy Creek. Residents from other area towns mingled with the locals as they crowded the large parquet dance floor two-stepping to a Rascal Flatts song. Neon lights from the oversized beer signs on the walls cast myriad colors over the dancers. Moments ago they'd returned to their table and he'd playfully given her chair a tug to draw her closer to his side. Now they sat together, Jackson nursing a beer while she sipped a frozen margarita.

"I've been to Smoky Joe's before but it's sure a lot nicer being here with you," Jackson said as he lifted two fingers in the air signaling to their waitress that they needed another round. "Do you see a lot of people you know here tonight?"

"Quite a few," she said leaning close to be heard over the music and chatter. "I've kept a fairly low profile since coming back."

"Because of the divorce?"

She nodded. "Mainly. Living in Dallas, I didn't worry too much about people finding out my business. It's a big city, but things are different in Sandy Creek. People make it their business to get all the gossip, ya know? Everyone knew when Grant and I married and certainly they all knew we divorced. Doubt they know the *why* of things but I figure they'll ferret out the information soon enough."

Jackson wrapped his arm around her shoulder and pressed a kiss to her lips instantly warming them and making her wish they could just leave now and head back to her now broken-in new bed. "Before I got to know you someone mentioned he remarried pretty fast."

Lori smiled a little, somewhat surprised by how that fact didn't really bother her anymore. She figured meeting Jackson had a lot to do with that. "Yeah, he did. That last year of our marriage we did a lot of marriage counseling. Looking back, I think my insistence on it was pretty stupid. He'd been seeing another woman that whole time. Naturally, I didn't know about that."

"Why was it stupid? You were trying to save your marriage." Jackson settled back lazily in his chair crossing his booted feet at the ankle. "I figure most people would have given up easily. Counted their losses and called up a good divorce lawyer. People have forgotten that marriage is a promise, a vow, and they give up before even trying to make things work. It's a damn shame."

Comparisons between Jackson and Grant were beyond ridiculous but it was amazing to her how insightful Jackson was compared to her ex. He was just deeper, more thoughtful about things and once again it occurred to her how similar she and Jackson were in the way they looked at life. "That's the way I feel about it, too," she said. "At least I know I tried to make a go of it."

Their waitress arrived at that moment and delivered their drinks just as the current song ended, giving everyone a break from all the noise. Suddenly they both looked up at the sound of Jackson's name being called. A group of Blue Moon guys stood off in the distance, all cleaned up and ready for a night on the town, such as it was. Jackson waved.

Looking at Lori, he settled his hand on hers. "I'm going to head over and say hi and get a quick report on what happened after I left the site today. Want to come?"

She shook her head. "No, you go on. Take your time."

"What? And leave you alone to fend off all these cowboys who want to dance with you? Hell, no. I'll be right back."

Lori felt the eyes of a number of people from Sandy Creek watching covertly when Jackson stood and gave her a sexy grin before walking away. No doubt they were speculating like crazy. Well let 'em look. She'd kept visits to town with Jackson to a minimum before, but now? She just didn't care. She was happy and believed Jackson was too.

Lori looked out over the crowded room and instant recognition ripped straight through her. She sat up straighter in her chair. As the strains of a slow ballad filled the room and couples began to dance again, she spotted Grant walking toward her, determination in his eyes.

Shit!

Lori did not need a confrontation with her ex. She was done with that and what the hell was he doing here? Lori hadn't seen him for a long time and she immediately noted changes that surprised her. He had circles under his dark eyes as if he hadn't been sleeping well. Grant was still a very handsome guy but there was a weariness about him she'd never seen before. Wasn't a new, young wife supposed to be the cure-all for male aging? Shoving snarky thoughts deep and with surprise propelling her to her feet, she cocked her head and managed to be cordial.

"Grant, hi, how are you? This is a surprise."

He hugged her. They weren't enemies. They'd known each other too long and too well, despite all the hurt and animosity at the very end of their marriage. Grant smiled. "It's good to see you. You look great."

"Um thanks. What are you doing here?"

"Came to see the folks. They said they ran into you not long ago."

She started to comment about his big news but instead scanned the crowd. "Where's Victoria? Did she come with you?"

Grant frowned, his jaw tightened. "No."

Lori studied his face and spoke cautiously. "I hear congratulations are in order."

"Congratulations?" he asked blankly. "For what?"

For what?

Weird.

"I understand you and Victoria are expecting." Under the circumstances she shoved bitter memories to the back of her mind. She'd tried to talk about starting a family so many times during their marriage but Grant had always shut her down. The time wasn't right, he'd insist. Let's wait awhile longer, he'd say. But she could be a grown up. "I'm very happy for you."

Grant looked at her for several long moments. "I'm not the father."

Huh? Lori stared and shook her head. Confusion whipped through her. From all accounts he was happy in his marriage. "But your folks said — "

Grant raked his fingers through his brown hair then shrugged. "I had a vasectomy eight years ago. Can't be mine."

A slap wouldn't have affected her more.

"You mean all those years ago you did this? You never told me. I would've known about it, Grant. You never once said — "

"I knew you'd throw a hissy fit so I took care of it while I was gone. You wouldn't have known a thing, Lori. Remember that two-week seminar I attended in Denver?"

"God! You're such a liar. I can't — "

Suddenly Jackson was there with his arm around her. "Hey, darlin'. Hope I'm not interrupting."

Chapter Seven

ର

Lori managed to wrap her mouth around a word or two. To say she was furious was an understatement. To say that she was hurt was tame. Emotions rose up to choke her but she managed an introduction.

"Jackson, this is my ex-husband, Grant Donovan."

Jackson reached out for a polite handshake and Grant frowned. He stepped back and looked from Jackson to her. "I'd heard you were seeing someone." Grant nodded sharply and turned to make his way back through the crowd.

"What the fuck?" Jackson took her arm and turned her to face him. To her horror, tears were swimming in her eyes. She blinked rapidly but it was no use.

"Come on, honey," Jackson said as he pulled her against him, led her through the crowds, and into the front foyer of the club.

Lori was so thankful the honky tonk was dark but the foyer of Smoky Joe's wasn't. Bright lights nearly blinded her. "Where are we going?"

"Outside. Hang on."

Before she knew it, he had led her through the front door and around to the dark side of the building. Totally isolated here she let go of her carefully held emotions and felt tears fall. Her hands were shaking. Jackson pressed her back against the wall and swiped at her tears with his thumb.

Lori looked up at him and saw the tension etched in his rugged face. A muscle worked furiously in his jaw. "I should kick his ass for upsetting you."

"No. No, it's not worth it. It's done."

He tilted her chin up and stared at her. "Do you still love him? Tell me the truth, Lori."

She could do nothing but be honest. "No. We're done. We've been over for a long time."

"Then I don't understand."

"I just learned tonight that he lied to me about something important."

"So he's a liar *and* an asshole."

A tiny laugh bubbled up. "You've got that right."

"Want to talk about it? Do you want to tell me what he lied about that has you so upset?"

She shook her head and sighed. "Not really. It's not important now and has nothing to do with you and me. I started over a long time ago."

Jackson moved his hand into her hair. Bending close, he brushed his lips across hers. "I saw him looking at you before."

"Before?"

"He sat there looking at you for a long time before he ever walked up. The bastard. I've never been a jealous guy but tonight I figured out pretty damn quick that you were different from the other women I've known. I was pissed. I wanted to plant my fist in his face. Then when I saw that he'd upset you, I almost lost it. He still wants you, Lori."

"He can't have me."

"That's good to know, darlin', because you are taken. You're mine." Jackson's kiss was savage, primal. He parted her lips with his tongue and swept deep, drinking her breath and causing pleasure to curl low in her belly. Sending his hands over her body as if he would possess every bit of her, he finally palmed her breasts until her nipples grew hard, puckering against the cups of her bra. He thumbed the hard peaks and sensation arrowed down her center to settle tightly in her pussy. Her panties went damp, the aching sensation further enhanced by the press of his cock as he rubbed it against her repeatedly. This wasn't the time and it certainly wasn't the place but her body had other ideas.

Jackson moved his lips over her jaw and whispered against her throat. "He can't have you and I want him to know it. When we go back in there, that fool will see you as a well-loved woman. Got that, Lori?"

Before she could speak much less think, he was unzipping her jeans. She knew she should say no, but she couldn't. She was wild for him and aching and suddenly having Jackson's cock buried deep in her needy pussy was the most important thing in the world. He thrust his hand into the front of her jeans, slid it past her silky panties to cup her bare flesh. Lori cried out as his fingers worked her clit then buried them deep into her drenched heat.

"Fuck me, Jackson!"

His jaw went tight as he reached into his back pocket for protection. In the distance she heard laughter and went still. Jackson kissed her quickly. "It's okay. They went inside. We're alone."

A thrill swept her. They could be discovered at any minute and she knew it. Her heartbeat sped apace with her need to be fucked while hidden away here in the dark. When Jackson slid the condom over his stiff cock, he stared into her eyes. "I'm gonna fuck you hard, darlin'."

"Oh yeah, do it."

He pushed her jeans over her hips until they settled just below her knees. Jackson tested the wetness of her pussy again, his eyes nearly black in the shadows and then he prodded her legs open as far as they could go considering the imprisonment of her jeans. She didn't know how he would manage this but then Jackson sent his arms around her, lifted her, pressed her against the wall and without preliminaries buried his cock hard and deep inside her. Over and over he pumped into her pussy teasing every nerve ending, pressing her G-spot until wave after wave of wicked sensation swept her. Lori sent her trembling fingers into his hair and over his neck. Then finally, knowing she would fall apart at any second, she gripped his broad shoulders absorbing each thrust of his eager cock. A scream built in the back of her throat but Jackson stopped it with his mouth, drinking it down as she came hard and long, a shudder ripping through her body. Immediately he stiffened. His cock jerked deep in her center as he let go too.

Kissing her quickly, he grinned down at her. "We'd better hurry. I figure we've pressed our luck as it is."

Laughing, up at him, she nodded and within moments they were zipped up and somewhat pulled together. Hand in hand they reentered Smoky Joe's. There wasn't a soul in the entryway, thankfully, but Lori eyed a long hallway that led to the restroom area.

She smiled up at Jackson, still feeling a little quivery from her orgasm. "I think I'll head into the restroom and freshen up a little bit."

Jackson nodded. "Me too. I'll meet you back here in about five minutes, honey. Will that give you enough time?"

Lori nodded as she headed down the dimly lit hallway and into the ladies room to clean up. When she studied her reflection in the mirror that hung over the sink, she noted the swelling of her lips. Smiling, she ran her finger over them and wondered if everyone in the club would figure out that she'd been kissing a great looking guy in the dark. The thought made her laugh. She hadn't done anything quite so naughty since, well, since when she and Jackson had played with those adult toys and broken in the new bed. What on earth had happened to her? Jackson had happened, that's what, and it was a good thing. Because of him, she had a new confidence in herself and her own sexuality.

Anxious to get back to him and ready to put the confrontation with Grant behind her, she drew her fingers through her tousled hair and put it back into some kind of order. When she felt somewhat fresher, she opened the door and had taken two steps down the hallway when someone grabbed her from behind and pressed her to the wall.

"What the hell do you think you are doing?" Grant said angrily, giving her a little shake. "You are making a fool of yourself over that character."

"Get your hands off me, Grant! How dare you?"

"Mom and Dad told me about this guy you've been seeing," he spat. "The whole damn town knows you are fucking this young stud. What are you trying to prove, Lori? You don't have to do this. I want you back. You belong with me."

"The hell I do! Get your hands off me. Right now!"

"Don't touch her!" Jackson's shout rang out. She heard the sound of his boots ringing on the floor seconds before he grabbed Grant and spun him away from her. Enraged, Jackson pulled back his fist then smashed it into Grant's face, knocking him flat on his back.

Jackson was breathing hard. Lori looked at Grant as he lay sprawled on the floor until he finally sat up and swiped at his bloody lip with the back of his sleeve. Lori took hold of Jackson's arm to hold him back.

Grant sneered, pointing his finger at her. "You are making a fool of yourself, Lori."

Silence fell for a second or two. Finally she shook her head and lifted Jackson's clenched fist to her mouth. She settled her lips there then stared at her ex. "No, Grant. The only fool here is you."

Amarillo was a hell of a long distance from Sandy Creek. After a fun-filled, action-packed weekend with Jackson's family, she should've been exhausted but instead she couldn't wipe the smile from her face. Despite the five-hour drive she couldn't shake the feeling of love and acceptance she'd felt from the Blue clan.

Lori was still smiling when she and Jackson neared her place.

"I swear, Jackson, it's been hours since that great meal but I'm still so full."

He laughed. "Dad wields a mean spatula and Mom whips up the best homemade barbecue sauce in the Texas Panhandle."

She rolled her head on the truck seat to look at him. Blue lights from the glowing dashboard accentuated his strong profile and Lori felt a blast of love for him fill her with warmth. "Now I know why you are such a grilling giant," she teased.

"Learned it at my dad's knees."

"I love your family, Jack, and it's obvious they adore you."

He reached across the space and took her hand as he turned up the long drive leading to her house. "They loved you, honey. I told you, you had nothing to worry about. They want me to be happy."

"And are you?"

"More than I could've imagined."

Lori's heart thumped hard in her chest. Was it possible he cared for her the way she cared for him?

He braked to a stop in front of the house and blew out a breath. "We're home."

"Do you mean that? Is that how you see my place?"

"Get unhooked and slide over here, darlin'."

Lori removed her seat belt and Jackson reached over to pull her close. Smiling, he kissed her. Anticipation filled her. "I think we ought to think about putting in that pool, you know, fixing up the backyard. I've also been giving some thought to a recliner for the living room."

"A recliner? Oh my God, Jackson, I can see you now. Flopped back in front of the television every Sunday watching football."

One dark brow arched high as he looked at her. "Yeah, the season starts in a few months. You have a problem with me watching football, honey? You know I promise to fuck you silly during halftime so what's the problem?"

"None. No problem. What are you trying to say Jackson?"

There it was. No going back.

Jackson's teasing smile faded. Reaching out, he cupped her cheek. "I've been thinking maybe I should move in here with you. It took being back in Amarillo to make me realize it just isn't home anymore. My house is just a house. Sure I love my folks but I've come to believe my place is here with you."

"Do you mean that, Jackson?" Joy filled her heart to nearly bursting. The pain of the last few years evaporated as if they'd never existed.

"I love you, Lori. I've never felt this way about another woman. If you'll have me, I want to build a life with you. I guess the big question remains, how do you feel?"

Laughing, Lori hugged him close, kissing his cheek, his chin, every place she could reach. "I love you too, Jackson. I'll love you always. Let's go shopping for that recliner!"

Hey Ladies! Just a post to let you know Jackson has moved in and we have a brand new recliner—just for him—sitting in the living room and a few days ago I found a great retail spot in downtown Sandy Creek. I think it'll be a perfect place to open my store. So while Jackson is busy pulling Texas Crude from the ground, I'll be stocking things and getting ready to open for business. In between, it'll be a hot time on the dusty plains for Jackson and me. *naughty grin* It's funny, not so long ago I was scared spitless to begin this cougar adventure. After the disappointment of my marriage ending, I pretty much thought it was all over for me but I've learned that happy ever afters DO exist. Lucky me! Starting over has never been so much FUN!

DRIVEN

Jayne Rylon

ဆ

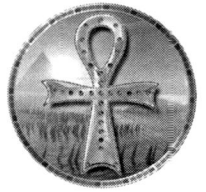

Dedication

ಐ

This book is double dedicated to Valerie Tibbs, graphic artist extraordinaire, who is crazy enough to have bought multiple copies of my stories in the name of friendship. Thank you for supporting me in so many ways. I hope you enjoy Lynn's story. This ménage is for you!

I'd also like to give a shout out to the girls I met in the bathroom of the Harrisburg, PA, airport when our flight was diverted from NYC. Thanks for offering to split a limo with me so we could all get to Broadway on time. The front row seats were worth it!

Author Note

ಐ

You'll find the women of Cougar Challenge and the Tempt the Cougar blog at www.temptthecougar.blogspot.com/

Trademarks Acknowledgement

ℬ

The author acknowledges the trademarked status and trademark owners of the following wordmarks mentioned in this work of fiction:

Blackberry: Research in Motion Limited

Camry: Toyota Motor Corporation

Google: Google, Inc.

Hertz: The Hertz Corporation

Jetway: Jetway, LLC

McDonalds: McDonalds Corporation

Peugeot: Peugeot Societe Anonyme

Sharpie: Stanford, L.P.

Superman: DC Comics

Wii: Nintendo of America, Inc.

Yankees: New York Yankees Partnership

Chapter One

ॐ

"Ladies and gentleman, this is your captain speaking."

Lynn Madison strained to hear the distorted announcement despite the shitty airplane speakers and the baby who'd been screaming since they'd taken off over an hour ago. She didn't blame the munchkin. She would bawl too if she didn't get that the gray clouds causing the turbulence, which bounced their regional jet across the sky, weren't as ominous as they appeared.

"We've been in a holding pattern, circling New York for the past fifteen minutes. Air traffic control just radioed. They're closing the airport until this cell blows over. No one's allowed in or out. We'll be diverting to Harrisburg, Pennsylvania but the delay shouldn't cost us more than an hour."

Groans of disappointment and frustration drowned out the sporadic whispers of concern proliferated by less-seasoned fliers. Lynn jumped straight to rearranging her tight schedule in her mind as the pilot droned on.

"We'll grab some fuel then wait for an update. If the situation changes, we'll let you know. We should be on the ground in about twenty minutes. Thank you for your patience. Be sure to keep your seat belt fastened; the air will be bumpy during our descent. Flight attendants, please prepare for landing."

Before the beady-eyed flight attendant could scold Lynn about stowing her netbook, she clicked to her browser window then hopped on the *Tempt the Cougar* blog she shared with a circle of friends. Her college roommate Rachel had introduced her to the group of erotic romance enthusiasts after Lynn had bitched about her bland sex life. The ladies had recommended several novels that had her eyebrows climbing and her fantasies growing spicier by the minute.

They'd quickly become very close, welcoming her into the fold and encouraging her to follow their lead in prowling for a younger man to seduce. She had to admit, the stories she'd heard since hanging around them had inspired some wicked fantasies.

Lynn envied the women who'd found love along with their wild adventures. But their proactive attitude in snatching the reins of their lives had resonated with her more than their steamy affairs. Enough to spur her to some serious introspection on what she wanted to do with the rest of her time on earth.

She'd set up a get-together with the members who lived in the tristate region while she killed time during her layover. She hadn't wanted to wait until next year's RomantiCon to meet them in person.

Thank God she'd splurged on the in-flight Wi-Fi.

LynnLuvs2Travel: Only have a few seconds, ladies. Flight is being diverted due to weather. Looks like I might have to bail on dinner. Was so looking forward to it! Sorry ☹ Expecting an update when we land. Fingers crossed I don't miss my connection to Europe!!!

Lynn sighed as she snapped the lid closed then tucked the netbook into her seatback pocket. Figured this would happen on the first day of her new life. The monumental changes she'd implemented had almost seemed too easy so far. Like blowing out the single candle that had topped the cake Rachel had baked for Lynn's fortieth birthday.

In the instant before she'd snuffed the flame, she'd wished her destiny were her own. No more wasted years, working on someone else's clock. Figuring out what she'd rather do, since retiring early would mean living in a cardboard box for twenty years or so until her investments kicked in, had taken a bit longer. But not much.

Three months later, she'd quit her job as a sourcing agent for a high-end retailer. Instant lightness had pervaded her soul when she turned in her resignation, reaffirming her decision.

After a dozen years of dreadful stays in spartan hotels, eating meat-and-potato meals or hauling ass through sketchy parts of foreign cities—all on the recommendation of her male counterparts—she knew better than most that a series of travel guides aimed at professional women going solo constituted an undiscovered niche in the market. It wasn't that the guys had deliberately sabotaged her, but her priorities ran more to a clean room, a spa and healthy meals than the number of strip clubs in a half-mile radius or a smoky bar with nonstop sports playing on a bazillion flat screen TVs.

Preoccupied with reliving the whirlwind of the past couple weeks, she was surprised at the squeak of the wheels meeting the runway.

As soon as she peered through the fogged plastic porthole to the tarmac, she abandoned hope. No fewer than a dozen jets kept their stranded plane company. Even if the sun shone bright at JFK in the next half-hour, the snafu had induced a logistics nightmare.

Sure enough, the pilot emerged from the cockpit to address the cabin face-to-face. "I'm sorry, folks, but things look worse than we originally thought. Traffic is being rerouted along the entire East Coast. We're going to let you head into the terminal until we receive a better estimate on our revised departure time."

Lynn's heart raced in her chest. She had lived well within her means despite her hefty corporate paycheck. The nest egg she'd accumulated had supplied her a shot at pursuing her dream but, in this economy, she'd had a hell of a time securing outside investors to back a no-name upstart. If the delay caused her and several hundred other people to camp out and compete for the limited vacant spots on cramped international flights, her itinerary could be ruined.

Everything hinged on making it to her starting point as scheduled. Train passes, local guides, connections, sold-out hotels...

The idea of all the lost work, not to mention cash for the original reservations and the last-minute bookings, had tears stinging her eyes. Would her old job consider rehiring her if this venture flopped? Probably not.

She gathered her belongings then filed down the stairs onto the tarmac for the march into the dinky terminal. On top of everything else, they had to be stranded at a two-gate airport with rudimentary facilities and limited options for connections.

Note to self... Include a chapter on travelers' insurance and the appropriate amount of time to leave between flights. Not that the six hours she'd allotted would help much in this situation. The insurance policy she'd selected would cover her flight arrangements if necessary but nothing could recoup the lost time. She'd have to drop chapters of her book.

As the herd of disgruntled passengers trundled up the ramp into the steel and glass building, which seemed out of place in the surrounding fields, they merged with the unfortunate occupants of the other impacted flights. A red-faced man doused in cheap cologne yelled into his Blackberry. He cut her off in his dash to hit up the airline representatives waiting inside. He rammed into her shoulder, knocking her oversized purse containing her netbook onto her elbow. The shifting weight threw her off balance on the slick surface.

Lynn skidded several feet toward the railing before a warm, muscled arm wrapped around her waist and a grumpy mumble washed over her earlobe. "Asshole."

She flinched, attempting to shy away. "What is wrong with people? I tripped."

One touch from an unknown man and she just about swallowed her tongue despite his rude treatment. *Lame!*

A carefree laugh replaced the foul temper she'd attempted to deflect. "Sorry, gorgeous. Not you. I meant that asshole who shoved you. He's lucky I don't kick his inconsiderate ass."

Her imagination ran wild at his tone—confident, worldly, bold, gallant but not too stuffy. The midnight voice colored by subtle hints of a Mediterranean accent inspired a million dirty thoughts that had her squirming. The broad hand on her ribs flexed so close to her breast she sucked in a gasp, willing her nipples to stop hardening beneath her thin, silk blouse.

"Damn, are you hurt?" He spun her into the shelter of his arms, his palms bracing her shoulders

So young! Heat blossomed in her cheeks. Here she was, lusting after a man at least a decade younger than her who probably thought himself a good Samaritan for helping his elder. As quick as she chastised herself, a naughty whisper invaded her embarrassment. *The Cougar ladies had scored men like this. Those lucky bitches!*

Hell, some of them had even managed to bag *two* virile studs.

"Let me help you inside."

Did he think her deaf and dumb on top of clumsy after that giant space out?

"I'm fine. Really." She shrugged from his hold, instantly regretting the loss of his touch. Her skin tingled where his fingers had rested. "Thank you."

"Any time."

She picked up the pace to avoid an awkward silence as he shuffled along next to her through the crowd, but he somehow managed to dodge a harried mom pushing a double stroller, a gentleman wrestling with a cello and a couple holding hands to keep even with her.

In her peripheral vision, she admired the agile maneuvers of his lean but built body. His black duffle, peppered with logos, rode against a trim hip covered in the dark navy denim favored by recent trends. The lighter creases around his upper thighs led her straight to dangerous territory. She jerked her gaze upward but had to cant her head pretty far to glimpse his unruly brown waves beneath a red baseball cap with something embroidered on the front.

His scruffy jaw couldn't obscure his sculpted cheekbones. The shadowed skin highlighted the contrast of his bright blue eyes. The impact of his stunning looks almost had her tripping again. It'd been fifteen years since she'd gotten her hands on prime beef like that.

Lynn Marie, how crass! Maybe the Cougars really were rubbing off on her.

"So, where were you headed?" No hint of exertion roughened his tone. Funny, her heart beat as hard as if she'd run a marathon.

"JFK."

"Me too." A grimace tugged his stunning mouth into a scowl.

They emerged from the Jetway into a tiny holding area crammed beyond capacity. Instead of wasting time at the airline's inundated desk, she headed for the departure board. Mr. Young-'n'-Sexy followed two steps behind. She adjusted her bag to cover her ass then tugged the hem of her skirt lower on her thighs when she sensed his stare on them. No use in advertising her sag.

Damn it, she couldn't remember the last time she'd fallen victim to an attraction so sudden and fierce. Of course, she had to waste it on someone out of her league whom she'd never see again after these five minutes fate had thrust them together passed.

The red status lights painting the departure and arrival board into a facsimile of something out of Amsterdam's infamous district had her heart plummeting. Every flight originating east of the Mississippi had been cancelled.

For three seconds, she forgot all about the hunk.

"Looks like we're going nowhere fast." The guy shoved his hat from his head, scrubbing his fingers through the thick mass of his luscious hair.

"I have five hours until my connection, maybe it'll clear up by then."

He scrunched his nose and gave his head a tiny shake but stopped short of contradicting her. Probably because he saw her fingernails gouging her palm around the strap of her bag.

"Maybe."

Lynn peered at the churning mass of people—all talking at once, calling loved ones or scrambling to make alternate arrangements—while she searched for a place to sit. Maybe if she could get online she would find some updated info. When two men in business suits abandoned a bench nearby, she plopped onto it. Electric sparks shot along her leg when the hottie perched beside her, their knees touching.

"I'm Sebastian, by the way." He tossed her a dazzling grin as he dug in his pocket for his neon green smartphone. When he leaned to the side for better access, he invaded her personal space in ways that had a riot of butterflies taking flight in her stomach. His chest, covered in snug gray t-shirt with faded charcoal designs, pressed close.

If she turned a teensy bit she could imagine herself in his arms. If she lifted her face an inch or two he would have easy access to claim her lips. Not that he'd want to. A man like him must have women falling all over him. Younger, more beautiful women. Women who'd have some clue of what to do with a sex god. Women who weren't afraid to go after what they wanted.

She cleared her throat then fished out her netbook. "I'm Lynn."

"Pretty. It fits."

Did she imagine the flare of desire in his amazing eyes? She could have stared into them all day if his phone hadn't chosen then to buzz as whoever he'd whipped off a text message to must have responded. Probably his girlfriend *du jour* or a booty call he'd stand up in New York.

The website for her airline had crashed by the time she remembered what she'd been doing. No doubt due to the thousands of people in situations as urgent as hers within a six-state radius. She clicked refresh then sighed as the browser's progress icon spun and spun. No hope for it.

While she waited, she tried to ignore the growling of her stomach drowning out the click of Sebastian typing fast and furious with his thumbs. In anticipation of her rich dinner at the swank Manhattan restaurant, she'd skipped breakfast.

"Will you hold my spot for a minute?" He patted the bench as he rose, leaving his bag behind.

Lynn couldn't resist teasing him. "Well, you don't look like a terrorist but I'm not sure I can vouch for the contents of your unattended bag."

"Gorgeous, you're welcome to peek at my underwear if you like but I won't stay away from the most beautiful woman in Harrisburg more than two minutes. Tops. You can time me." She had no doubt he intended the racy implications of his smoky tone when he paired it with a wink that melted her insides.

Her tongue almost dragged the floor as she watched his tight ass flex in time to his strut until he faded into the crowd.

Screw the airline's site, she needed reinforcements. Fast.

LynnLuvs2Travel: OMG! Still stuck in the airport, no hope for making dinner. Hottest guy ever rescued me from splattering on the runway. Now sitting next to me since he's heading to JFK too. You all are a bad influence! I can't stop thinking about what he'd be like in bed. Blue, blue eyes. Body to die for. Sexy accent. Killer smile. God, he even smells good.

I think I might have had a mini orgasm just looking at him. Too bad he's probably not even thirty yet.

She'd barely hit the send button when a flashing box with Rachel's name appeared on her screen like magic.

Rachel: Make lemonade!

LynnLuvs2Trvl: Yeah, I'm thinking of heading to Hertz to rent a car. Pulled up driving directions. I think I can make it if I go right now. Checking the budget first but...that's what credit cards are for, right?

Rachel: LYNN!!!! I meant your stud! This is exactly what you need. Someone to help you shake things up. Match your love life to your new career.

LynnLuvs2Trvl: What? Are you kidding? I have so much riding on this trip. I can't risk it on a guy who's not going to give me the time of day.

Rachel: You know I respect the hard decisions you've made lately, sweetie. But really, you're not going to be happy until you go for broke. It's not only your job that stifled you. It was those boring men you dated. You have to stop settling for safe.

LynnLuvs2Trvl: Maybe, but not now.

Rachel: Then when? I haven't heard you talk about a man like that in...well...ever!

LynnLuvs2Trvl: It's crazy. From the first moment he touched me, my system went haywire.

Rachel: I know exactly what you mean. It's like that for me with Ethan. Please don't throw that away. Please. Go rent your car. But...ask him if he wants a ride! I bet you a triple chocolate sundae he says yes so fast your head will spin.

LynnLuvs2Trvl: Drive four hours with a complete stranger? Have you lost your mind?

Rachel: It's possible. Trust your instincts. You always have been a good judge of character.

LynnLuvs2Trvl: You're corrupting me. I can't believe I actually considered that for two seconds. No way, Rach. Sorry, I have to go. Have to get this mess straightened out before all my plans are ruined.

Rachel: Okay, sweetie. I hope it works out! And if you miss your flight, then I hope he has a twin brother and you let both guys sweep you off your feet to live out your wildest and craziest ménage fantasies. Come to the dark side. Go Team Cougar!

LynnLuvs2Trvl: LOL Love you, crazycakes.

Rachel: Love you too. Let me know how it goes.

Chapter Two
୫୬

"Either you found out our flights are on track again or your boyfriend sent you one hell of an email." Sebastian cursed the unfamiliar jealousy streaking through him over the naughty grin decorating the sinful lips of the woman he'd just met. "Since I didn't hear any cheering from the rest of these folks, I'm betting on the boyfriend."

Damn though, she'd drawn him to her like the strongest magnet on earth. Something about her sang to him, irresistible and potent. Sure, she was smoking hot. Fine. Her ash blonde hair framed her elegant face in soft curtains and her mile-high heels accentuated her long legs, but that alone couldn't account for the hard-on straining against his designer jeans. Freaking sponsorships. He hated wearing the uncomfortable style but it paid his most extravagant bills.

Granted, he seemed tame compared to some of the celebrity bad-boy drivers, but he knew how to have a good time when the mood struck. He'd had flashier girls than Lynn throw themselves in his direction, but something special had happened when he spotted her. Older than him, sophisticated, classy and so different from the women he fucked around with—he couldn't stop imagining what she'd look like laid out on his king-sized mattress, wearing only that smirk.

Best of all, she didn't seem to recognize him. The chemistry between them had nothing to do with his money, his racing or the ridiculous hype his marketing department cooked up. Unbelievable. He wasn't about to let her get away unless she'd already been spoken for. He didn't cheat and he'd never sleep with someone else's woman, no matter how bad he wanted to.

Well, without the guy's permission anyway. There had been a few times... His mind conjured a vivid image of Lynn sandwiched between him and his navigator Mark as they ravished her bold curves.

He had to shake his head to clear the ringing in his ears when he realized she'd answered him but he'd missed her response. A woman like her would never be into the nasty games he'd played with the groupies who'd made for an easy feast in his younger years.

"I mean, I've been in relationships of course." He grinned when a blush stained her cheeks. She grimaced then sputtered, "Just not at the moment."

"Nice. Then I don't have to worry about someone hunting me down for buying you dinner." He adjusted his cock as discreetly as he could when he sat, but the confining jeans wouldn't hide his obvious arousal if she so much as glanced at his crotch again.

She groaned. "Don't tease. There's nothing open in this hellhole, is there?"

"Nope. The lone McDonald's is on the other side of the security checkpoint. They're not letting anyone through. But your stomach's growling loud enough I thought I was on a safari. So, I brought you a three-course vending machine banquet." Sebastian hoped she wasn't too prissy to pig out on junk food with him. He hadn't needed to worry.

"Please tell me you scored some of those tiny powdered donuts."

"You'll have to wait and see. First up, the amuse-bouche." He handed her a bottle of water before he presented a bite-sized caramel with a flourish.

"I think I love you," she sighed.

When she reached to take the morsel from his hand, he withdrew. "Uh-uh. This is a fixed menu for two."

He unwrapped the candy then held it between his fingertips a few inches in front of her mouth. Lynn rolled her eyes then accepted his silent dare instead of telling him to fuck off. She leaned forward until her exposed cleavage had his mouth watering then wrapped her lips around the treat and bit it in half. A thin line of caramel stretched. It broke, leaving a sweet trail at the corner of her mouth.

Sebastian would have given the entire payout of his next race to lick it off but he'd pushed his luck enough already. He swiped the gooey mess from her lips then brought his thumb to his tongue along with the other half of the caramel. The flavor of her skin surpassed the sweetness of the candy.

"Mmm, delicious."

Her regal neck flexed as she swallowed, making it far too easy to imagine her throat working around him instead. He groaned.

"Looks like I'm not the only one with a sweet tooth."

"You have no idea." The rough tone of his voice surprised him. He shook himself, trying to find some restraint. He couldn't bear to frighten her off.

"Next up, the main course. He slid the bundled beef jerky and cheddar cheese from his pocket then offered it to her. When he ripped open the packaging, a loud gurgle drowned out the crinkle of plastic. "Damn, no screwing around. You're really hungry. It sucks that they've cut all the snacks out of your domestic flights."

She didn't argue, accepting the meager offering with a murmured, "Thanks."

After she chewed and swallowed a hunk of dried meat, she asked, "Is there still a land of free munchies? Where are you from?"

"A tiny village on the Amalfi Coast."

"Which one?" She popped another nugget into her mouth. Such contrasts. An all-business skirt and blouse in dove gray and pink matched her perfect French manicure but couldn't detract from the hints of wicked mischief flashing in her eyes or her ability to enjoy the simple pleasures he'd brought her.

"Oh, nowhere you'd know."

"Try me." Her arched eyebrow made him sorry to squash her rebelliousness when he proved her wrong.

"Erchie."

"Ah, yes. Often overlooked. Closer to Salerno than Sorrento. It's actually one of the stops on my itinerary."

"You're kidding! What are you planning to do there?"

"Write travel guides. For women. Alone." She blushed then studied the tiles as though embarrassed for not having a companion. "At least I hope to. I quit my job to give it a go."

"No shit. You'll have to stay at my mother's bed and breakfast. The rooms are small but cozy and she cooks the best pasta in all of Italy. She'd make any *ragazza* feel right at home as long as they don't mind her talking their ears off or going into town to gossip with her friends."

"That sounds perfect." Her smile lit up the gloomy terminal. "But I'm sure she'll be booked solid this time of year."

"You can have my old room. She refuses to rent it out in case I'm able to make it home in between events. Like I'd mind crashing on the couch for a night or two. But she won't hear of it." He chucked as he thought of the horror on his mother's face when he'd proposed the idea last.

Truth was, though he'd spent his youth ticking off the days until he could escape his lazy village to someplace urban and fast-paced, lately he longed for the peace he'd known while lounging on the beach, swimming in the jewel blue waters of the Mediterranean or fishing with his father before he'd lost his battle with cancer. "Depending on the timing, maybe I could meet you there."

The thought of this woman in his boyhood bed had his molars throbbing as he ground them to dust. It only got worse when she licked salt from her fingertips, one by one.

"I couldn't ask you to do that." She chuckled.

As though it would be any kind of imposition.

"What events were you talking about? What do *you* do?"

"Ah. I drive." He relished the dilation of her pupils when he revealed the pack of donuts he'd stashed behind his back, feeling only a little guilty for distracting her. He didn't want to ruin their casual exchange. People always got weird when they found out. "Dessert?"

"Oh yeah. I never pass it up. If you couldn't tell." She nibbled one side of the cake ring he shared, paying no mind to the powdered sugar snowing onto her clothes.

"Me either."

Her gaze snapped to his, searing him with her green laser stare for several moments before she steered the conversation to her original goal. "So...you drive. A taxi?"

"Not exactly."

"Then what, exactly?" She refused to surrender. He loved that.

"Rally cars." He shrugged, hoping to play it off. It didn't mean as much in the States where the sport had never grown popular.

"Wow! A racecar driver."

Sebastian tamped down the pride attempting to flair at the approval in her voice.

"That can't be an easy thing to pursue. I mean, doesn't every boy dream of speed? I wish I'd refused to give in to reality when I was your age."

He laughed out loud. "My age. *Dio*, you make it sound like you're a hundred years old. Bust out the 'whippersnapper' or maybe 'kids today', why don't you?"

"Come on, you're what...twenty-five?"

"Twenty-eight."

"I turned forty this year!"

"Though some things get finer with age, it's still just a number, Lynn." He studied the pinched corner of her lips. She frowned as she swallowed the final crumbs of the donut. "You're free now and going after what you want. That's all that matters."

He cursed under his breath when he reminded her of their situation. In an instant, she morphed into a bundle of tension.

"What am I doing? I have to get out of here. I need to make it to New York." She glanced at her watch then checked the board once more as though expecting a miracle. "There's no way I'll make it if I wait for the flight. Will you watch my things for a minute?"

"Can I peek at *your* underwear?"

"Hell no!" A chuckle broke from her as she pressed a palm to her cheek. She began to turn then came closer instead. "I don't wear any."

Her scandalous whisper reverberated through his chest straight to his straining erection as he watched her float away. Her unpracticed flirting turned him on more than the skilled seduction he'd enjoyed from women in the past. He couldn't take his eyes off her as she sashayed toward the counter where the line had died down some.

Sebastian didn't notice the hyper child running past until it was too late. The kid skipped from black tile to black tile, lassoing his ankle in Lynn's purse strap. Tangled, the child and the bag crashed to the floor. Sebastian reached out to make sure the boy hadn't hurt himself but the child's mortified mother beat him to it. When she'd assured herself the kid was fine, she started a lecture on public behavior with, "Tommy John Andrews…"

Ouch! He'd always hated it when he earned a full-name reprimand.

With a wink at the boy, he gathered the scattered contents of Lynn's carry-on. He set her netbook on the bench then reached for the books that had tumbled free. The graphic covers had him doing a double take.

Holy shit! That couldn't be what it looked like.

Yet, sure enough, when he scooted the first one closer for a thorough inspection, he confirmed the *two* men depicted both had their hands beneath the skirt of the women between them.

His pulse spiked, maybe even skipped a beat here and there. The thick paper swished as he thumbed through the novel, picking out juicy scenes to browse. Lynn moved up from gorgeous, sweet and funny to his dream woman in a matter of seconds.

Passionate possibilities flooded his mind. Had she ever tried ménage? Bondage? Or even the raw, primal sex for two filling the pages in his hands? He doubted it. Hell, the woman had nearly choked on a tiny tease over going commando.

He would love to show her all she had missed.

When her netbook dinged from near his ear as he crouched on the floor, he jerked hard enough to bang his knee under the seat. "Sorry," he mumbled to the grouchy man he'd jarred from a nap.

Guilty much, Fiori?

The flashing icon in the system tray caught his attention. His finger moved toward the touchpad despite his attempt to restrain himself. Shit, that'd never been his strong suit.

The new email contained a link to comments on a blog. He clicked before his conscience could catch up with his caveman instincts.

Tempt The Cougar. He didn't realize he'd started grinning like a madman until his cheeks ached. His gorgeous crush hid more than she let on. So she thought he was sexy? Good to know.

Sebastian scanned the posts. He must have done something really, really good—like saving the planet good—in a previous life. Lynn and her friends were into younger men. How about that?

Sam: Do it, Lynn! Or, should I say, do him?

Autumn: Ohhh, does he have any cute friends?

Stevie: Sneak us a pic with your phone!

Larissa: Back off, Cougars. You all have studs of your own. I understand being cautious, Lynn, but there's a difference between that and isolation. If you can, see where it goes. It's okay to have fun every once in a while. Rawrrrr!

LynnLuvs2Trvl: Hey, ladies. Lynn stepped away for a minute. I promise I'm not a serial killer. Your friend is beautiful. The attraction is not one-sided. You can check me out. My name is Sebastian Fiori. I'm a rally car driver for Driven Wild. Go ahead, Google me. I can give you references...'cause I'm telling you now, I'm interested in fulfilling her fantasies. Maybe you could put in a good word for me?

Darci: Holy crap! She wasn't joking. You're HOT!

LynnLuvs2Trvl: Uh, thanks.

Rachel: If you hurt her, we will hunt you down. My fiancé is a cop.

LynnLuvs2Trvl: She's safe with me. I swear it. She'll call you when we get to NY. Give me four hours before you release the hounds.

Rachel: How are you going to get there?

LynnLuvs2Trvl: I have a plan, don't worry.

Chapter Three
ဆ

"Excuse me. I realize you're swamped right now but I have a flight to Europe to catch in less than five hours. Can you give me any estimate at all of how long it might be before we're en route?"

"Sorry, ma'am." The freckle-faced kid made her feel ancient. "I'm not supposed to say."

No use in hassling the guy. She'd worked her share of shit jobs in her college years. "I understand. Thanks, anyway."

Just as she turned, the kid whispered, "But...if I were you, I'd go for a rental car. With this mess, you'll be lucky to snag one. If you can though, the drive's only four hours or so. If traffic's not bad, you'll make your flight. That's more than I can promise if you hang around here."

Lynn nodded. "That's what I thought."

"Let me call for you. I have the number on speed dial." He tapped the monstrous phone on his desk then waited a beat before asking, "Hey, Russell, can I make a reservation for a passenger? I'm going to send her right over to you."

She held her breath as the kid listened. Then sighed when he cursed under his breath.

"Nothing at all? Not even to carpool up to JFK?" Another pause. "Yeah, trust me, you should see things in here. It's a zoo today. I don't get paid enough for this. Not your fault, man. Thanks."

He didn't meet her gaze as he replaced the handset in the cradle as though he expected her to rant and rave.

"It's okay. I appreciate you trying." Lynn couldn't prevent her disappointment from shading her tone.

"Want me to see what's available for standby, maybe we can reroute you?"

"There's not enough time..."

Lynn jumped when someone cupped her elbow. Without looking, she recognized Sebastian's scent and the gentle yet firm way he ensnared her. She leaned into his hold as her knees turned to jelly.

"That won't be necessary. I've made other arrangements for us."

"You did what?" Her hackles rose. She hadn't fought to break every single confining influence in her life only to let some stranger start making her decisions.

He ignored her outrage. "Could you please have our luggage forwarded to our final destination?"

Sebastian passed a torn corner of paper with an address scribbled on it over her head. She concentrated on closing her gaping mouth and relaxing her contorted face in case it stuck like that. As if she needed more wrinkles!

"Yes of course, Mr. Fiori."

She whipped around to face the attendant. Obviously rally car racing meant more than she'd realized. Her young coconspirator stared at Sebastian as she imagined he would Superman or maybe one of the Yankees.

"How do you know where I'm headed?" The squeak came out an octave above her usual tone.

"Your friends told me you're starting your trip in Paris. I'm on my way to France for a rally. By the way, Rachel says to have a good time." He had the balls to wink at her.

She sputtered, trying to find the anger she knew should raise her blood pressure over his violation of her privacy. Still, none seemed to materialize. Had he opened the door to her fantasies? Could it be so horrible to accept his offer if it was what she would have chosen anyway?

At least she didn't have to face humiliation. When he'd discovered the blog, he could have left—could have walked away without looking over his shoulder. But he hadn't. He'd come to claim her.

"I'd love to get to know you better." His knuckles skimmed her cheekbone, sending a rush of anticipation through her. "Besides, it's the only way you're going to make it on time. I promise not to bite. Unless you ask nice."

Before self-doubt sabotaged her instincts, she nuzzled his fingers then turned her face to nip one. "Let's go then. Don't want to miss our flight."

She'd forgotten about their audience until the young man cleared his throat. "C-could I get your autograph?"

"Sure. What's your name?" Sebastian worked a silver Sharpie and a glossy collector card from his back pocket.

"Jim."

Holy crap. He'd come prepared. She gawked at the image of him posing in a full-body racing suit. It shouldn't be possible for one man to look that sexy.

Sebastian jotted a quick note then signed the thick stock. "Nice to meet you, Jim. Thanks for taking care of the luggage."

"No problem. This rocks!" The two guys bumped fists, a trend she would never understand. Still, she didn't linger on the generational difference between her and Sebastian. How could she when he made it effortless to stay near him?

They waved as they left the counter. She attempted to unburden Sebastian by reclaiming her carry-on but he refused to let her shoulder it, instead, stacking it on top of his own duffle. When she drifted near the rental car kiosks, he draped an arm around her waist then steered her toward the terminal exit instead.

"You got a car already?"

"I didn't have any luck with the rentals either." He frowned. "We're going to have to let someone else drive."

"What do you mean?" Her eyes narrowed a moment before they made their way outside. "Sebastian! You can't hire a limo for a four-hour drive. It's going to cost a fortune!"

"You want to make our flight, gorgeous?"

She sighed. "Let me pay for half."

"No need." When she would have objected, he silenced her by pressing his lips to hers, catching her off guard. Any possible argument evaporated from her brain as she soaked in the heat of his embrace. Her palms landed on his sculpted chest. His long fingers supported her neck while his lips sampled each of hers then traced the seam between them. She gasped at the sensation, parting for his gentle exploration. Instead of pressing his advantage though, he retreated.

Dazed, she didn't understand him at first when he murmured, "This one's on Driven Wild. They need me there for the time trials. Ride up to New York with me. I want to get to know you better."

She wondered exactly what he had in mind when his palms skimmed over her shoulder then along the length of her back until he stopped a fraction of an inch short of her ass. The old Lynn would have waited to see what developed. The new Lynn didn't have that kind of patience.

No more wasted time, remember? "Does getting to know each other involve talking or making out?"

She bit her lip as she hoped he understood she couldn't quite go for broke yet. What she really wanted to ask was, "Are we going to get it on in the limo?"

What would she do if he expected them to mess around? Would she run toward the waiting car or away from it? She couldn't say for certain, but she knew which option her soaked pussy voted for.

"I'm yours for the ride, gorgeous. Whatever you like, I'm here to please. No pressure either way. No judgment and no hard feelings."

The chauffer rounded the car then held the gleaming door open as they hashed out the details of their arrangement. Sebastian inched forward, nudging her toward the waiting vehicle. She'd never faced temptation so strong before. Not one reason to refuse him came to mind.

Lynn surrendered. Her forehead rested on his chest as she agreed, "Let's go."

"You won't regret it."

Lynn smiled across the intimate space at Sebastian as he described growing up in one of the most beautiful places on earth. Eyes closed, he tipped his head into the rest. His legs splayed on the supple leather bench seat. An empty flute held the remnants of the champagne they'd split. Though it hadn't yet been an hour since they'd left Harrisburg, the steady clip of miles rolling by felt like sand pouring through an hourglass.

Their legs pressed together from knees to feet. They'd both kicked off their shoes once they'd settled into the plush limo. His socked toes rubbed against hers then up to her ankle idly as they talked, hopping from subject to subject.

Considering their age differences, they had an amazing amount in common.

"What's your favorite food?"

She blinked while her mind caught up to what he'd asked. "I love spaghetti."

"Me too," he grinned. "It's sort of required by my birthright."

"White wine or red?" she countered.

"Red all the way."

"I agree." She smiled.

A horn blast jolted her from their exchange. Sebastian cursed then peered out the window as streams of traffic passed them on the left. The knuckles of his hand turned white where they rested on his knee.

"It really does bother you not to drive, doesn't it?" Lynn covered his fingers with her own, loosening their grip. God, his hands were huge compared to hers. So strong.

"Stupid, right?" He shook his head in chagrin.

"No, not when you're so highly trained. I can understand how it would make you anxious." She massaged his ultra-tense thigh muscle until he relaxed a smidge.

"If I were up there, I could get us to New York in two hours flat."

"But then we'd have less time for...this."

He leaned forward, resting his elbows on his knees until she couldn't evade his piercing gaze. "Distract me?"

"How?" Lynn gulped.

"Come sit here while we talk." He patted the seat beside his hip.

Tired of tiptoeing around the chemistry threatening to blow them both to smithereens, she did one better. She crawled onto his lap. He smiled as he reached for her. The bulk of his shoulders filled her arms when she wrapped them around him before letting him tug her the rest of the way over him. Soft fabric teased her thighs as her skirt rode higher. She settled, kneeling with one leg on either side of his trim hips.

Sebastian shifted forward to give her room to explore the broad expanse of his back with her greedy hands. His abdomen fit tight against her. The pressure of his hard-on imprinting on her belly had her sucking in a breath. The expansion of her chest melded her hard nipples to his solid pecs. She squirmed beneath the weight of her arousal, hoping to get it under control.

No such luck. She moaned aloud.

"You're so responsive. That's such a turn-on." He stroked her hair, making her glad she'd taken the extra time to blow-dry and curl it with her fat, round brush before packing the last of her toiletries this morning. Somehow it had felt like a special occasion. "And so gorgeous."

"And almost twice your age. Do you go for older women often?"

"Never before you. You're everything I was looking for but didn't know I wanted. It's not a pick-up line or something. You're so damn refined compared to the women I've dated. But not stuck-up or snobby. More like...graceful, elegant, mature and reserved."

His genuine awe erased her self-consciousness.

No answer came to mind when his full lips mesmerized her. She swore the flavor of him from the airport lingered, mingling with the champagne they'd drunk. Delicious. She craved another taste.

The greenish-blue of his eyes reminded her of the Mediterranean waters he'd described with heartfelt sentiment, rivaling the greatest poetry she'd ever read. With the addition of the heat in them, she half expected them to steam up.

Unable to resist a moment longer, she buried her fingers in the unruly locks of his thick brown hair then captured his mouth. This kiss held no hint of the gentle coercion they'd shared earlier. No, this time she pillaged, taking what she wanted while he gave as good in return.

Euphoria washed over her, urging her to ride the wave. For the first time in her life, she understood what the word "lust" really meant. When she ground her pelvis into his, he met the motion with a thrust of his own, stroking her aching core with his denim-encased hard-on.

That's when she heard the *whhhhp* of something ripping.

"Oh my God. Did I hurt you?" She would have scrambled off him but he still had one arm wrapped around her.

Instead of shrieking in pain, he laughed. And laughed. And laughed.

"What's so funny?"

When he collapsed against the seat, leaving a wedge of space between their torsos, she saw it too. Lynn slid to the floor between his knees to get a better look at the split seam in the crotch of his jeans.

"Fucking sponsors. These damn things were about to castrate me."

Afraid her eyes might bulge out of her skull, she couldn't help herself. She traced the frayed edge of the hole—where his olive flesh peeked from beneath the confining packaging—with the tip of her index finger.

"You're not wearing underwear either," she whispered.

"Never do," he growled behind clenched teeth. "I'm getting rid of these before the button gives way and puts your eye out. Safety first, gorgeous."

"Let me." She brushed his hands away from her target. When their fingers skimmed his erection, he hissed.

"Hurry."

Lynn shoved his gray t-shirt up his six-pack abs to expose the waistband of his jeans. She wrestled the button at the top of his fly. It gave way, tearing the zipper open as well.

"Ahhh." Sebastian groaned as she relieved the pressure on his straining cock.

He had her previous lovers beat by a solid three inches. Her mouth watered at the sight.

Together they peeled his jeans from his hips. He lifted to help her strip them off then sat, unashamed and primed, before her. She peeked up at his face from her place on the floor, her lashes lowered.

"Whatever you want," he murmured.

"I want you."

Chapter Four

∞

Lynn licked a trail from Sebastian's knee along his thigh. She nipped the ridge of muscle in his quad. While she slaked the urges drowning out every practical facet of her nature, she watched him shuck his shirt in her peripheral vision.

The man was in his prime, no doubt about that.

She reached up to trace the contours of his abdomen as it flexed in time with his uneven respiration. Still, he didn't goad her or make any move to take control.

The freedom to explore, to do as she pleased, had her heart racing almost as much as the attraction rushing through her veins. A wicked impulse prodded her to tease him further before rewarding his patience.

Scant inches from his erection, she turned her head to let her breath wash over his balls. Then she rocked onto her haunches. Sebastian's hands fisted on the seat beside his thighs. True to his word though, he didn't pressure her to continue.

"Thank you," she whispered.

Disappointment dulled the hunger in his eyes though he tried to hide it with a half-hearted smile. When she spun around, coming to her feet with her hands braced on the opposite seat, his stare blazed once more. Tapping a reservoir of brazen sensuality she hadn't known she possessed, she rocked from side to side, causing her skirt to flash glimpses of her bare ass and pussy, if the cool breeze was any indication.

Even the chilly air didn't stand a chance at tempering her arousal. The moisture coating her thighs probably glistened in the fancy halogen lighting of the cabin. Hopefully it didn't highlight her flaws as well. If it did, Sebastian didn't seem to mind. He groaned when she tucked her fingers into her stretchy waistband then shimmied until the fabric pooled around her bare toes.

"Gorgeous."

She snuck a glance over her shoulder. His hand had migrated to his crotch where he alternated cupping his balls and stroking his magnificent erection, which seemed to have swollen to greater proportions. She licked her lips when she caught sight of the defined ridges of his veins. They'd feel amazing tunneling inside her.

The low, rock beat filling the car set the perfect rhythm for her striptease.

She spun around then sat, mirroring him on the opposite seat. Her spread legs presented him with her bare pussy.

"You shave," he panted.

"Wax."

He scrunched his eyes closed for a moment as his hand hesitated in its circuit along his hard-on. A feline grin tugged one corner of her mouth upward. Power had her head spinning double-time. Her heavy breasts demanded to be freed from the confines of her bra.

Lynn flicked her fingers over the bottom button on her blouse, releasing it. Then she did the same for the top closure. She worked her way toward the middle, running her hands over her flaming skin to soothe some of her restless energy but only ended up escalating the frenzy of desire burning within her.

She continued until one single point held her shirt closed over her chest.

"You're killing me."

"Me too," she rasped as she approached him once more. She bent over so his face nestled in her cleavage. The coarse stubble of his sparse shadow rasped the soft mounds of her breasts.

"Undo it," she demanded. When his hands wandered up her sides toward his goal, she covered them with her own, squeezing gently. "No, with your teeth."

Sebastian complied. He latched on then yanked the panel until the button flew off. Then he licked and bit her breast as he rooted around the edge of the lace cups, working her nipple free.

Wet heat surrounded the hardened tip as he drew on it with lazy pulls of his lips. His tongue flicked over the flushed peak, causing her toes to curl in the carpet. He devoured her with honest yearning so intense it stole her breath.

Lynn shrugged out of the blouse then reached behind her back. She unclasped her bra, letting it fall to the floor. The hand she braced on his shoulder steadied her while she indulged his appetite, allowing him to feast on her breasts until she saw stars. Her thighs rubbed each other as she attempted to relieve some of the pressure building between her legs.

She needed more. Had to have him touching her.

A slick pop marked the exit of her nipple from his mouth when she retreated to the seat behird her. She propped her legs up, exposing herself completely to the young, virile man before her. Her heels sank into the cushion.

He didn't need her to spell out her wishes. Goose bumps rose on her arms when he made a predatory lunge toward her. Agile, fit and determined, he stole her breath.

The span of his long fingers cupped her thighs as he pushed them higher and farther apart to make room for his broad shoulders. Without a moment's hesitation, he buried his face in her soaked pussy.

"*Dio*, you're so hot. *Molto dolce, bella.*" She didn't speak Italian but she understood the language of his touch, the urgency in his tone as he mumbled against her swollen flesh. The vibration of his praise added to the ecstasy of his manipulation.

His tongue traced the rim of her opening as his lips sipped the dew from her labia, working steadily upward toward her clit. Her fingers clenched on his shoulders and back, urging him closer. Desperation drove her to rake her nails over him, forcing him to take more, but he didn't seem to mind. Instead, he redoubled his efforts, losing the hint of playfulness he'd had before.

A moan escaped her chest when his teeth skimmed her sensitive skin. He positioned one of her thighs on his shoulder as his hand journeyed inward toward her throbbing pussy.

"Yes! Sink your fingers in me. I want to be filled." The stark honesty of her expressed desires startled her. Sex had never been this good—this raw or this powerful—for her. He allowed her to fulfill the sensual potential she'd given up on reaching.

The tip of one finger swirled through the juices streaming from her as he concentrated the flicks of his tongue on the area surrounding her clit. The indirect stimulation eased her into the full-on pressure of his lips.

Fireworks exploded in brilliant shades of red and gold behind her clamped eyelids. She forced herself to open them so she didn't miss a moment of Sebastian's expert seduction.

He worked his digit inside her by degrees until the knuckles of his other fingers settled into the valley of her ass. Pleasure tightened every muscle of her body, causing her to hug his embedded hand. The ripple of her channel around him elicited a moan from each of them.

Shocks of bliss fizzled up her spine as he moved within her. Each wiggle of his tongue on her clit pushed her higher. She couldn't stand to toe the edge of orgasm much longer. The surfeit of rapture would drive her insane.

Lynn gripped his hair in her fist, aligning him with the one spot sure to set her off in seconds. "Make me come, Bastian. Now."

He growled as he delved deeper, his finger rotating to press her G-spot against her pelvic bone. Then his lips surrounded her clit, his mouth doing something magical to her pussy. She fucked his face without restraint. He followed the arc of her hips with enthusiastic laps of his tongue.

The flex of her pussy around him forced more lubrication onto his hand. He groaned when it eased his way, allowing him to sink a little deeper. The echo of his praise for her uninhibited display shattered her. Spasm after spasm threatened to rip her apart.

When she thought the climax couldn't get any stronger, he rubbed the rough patch inside her, renewing her orgasm. She screamed his name as he continued to eat her, wringing every last drop of passion from her.

He read the slowing of her contractions, bringing her down easy from dizzying heights. No man had ever been so in tune with her body. Boneless, she sagged in his supporting grasp, attempting to catch her breath.

"Gorgeous," he whispered in between butterfly kisses on her thigh, mons and stomach.

She couldn't summon the energy to move, though kneeling on the floor had to be uncomfortable for him. "Hold me?"

Lynn didn't have to ask twice. Sebastian scooped her into his arms then twisted so he rolled onto the seat on his side. She curled into his chest, their legs scissored. The glimmer of her pleasure on his lips enticed her to lick it off. She sampled the arousal he'd inspired when she fused their mouths together. One part him, one part her—the recipe made for a scrumptious result.

Despite the hard-on branding her hip, he attempted gentleness. He caressed her jaw while he nibbled her lips. But sexual tension radiated from him. If she didn't plan to restrain her desires, why should he have to?

Months of abstinence ensured her lust couldn't be wiped away by the initial relief her monumental orgasm had provided. Not with the promise of more arcing between them.

"Do you have any condoms with you?" she whispered, nearly begging.

"There's a whole box in my bag."

"Get them."

While he rummaged through the duffle on the floor beside his head with one hand, he asked, "What's your favorite position, *tesoro?*"

"You ask a lot of questions."

"Want me to find out some other way?" The fingers of his free hand splayed across the small of her back, his thumb tucked under her hipbone. "I could investigate."

"I'm more interested in you. What do you like?"

"Anything. Everything. It depends on the moment, the woman and my mood. Right now, I'd love for you to ride me. I want to watch your tits bounce while you fuck me. The liberation shining in your eyes is addictive. Sexy."

Lynn grabbed the condom he proffered. She moved to the edge of the seat so he could flip to his back. The foil wrapper tore easily when she held one corner between her teeth. Before covering his shaft, she bent to sample the pearly liquid beading in the slit on the head of his penis. She would have taken him in her mouth, savored his heat and musk, but Sebastian edged away.

"Not this time. I won't last." He wrapped his fingers around her wrist then guided the condom closer. "Cover me."

She did as he asked. The thin latex rolled over his cock with some effort. Her hands stroked his length, marveling at the solid mass of his erection. She could play with him all day. But when she caught sight of his agonized face, she realized how much she'd tortured him already.

The bunched muscles of his thigh flexed against the inside of hers when she swung her other leg over his waist. Tipping forward, she plastered them together, chest to chest and pelvis to pelvis. They both gasped at the full-body contact.

Sebastian's arms came around her, his hands wandering to her ass. He grabbed the cheeks, his fingers sinking in as he spread them. She slid her hips forward then back, stroking his length with the wet lips of her pussy. The head of his erection nudged her clit when it jerked beneath her in time to his pounding heart.

She planted her hands on his chest as she humped him shamelessly, lowering her lips to his for a scorching kiss. On each pass, she increased the swing of her hips until the tip of his cock lodged inside the mouth of her pussy, on the cusp of entering.

The pressure had her sighing, anticipating the moment when his penetration would burn her as he stretched her wide.

"Take me inside you," he growled.

They moved at the same time, she rocked her hips up and back while he thrust from below. The head of his cock parted her slick flesh, joining them for the first time. The universe seemed to stop as their eyes met and held.

Sebastian smiled. Then he wrapped his hands over her shoulders and tugged her toward him. Lynn moved in tandem, fitting them together, inch by inch. When he'd made it about halfway, she kissed the exposed sinew of his throat before lifting her torso upright. Her ass rested on her heels as her hands fell back, one on each of his tense thighs. She locked her elbows, using gravity to shove him into her the rest of the way.

When he packed her full, she paused, staring into the depths of his eyes, trying to catch her breath while bands of desire constricted her chest. Had anything ever felt this good?

"Gorgeous, *tesoro*." His hands cupped her presented breasts, thrust forward by her position. "You fit me perfectly."

His cock felt so hot inside her, setting off mini explosions in her abdomen. She bucked, trying to soothe the arousal but only amplified it instead. He impaled her, every nerve ending in her pussy aware of his presence. The contours formed by the ridge of the head and his veined shaft rippled over the spongy walls.

Every rock of her hips dragged her clit across the pad of muscle above his cock.

"That's it. Fuck me." He pinched her nipples, rolling them between his thumb and forefingers. "Ride me hard."

He made it so easy to take what she wanted. Lynn found herself bobbing on him, pounding his length inside her as deep as he could reach. She leaned farther back until the head of his cock nudged her just right every time she forced it through the constricting rings of muscle at her entrance.

Close now, she fucked with less accuracy and more passion. Their bodies expanded and contracted to keep him lodged inside her. Every time the head of his cock locked with the mouth of her pussy, she moaned then relished the long glide of him coming home.

Each muscle in his body tensed, quivering. His sweat-slicked chest, his amazing abs, even the thighs she clenched in her death grip, gathered. Knowing she affected him—that she could stretch him on a rack of desire as inescapable as the one she found herself bound to—was more than she could bear.

The knot of her clit tapped him as she buried him deep then rocked in quick, shallow arcs.

"Lynn. Damn it." Sebastian fought the pleasure she gave him, but when she added a circular grind of her hips to every stroke, he lost. "Going to come."

His hard-on flared inside her as the first hints of her orgasm bubbled in the depths of her abdomen. Every ounce of pleasure she gifted him returned to her double. She reached behind her back to cup his tight sac, holding his balls in her palm.

He roared with satisfaction at the same time the base of his cock jerked against her fingertips. Imagining the rush of his cum filling the condom he wore—combined with the pressure on her clit and the equipment overflowing her pussy—triggered her orgasm.

Her pussy milked him with rhythmic pulses. The relief she experienced went deeper, felt more substantial, with him inside her. Joining her. The grunts he made and the flex of his cock extended her pleasure until she collapsed, limp, on his chest.

Even then, the occasional aftershock vibrated through them, making them both sigh and moan. Though she couldn't imagine moving a muscle, Sebastian seemed rejuvenated. Unable to lie still, he petted her back, stroked her ass, kissed her cheek and played with her hair.

When his half-hard cock slipped from her, he shifted her to the side to take care of the condom. She didn't realize what he intended until the blast of fresh air pebbled her nipples.

She laughed. "Did you throw that out the window?"

"What else was I supposed to do with it?" He shrugged then grinned. "Hope the people behind us were following at a safe distance."

A cotton undershirt dangled from his fist when he knelt by her side once more. She blushed when he spread her legs to dry her before plucking her skirt off the running board.

"Now you're turning shy on me?" He helped her dress before rummaging in his duffle for a change of clothes.

"It's not every day I meet a young stud then assault him in a limousine."

He had no answer for that. She supposed it might not be so far out of the realm of ordinary for him.

"I wish we had more time to lounge naked together. I would love to hold you. But that might be hard to explain if we were in an accident. My mother would not approve." He winked, some of his earlier lighthearted nature emerging from the haze of sensuality that had obscured it.

Once their appearances had been returned to order, he rejoined her on the seat, snuggling close. Still, she found she couldn't let that nagging thought go. She refused to smother her curiosity a moment longer.

"Have you ever done something like this before?"

"Like what?"

"Fooled around with someone you just met?"

"Yes."

She nodded. "I figured."

"But it was never like this, Lynn. Those times were about scratching an itch with girls who sought a notch on their bedpost—wanted to say they fucked Sebastian Fiori. Not me, my name."

He couldn't obscure the bitterness underlying his resignation.

"If it makes you feel better, you're a no-name to me." She smiled. "Or at least you were. I'll never forget you now."

"Same here, gorgeous." His fingertip traced her brow. "I kind of got the feeling this is some kind of experiment for you. I'm glad I was in the right place at the right time. Luckiest day of my life."

"You think I'd have done this with any hot guy I met?" She started to sit up but he tucked her closer. "Bastian, that's not true. Believe me, I have lots of fantasies. Yes, one of them was to take a younger lover, but I've never wanted to make one come true as much as when I met you."

"Tell me about the books in your purse. Are they about things you want to try? Or simply something to dream about?"

Ridiculous, considering what they'd done, she blushed again. "I guess they're a hot fantasy. Not something I ever expected to experience but something to wonder about. Sort of like winning the lotto. Part of the fun of buying a ticket is imagining what you'd do with the winnings because that's as close as you'll ever get, you know?"

"I suppose." He nuzzled her neck. "I've never bought a lotto ticket. If I want something, I try to figure out how I can get it myself."

Admiration for her lover flared in her chest.

"Someday, I hope I can say the same."

"What if I know a way you can? At least with these…"

"Mr. Fiori, we're nearing JFK. Which gate do you require?" The chauffer buzzed through the tinted glass partition on the intercom.

Lynn's heart bottomed out. Her time with this incredible man had expired. Sure, they'd be on the same plane, but now she had no doubt he'd be flying first class with flight attendants hanging on every request while she suffered through the nine-hour journey squashed in coach. If she got really lucky, she'd be seated between an armrest hogger and someone intent on talking her ear off when all she wanted to do was relive these past four hours, over and over.

"Terminal three, gate eleven," she supplied. At the same time he said, "Terminal four, gate nine."

Oh no! They weren't on the same flight after all. She'd have less than five minutes to say goodbye as the first airport signs zipped past the window.

"Terminal four, please," he repeated for the driver then clicked the channel closed and cleared his throat. "Lynn, I told the airline to release your seat, that you'd made other plans. The flight was oversold even before the weather jacked stuff up. They were looking for any reason to generate free spots."

This time he couldn't hold her when she shoved away from his betraying warmth. "Who the fuck do you think you are? I gave up everything I know for this opportunity. You think you can make decisions for me after knowing me for less than five minutes?"

"Listen, please." He held his hand out, palms facing her when she contemplated chucking her shoe at him. "It's not as bad as you think. I wasn't sure if we were going to make it here on time with the traffic. Look, it's already six forty-five."

She hauled her cell from her purse then dropped her head in her hands. Hormones had distracted her when she could least afford it. He was right. Even if she'd run or found a trolley to drive her, she would have had a hard time making it to her gate before they released her seat for the international flight.

"So why'd you bother with all this nonsense?" She waved at the decadent car. "You were that sure you'd get in my skirt?"

"Not at all."

She crossed her arms over her chest, trying to ignore the husky note to his voice. Like she gave a crap if she'd hurt his pride.

"I made other arrangements for us. I'm sorry, I should have asked but I didn't think you'd accept. Not until you knew me better. I didn't plan for this to happen, but I'd be lying if I said I didn't hope." A ghost of his previous smile returned. "I still think you're gorgeous."

Anger at his ability to melt her insides, even now, had her snapping at him. "Cut that out. Tell me how I'm getting to Europe."

"On the team's private jet."

Had she heard him right? "Private jet?"

"Uh, yeah. I came to the States with my navigator Mark. We checked out a few brake suppliers we're considering changing to. After that, he went to visit some family while I did a little sightseeing. I was meeting him here for the flight to France."

"You're making a transatlantic flight on a private jet." She couldn't stop herself from repeating herself even though she knew she sounded ridiculous.

"Yep." He grinned. "Are you impressed yet? I'm kind of banking on that, you know?"

"Holy crap." She shook her head. "And you're sure it's okay for me to come along?"

"I cleared it with our owner. And Mark." His lids grew heavy as he stared at her, the embers of their lust glowing a little brighter for a moment. "He's looking forward to meeting you."

"What did you tell him about me?" Suspicion had her pulse picking up speed with every beat of her heart.

"Enough." Sebastian scrubbed his hand through his hair before settling her onto his lap once more. Shock numbed her too much to fight. Besides, his touch calmed even when it should have repulsed. "If you just need a lift, we're more than glad to help. If you want to check out the private cabin with me, that's even better. And if you want to reach for your fantasies, win the lotto…well, you're holding the ticket. All you have to do is cash it."

She couldn't deny the pressure of his cock, hard once more, against her thigh.

"You'd be okay with that? Sharing me with your friend?" Part of her became horny as hell as she considered the possibility, but part of her cried that he didn't want to keep her for himself. Stupid, considering they'd met mere hours ago. How could she think their affair could be more than a simple fuck?

"I'm not going to lie, *tesoro.* I've done it before. But…" He shook his head. "It's fine. If that's what you want, it's fine. More than fine." His fingers clenched on her hip and knee.

"How much time do we have before take off? When do I have to decide?"

"It's not an ultimatum. Fly with me. See what develops, okay?"

They pulled up to the curb as he pressed a gentle kiss to her lips. She nodded but she already suspected their voyage could have only one destination. It wasn't every day someone held a golden ticket.

What a waste it would be not to use it.

Chapter Five

જી

The driver opened the door then handed her out. Was it too much to hope for an internet connection in the terminal?

"We have to be on board in twenty minutes. I'm going to check on our luggage. Why don't you call Rachel and let her know you're okay? I'm a little afraid of your friends." He joked but she caught the serious kernel in his eyes.

He'd lobbed her a perfect excuse to get some advice and she would grab it.

"Thank you." She hugged him tight. Maybe he'd gone about things all wrong, but she could admit to herself that she'd have been royally screwed—and not the fun kind—if he hadn't done it. "I'll meet you at the gate in fifteen minutes."

Lynn found a bench in a quiet corner. This terminal had a much classier feel than the cramped, utilitarian commercial wings. Her finger tapped the icon for Rachel in her contact list. Unsure if the thing had even rung, her best friend's shriek almost destroyed her eardrum.

"Tell me everything! Are you okay? What's going on?" In the background she thought she heard Ethan trying to calm his fiancée.

"I'm good. Everything's good. Great really." She hesitated.

"Are you sure?" Rachel pressed.

"Yes." The aura of her sexual conquest had been tainted by her doubts. "It's just...well, Sebastian has a bad habit of acting before asking. He's done it twice in the nanosecond I've known him."

"Did he hurt you?" The *shwing* of her friend's claws coming out rang through the line.

"No, that's not it. But he trampled my pathetic attempt at being in charge of my destiny."

"That's the price you pay for having a hotheaded, younger man in your life. You just met. He doesn't understand what you've been through yet. But there are definite bennies too. Speaking of...did you fuck him?"

"Rach!" Ethan's outrage traveled over the line.

"Uh..."

"You did! I knew it! God, he's smoking. And really good at his job. I researched him for you. He's won the title in his class the last three years in a row."

Why should Lynn feel any measure of pride over that? It wasn't as if she'd had a hand in it. Still, something inside her glowed for him.

"I only have a few minutes, Rach. I'm flying to France with him on his team's private jet."

"Holy shit! He's hot, successful, good in bed *and* he has access to a private jet? You bitch!"

Ethan mumbled in the background. Something about the *Kama Sutra*.

Lynn really didn't want to know.

"I never said he was good in bed." She'd burn in hell for implying he wasn't.

"Whatever! I can hear it in your voice. Okay, okay, I'm under control now. What the heck do you need me for? Sounds like you've got things well in hand."

"He..." She had to stop and clear her throat before starting again. "He found my books. There's going to be another guy with us. His navigator. Sebastian implied they're into *ménage*."

Nothing came across the line.

"Hello?" She peered at the display on her cell, which claimed to still be connected. Not now! She banged the thing against the heel of her palm. "Rachel? Can you hear me?"

"Sorry. Still here. Just... Whoa."

In all the years they'd known each other, Rachel had never been at a loss for words before.

"Is that a good 'whoa'? Or a bad 'whoa'?" Panic started to breed self-doubt.

"It's a just-wait-until-I-post-this-on-the-blog whoa. I know you, Lynn. If you didn't feel it you would have kicked him to the curb already. The fact you're considering means you really have something going. To be honest, I'm more concerned about that. What are you going to do after tonight? Are you going to be able to walk without getting hurt?"

"I—I don't know. It might be too late for that already." She wished she could put the world on hold to think things through. Then again, hadn't that always gotten her in trouble? Maybe it was time to let go and trust her instincts. "I think I'm going to do it, Rach. If there's a spark between us, I'm going to go for it. I'll figure the rest out later."

"Good for you. Enjoy yourself. Email me when you can so I know you're all right."

"I will. Thanks." She closed her phone with a snap. The digital clock on the front reminded her no more than five minutes of her reprieve remained. No way in hell would she meet Sebastian's friend looking like a something that'd been strapped to the hood of their racecar for a dozen rough miles.

She hustled to the restroom to freshen up.

* * * * *

"Dude. Quit pacing, you're driving me nuts."

Sebastian glared at Mark, the ungrateful bastard. Didn't he realize how much they stood to lose? Letting Lynn out of his sight had been a gamble, but he'd nearly pushed her too far by rearranging her schedule. Maybe she'd tell them to fuck off. "What if she doesn't show?"

"She'll come. You said this trip is important to her, right? There's no other choice today. I came through the main hall from my connecting flight. It's wall-to-wall in there."

He didn't dare tell his friend how bad he hoped Lynn returned because of him—the hell with the lack of alternates. He'd never live that down. At least not until the man had met her. Sebastian found it hard to believe anyone could resist Lynn. How she'd made it this long without some guy claiming her boggled his mind. Unless she didn't want to be tied down.

"Hot damn, is *that* your lady?" Mark looked like a kid in a candy store as he watched Lynn approach.

"Uh-huh." She had gotten even more gorgeous in the past half-hour. He'd swear to it.

"Good eye, Fiori."

"It's more than that, asshole." He regretted the fire in the rebuke when his friend turned to face him, eyebrows raised. Maybe this hadn't been one of his best ideas.

Too late to rescind his offer—not that he'd deny Lynn a chance to explore her fantasy—he reached out to buss her cheeks before making introductions.

He ignored the urge to snatch her away as she hugged Mark in greeting. When her luscious breasts pressed against his friend, she might as well have waved a red flag at the poor sucker. No way could the man resist her stacked frame if given half a chance.

Mark had been his second-in-command since their junior racing days a decade ago. His best friend understood what Sebastian wanted when he lingered instead of clambering onto the plane.

"Very nice to meet you, Lynn. I'll see you two on board. Gotta make a call before we take off." He wore a shit-eating grin as he practically skipped into the Jetway.

"I was afraid you'd run." No use in beating around the bush.

"Me too." She patted his chest then fixed some imaginary wrinkle in his collar before she whispered, "But I couldn't. I would regret it the rest of my life. Not knowing what might have been. I have to say this though. No more stealing my thunder. Only *I* say what goes with me."

"There are no expectations, *tesoro.*"

"I'm hardly your treasure." She smiled despite her protest. When she'd translated the term on her phone, his sweetness had caused a warm glow to spread through her.

"Let me be the judge." His thumbs brushed her cheekbones as he bent to kiss her. Long, lingering glides of their lips lulled his anxiety. Everything would be fine as long as she went with him. "Whatever happens…"

He stopped short of promises he didn't think she'd welcome. This should have been a one-night stand. If a fancy one. So why did it feel like the start of a relationship to him instead?

Before he could crack a tooth on his size-eleven sneakers, the flight attendant hailed them from the open door. "Excuse me, Mr. Fiori. The captain is calling for you to board at this time."

"Thanks, Marcy." He nodded to the woman before returning his focus to Lynn. "You ready?"

She grabbed his hand then matched her stride to his as they crossed the threshold in synch. The door locked behind them. There could be no turning back now.

Lynn gasped when confronted with the opulence of the private jet. If the limo had been a giant step up from her Camry, the sleek lounge and dining areas of the aircraft were light years ahead of the standard commuters she'd flown in. Afraid to stain the pure white carpet, she toed off her heels near the entrance.

"Talk about leg room!" A giggle escaped before she could squash it. Unbecoming of a forty-year-old woman, she thought. "I could do cartwheels in here."

"In that skirt, I don't recommend it." Sebastian winked at her.

"Aw, come on. Don't ruin all my fun, *amico.*"

She grinned at the easygoing man who'd introduced himself as Mark. A few inches shorter than Sebastian, he had muscles galore. His sandy hair complemented chocolate eyes and olive skin, giving him an appearance that could have come off as boring but definitely did not. His sense of humor sparkled, adding charm to everything he did.

For a situation with a high awkwardness potential, he made her feel right at home.

"But if naked gymnastics are out of the equation there is dinner to look forward to. As soon as we reach cruising altitude. Don't know about you kids but I'm starving. Let's strap in so we can get this show on the road."

The unorthodox seating arrangements threw her. Where exactly did one sit for takeoff? Not in the dining room chairs bolted to the floor, right?

"Join us over here." Sebastian led her to a double lounger, similar to a loveseat. Puffy cushions camouflaged standard airplane seat belts tucked in the seams. They settled onto the chair as Mark claimed the single version, facing them.

The safety spiel played on the huge flat screen at the top of the bulkhead, but all of them had traveled enough to recite it by heart if they chose. Sebastian reached across her waist to grab hold of the buckle then snapped her in. The heat of his touch set her on fire.

For too long, she'd sacrificed her personal life for her career. After two years of clinical orgasms, thanks to her purple, bead-filled, rabbit vibrator, their bout of wild sex had affected her like an alcoholic falling off the wagon. And she was ready to binge.

140

Lynn didn't realize she and Sebastian had locked gazes until the flight attendant fractured their shared intensity. "All set here?"

"Yes, thanks." Mark answered for them when Sebastian cleared his throat.

"I'll be serving dinner as soon as the captain allows, as you requested. Will you need service before then?" Half Lynn's age, the leggy bombshell made delicious eye candy, but neither Sebastian nor Mark paid the woman much attention.

"If something comes up, we'll ring. Otherwise, go relax up front." Sebastian dismissed the young beauty without looking away from Lynn.

The power of the men's interest had her head swelling by the second.

The engines roared as soon as the woman disappeared behind the curtain separating their space from the galley and crew.

"We've got trivia, movies, some books on the shelf over there and even video games. Seb plays a mean Wii tennis." Mark diffused the tension radiating between them as they inched toward the top of the runway.

"I'm more into the yoga in Fit myself."

"You can actually pull that shit off? Seb and I tried it once but we called it quits when he busted his ass in a lame excuse for the tree pose. Funniest damn thing I've seen." He paused to give his jaw an exaggerated stroke. "Though it might have had something to do with the case of beer we drank before that."

He laughed, the infectious delight drawing a mirroring grin from her.

"*Dio*, you swore you'd never use your powers for evil." Sebastian squeezed her thigh as he gave Mark shit. Unable to resist touching him, she laced their fingers then tipped her head, content to rest against his shoulder, which rocked a bit with his chuckles.

"Tired, *tesoro*?"

"It's been one heck of a day." The engines revved as the captain announced their position as first for departure.

"Damn straight," Sebastian muttered before nudging her chin toward his for a taste of her lips. What seemed like an innocent gesture at first morphed into something serious when neither of them could stop at a tiny peck. They leaned toward each other, angling their faces for better access.

Lynn couldn't say for sure if the concentrated lust of his kiss or the g-force of the jet accelerating down the runway caused her stomach to do more summersaults, but thirty seconds later she soared. She savored the cinnamon flavor of the candy he must have eaten and allowed herself to relax. Despite the short time she'd known him, she realized she trusted him. If she didn't, she never would have gotten on board the plane, or with his plans.

He coaxed her to take his tongue farther into her mouth as he seduced her with broad sweeps of his lips. The perfection of the moment flowed over her, making her dizzy. Her equilibrium shifted as they circled higher and higher above the receding earth. Could she reach for the stars? From here she felt closer than ever before.

She opened her eyes. Sebastian watched her, absorbing every nuance of her reaction. In the limo, she'd acted with pure, desperate need. She'd taken what she wanted. Now she craved something different. Something riskier.

While staring straight into the depths of his stare, as blue and endless as the ocean, she let go of her doubts and fears. She melted into his open arms, allowing him to cradle her exactly as he liked. He might have made fewer revolutions around the sun than she, but he had a hell of a lot more experience than her zilch when it came to no-strings affairs. He could make her burn.

A growl rumbled from his throat. His fingers tensed where they massaged her scalp, mussing her hair.

"So sexy." Mark's smoky timbre startled her. She'd forgotten he existed. Tingles magnified when she thought about the show they put on for him in his front-row seat. "That's right, *cara*. Let Seb take care of you. He will. *We* will, if you let us."

A soft moan betrayed her.

"Watching you make out is getting me hard."

Sebastian couldn't remain unaffected in the wake of Mark's taunting. He nipped her lip then sucked away the sting. Their chests rose and fell with uneven gasps, melding the side of her breast to his forearm in sporadic bursts. She arched, seeking more contact.

"*Seni*, Seb." Mark's foreign direction soothed her universal dilemma when her lover responded, shifting his hand to cup her breast.

His thumb brushed her nipple, coaxing it to tighten beneath his strumming. Grateful for the relief, she snuck a glance in Mark's direction. His dilated pupils fixed on the intersection of Sebastian's skilled fingers and her satin blouse, which covered the heavy globes of her chest. The long, dark lashes surrounding his eyes swept his cheeks with each of his languorous blinks.

One of his hands gripped the armrest hard enough she feared he might bend it. The other cupped the bulge in his pants. His lips parted when he blew out a breath between clenched teeth.

Sebastian relinquished control of her mouth to allow her greater flexibility. She basked in Mark's approval until bursts of ecstasy wrenched her attention to the man feasting on her neck and collarbones. When she reached for her seat belt to free herself, he gripped her wrist.

"Let him play, *cara*." Mark took the devious bastard's side then upped the ante. "Put your hands inside the belt."

When she could force her brain to process his command, she hesitated less than half a second before complying.

Sebastian grabbed the free end of the canvas strap and yanked. She squirmed but didn't get far. Her thighs fell open, begging for relief from the pressure he amplified with every touch.

"*Grazioso.* So pretty." Mark groaned when Sebastian worked her skirt up to her waist.

"Let me see *you*, Mark." She froze when the breathy request slipped past her guard. Would it upset Sebastian? She had no idea what to expect. What were the rules here? So unlike anything she'd done before, she hadn't bothered to ask before diving in headfirst, praying Sebastian would be there to catch her.

"I can't," Mark rasped.

She shouldn't have worried. Sebastian paused to grin at her. "You hear that? You're driving him insane, gorgeous. If he puts his hand in his pants right now, he'll come so fast and hard we'll go supersonic."

"He's not the only one." Her head bounced against the rest, her hips rising toward the devious fingertips drawing circles on the inside of her thigh. So close…

"Challenge him, gorgeous. I want to see which of you can hold out longest."

"What's the prize?" The wicked streak she'd embraced grew wider by the moment.

"Winner gets to decide what's for dessert tonight." Sebastian's rough whisper made it clear he had something more decadent than triple-layer chocolate cake in mind.

"Anything they want?" Endless visions of what she'd request—the two men focused on her, both kneeling between her legs, lapping at her soaked pussy, taking turns fucking her into oblivion—overrode her reservations.

"Anything."

"Take your cock out, Mark."

"I love it when you turn bossy." Sebastian nuzzled her jaw.

She smiled. "Me too. Who would have guessed?"

The rustle of Mark shifting for better access drew her attention to him once more. He shoved his t-shirt high on his chest then slid the zipper carefully over the tent in his pants. A rock of his hips accompanied an agile swipe of his hands, which thrust his jeans and boxer briefs to the tops of his thighs. Just low enough to allow his erection to grow upward along his abdomen.

"Impressive." She licked her lips.

"They don't call us Italian stallions for nothing." He winked then grimaced. "But I've got nothing on Seb."

"Mmm." Lynn sighed as she remembered how he'd stretched her. The memory put her in jeopardy of losing their bet before it'd begun. "No fair. That was a low blow."

"Anything goes."

"In that case...wrap your hand around your hard-on. Show me how you jerk yourself off. Long, full strokes from the base to the tip. No skimping."

"Fuck, yes," Mark muttered as he obeyed.

She relished the thrill even as it drove her closer to the end of their match. Arousal bubbled within her, making it hard to catch her breath. Sebastian didn't help any when he walked his fingertips up her thigh to pet her swollen pussy. She gasped.

"Oh yeah, take that." Mark's strained chuckle didn't last long.

"Use your other hand. Play with your balls."

Sebastian looked between them with a grin. "You two aren't screwing around. Good thing, probably twenty minutes or less until Marcy brings dinner. If no one wins before then, *I'm* taking the prize."

"Get your fingers inside her, Fiori. I'll share the reward with you," Mark promised. When Sebastian didn't move quick enough to suit him, he snapped, "Hurry up."

Lynn cried out when her lover's long fingers glided through the ample lubrication dripping from her slit. Three thick digits invaded her clenched rings of muscle until the pad of his palm pressed her clit. "Bastian!"

She attempted to sit still, to keep from writhing on him, but the temptation overpowered her logic. Her hands fisted on either side of her spread thighs, trapped by the strap. Thank God, or she might have yanked Sebastian closer and come on the spot.

"She's so tight. Wait 'til you feel her pussy on your cock. Amazing."

Mark groaned, "Whose side are you on, dude?"

The navigator's hand sped up, making a wet, slapping noise each time he passed over the slick head of his cock.

Instead of answering, Sebastian scissored his fingers inside her, stroking the walls of her pussy until he hit a particularly sensitive spot. She shrieked then trembled, her thighs tensing to try to align his touch once more.

"Oh yeah. Come for him, *cara*." Mark panted. "I can smell your sweetness from here."

"So close." She could surrender now if she wanted. Why didn't she want to again? The promise of a brilliant orgasm weakened her resolve. Rhythmic pulses began to squeeze her around Sebastian, making him work to maintain his pattern of invasion and retreat.

"Me. Too." Mark grimaced. His hand added a twist near the top of his stroke now, rubbing the underside of his cock with the pads of his fingers. His muscles strained, making him look every bit a Roman god straight out of legend. Soon she could have him. Have them both, fucking her together.

Positive she'd lose their challenge in the next moment, Sebastian shocked her by removing his hand from her clit, though he continued to pump his fingers inside her. She cried out as she receded a tiny step from the ledge of ecstasy. With Bastian's hand blocking the view, Mark couldn't tell. Not that he could see well through the slits his eyes had become anyway.

The younger man's hand flew over the straining flesh of his cock for two more seconds before his entire body went stock-still.

"Oh. Fuck," he grunted then his abdomen rippled in a wave of lithe muscle before stream after stream of milky cum poured from the purple tip, glazing his hand, his six-pack and his balls.

The erotic sight had her trembling. Sebastian's fingers slid the fraction of an inch over to the perfect spot he'd abandoned then flexed as he shifted her pleasure into high gear. She bucked against him, rubbing herself shamelessly on his hand. He couldn't deny her now.

The ragged moans echoing from Mark as he wrung satisfaction from every pulse of his orgasm sealed her fate. She exploded, clamping her legs shut to keep Sebastian right where she needed him. Her spine arched, exposing her mouth to him. He didn't waste any time claiming her. The sensual kiss guided her through the tumultuous passion battering her senses until she sagged against the seat, huffing as though she'd run a marathon.

He rubbed their noses together then separated them to bring his drenched digits to his mouth, humming with approval at her taste. When he'd cleaned every last drop of honey from them, he leaned close to whisper in her ear. She hardly heard him over the ringing in them.

"I'm always on your side."

Unsure of how to respond, she stared into the pools of desire in his eyes as he arranged her clothes and released her wrists. The flight attendant saved her from answering when she announced from the doorway, "The captain says you can move freely about the cabin now. I'll have your spaghetti ready in five minutes."

Mark flung aside the pillow he'd used to shield his lap from the woman's view, though she'd have to be a moron to have missed the flush bronzing his skin. He crossed the gap between them then kissed Lynn's cheek. "I gotta get cleaned up first. I'm starving. But don't worry, I'm saving plenty of room for dessert. Nice game."

When he ambled into the restroom near the rear of the plane, she turned to Sebastian with wide eyes.

"*Buon appetito, tesoro.*"

Chapter Six

❧

"That was delicious." Lynn folded her hands over the linen napkin in her lap. "I still can't believe you arranged my favorite meal on such short notice."

"I'm glad you enjoyed it." Sebastian smiled as he sipped the last of his wine. They'd finished eating over half an hour ago but none of them had budged from the frosted glass table where they shared great conversation and lots of laughs.

Mark had regaled her with stories of their adventures over the past ten years on the circuit. Though he'd probably edited out the worst of the tales, she couldn't believe some of the things the two of them had been through together. It made her realize how much she'd lost out on while dedicating herself to climbing the corporate ladder.

"What's that look all about?" Sebastian nudged the base of her chair so the seat swiveled in his direction from her position between the two men.

"Nothing." She shrugged. "I guess I'm a little jealous, that's all."

"Because you always wanted to be an international racing sensation?" Mark teased from behind her.

"Not exactly," she chuckled. "More like I've always wished for the freedom to go where I wanted when I wanted, to see the world and do what I love."

"You're on your way now, right?" Bastian scooped her from the molded bucket chair onto his lap.

"Yeah, I guess I am." She snuggled against his chest as she recounted all the changes she'd made in the past months then wondered why the thought of striking out on her own didn't thrill her quite as much right then.

"You're going to do great, gorgeous." His hands glided across her back, rubbing the tension from her. The combination of the wine flowing through her and his gentle care had her relaxed in no time. She didn't even flinch when the flight attendant came to clear their dishes.

"Is there anything else I can get for you?"

"We're good, thanks." Sebastian's chest rumbled beneath her cheek with his dismissal. "We won't be needing service until breakfast. Say, an hour before we land?"

"Enjoy the rest of the flight then."

"Oh, we will." Mark uttered the remark under his breath. For their ears only.

Desire flared in her gut. Would they really give her what she yearned for most—the room to stretch her wings and explore without judgment or recrimination?

Yes, they would. The certainty blossomed in her.

Anxious to repay their generosity, she peeked up from her perch. "No more games, no messing around. I want you."

She trailed her fingers over Sebastian's cheek then turned to include Mark. "And you. Right now."

"Who am I to keep a lady waiting?" The navigator rose from his chair across the table then whipped his shirt over his head. The flex of his ridiculous muscles entranced her until he popped the button on his jeans.

Lynn hopped off Sebastian then grasped the hem of his cotton shirt. She tugged it up then over his raised arms. She stood there a moment, memorizing every curve and the play of the soft light on his tan skin.

"What will you do with us, *tesoro*?" Calm, collected and ready for anything, he challenged her to shock him with that curious stare.

Instead of answering, she swayed from side to side as she peeled her blouse from her shoulders then shimmied out of her skirt. Lynn rolled the stockings down her legs, loving the hunger in Sebastian's gaze.

A hiss escaped from between his clenched teeth.

The sound had her smiling when she turned to slip her underwear off, granting him a clear view of her naked ass and back. In the distance, she heard Mark rummaging through the duffle he'd stowed behind their take-off seats.

"Stand up, Bastian." When he did as she commanded, she knelt before him. She'd never had such an overpowering urge to give someone pleasure as she did right now, with this man. After all, he'd taken care of her earlier while seeking nothing in return. She had no doubt he'd do it again now if she were selfish enough to let him.

His hands toyed with the strands of her hair but didn't grab hold, didn't force her in any direction. He waited, with supreme patience, while she counted to ten to keep from begging him to fuck her on the floor. Two minutes of ecstasy wouldn't satisfy her this time.

She eased snug denim from his trim hips, staring as his half-hard cock bobbed along his thigh. Her hands rose, bracing her weight above his knees. Then she dipped her head to take him into her mouth.

"*Dio!* Yes." Light draws of her lips on his lengthening shaft had his breath rushing out in great gasps. She smiled around him as she watched his reaction from beneath her lashes. Working him gently, she eased his length to the back of her mouth, relishing every taste. While she encompassed him with wet heat, she reached out her tongue to lick the raised seam of his sac.

"Damn, sweetheart." Mark's palms landed on her shoulders when he zoomed in for a closer look at her handiwork. "I bet that feels fucking great."

"Does." Sebastian's groan sent a thrill along her spine. She'd learned a thing or two in her sexual encounters she would bet the young hussies they'd been with hadn't bothered to pay attention to yet. Not every man wanted a woman to eat him alive.

Her palms glided up his ripped legs to squeeze his ass. Then she nudged him toward the table. When he caught on, he turned as she came to her feet, keeping his cock buried to the hilt as he reclined. It slid against her tongue. She moaned, causing him to jerk harder in a vicious cycle of arousal.

Bent at the waist, she remained in the perfect position to continue laving him. Sebastian sprawled on his back on the table with his gorgeous ass resting on the edge. She settled between his splayed thighs. He propped each foot on the seat of a chair on either side of her to provide her with easy access. She spread her legs then arched her spine to present herself to Mark.

"You want me to fuck you, *cara*?"

She moaned around Sebastian's shaft, now rock-hard and heavy between her lips.

"Good thing I grabbed these." The crinkle of a wrapper tearing couldn't distract her from her mission.

Lynn relaxed her throat, easing Sebastian farther in until her lips rested on the trunk of his body.

"So good." His hands latched on to the edge of the table beside his tense thighs, allowing her to take her time in torturing him. "You're killing me."

She giggled around him. But not for long.

"Help me out, Mark." His strained plea shot straight to her pussy then up to her heavy breasts, dangling beneath her. "Distract her. I don't want to come like this. Not yet."

He might not want to crash into orgasm, but she sure as hell did. Two young studs would be able to keep up with her all night long if she wished. She didn't have to stifle her reaction as she sometimes did with men her own age.

The head of Mark's cock nudged her slippery vulva, seeking entrance. Each glancing press of his latex-encased shaft had her rocking back to greet it. He teased her, rimming the mouth of her pussy with the blunt head until she thought she might scream in frustration.

Then he notched the tip against her. She clamped down, kissing it with her steamy flesh.

He groaned, blanketing her spine as he reached for her shoulders. When he had her pinned where he liked, he lunged, impaling her on his beefy erection in one fluid thrust.

Stars exploded in her vision. Her eyes flew open, locked with Sebastian's, letting him witness her overwhelming pleasure. A rush of adrenaline left her soaring as one man fucked her while the other watched. She'd expected the experience to be phenomenal, but nothing could have prepared her for this high.

"Yes, gorgeous." Sebastian groaned. "Surrender to it. Let him take you all the way."

Mark's arms came around her—one below her breasts and the other above her hips—when her legs trembled, threatening to collapse. The fingers of his lower hand splayed over her mound, teasing her clit.

A miniature shockwave emanated from the site of his impact. Instincts had her lips curling over her teeth to protect Bastian from her desire. She sucked him harder, her tongue swirling over the ridge on the underside of his cock. Nothing could compare to his pre-cum busting over her taste buds while his friend tunneled deep and slow but steady inside her.

"*Tesoro*, stop." He panted. "Give me a minute."

She shook her head in disagreement, his hard-on slapping the inside of each of her cheeks in the process. Another spurt of his musk splattered on the roof of her mouth.

Mark ground into her harder when he realized what she intended. "Oh yeah. Make him come for you. Swallow him. He won't be able to resist."

Lynn gave Bastian one last lick then glided to the root. His bulging head opened her throat and she gulped around him. Thank God she didn't have a gag reflex.

Mark increased the pace of his fucking, pairing each stroke with a tap from his finger. Her entire body gathered, suffocating his implanted cock.

When Sebastian's heels drummed on the plastic chairs, his head thrashed from side to side. Then his glorious body arched off the table, accompanied by a shout. His contracted balls bobbed against her lips as they pumped his semen down her throat. The elation at conquering his resistance pulled her with him into the maelstrom of passion and surrender.

She came so hard on Mark's cock, she didn't know how the other man kept moving within her. For each pulse of her muscles, she swallowed another draught of Sebastian's seed. After what could have been seconds, or minutes, she purred around his semi-erect flesh.

"You two alive over there?" Mark continued to tunnel inside her throbbing channel.

"Mmm."

Bastian shivered when she moaned, his cock twitching in her loose hold. He levered onto his elbow for a better view then petted her hair as he caught his breath. "That…was the *best* blowjob I've ever had. *Dio,* how can I want more?"

Lynn smirked when his penis began to inflate beneath the gentle laps of her tongue. She let him slide from her mouth for a moment, nuzzling his balls instead.

"That's so hot, *cara.*" Mark withdrew his cock then used it to tap her clit until the ultrasensitivity transformed into renewed desire. Once it had, she ground herself on him again. Satisfied, he slid home, screwing her with short, fast jabs that stoked the embers of her climax. "You're not afraid to take what you want."

"Be gentler with her, Mark." Sebastian would have squirmed away from her if she hadn't increased the suction on his testicle.

"No." Her garbled response was clear enough. "Harder."

"You're sure?" Mark stalled, waiting for confirmation both from her and his best friend.

"Now!"

"Sorry, gorgeous. You're the boss." Sebastian grimaced then nodded at the other man. "Give her what she wants."

"You better get back in the game. Need to tag you soon. Not gonna last." In fact, Mark's breathing had already become erratic and his hands moved to grope her breasts. The pressure on her hard nipples felt divine.

"You love driving us wild, don't you?" Bastian traced her mouth around the edge of his balls.

"Mmm." She gasped as Mark's blunt dick hit a sweet spot.

"Right there, *amico.*"

The guys' coordinated efforts had her entire body compressing again. She'd never been so turned-on in all her life. Their expert lovemaking blew her mind. Mark bent lower then bit her shoulder. His abs slapped her ass faster and faster, but the stud ground his cock against her G-spot each time until she couldn't resist a moment longer.

She abandoned Sebastian's rejuvenated hard-on to scream out her pleasure. Mark slammed inside her one final time then poured his release into the condom he wore, all the while muttering things she couldn't understand but didn't need to.

All that mattered was the fire raging in Sebastian's eyes when she glanced up at him.

"Come here." He tugged her onto the table with him, her knees straddling his trim hips, to claim her mouth. And no matter how his best friend had pleased her, something about kissing this man held more significance. The attraction flowed between them, instant and powerful.

"One more," she whispered against his lips, feeling greedy.

"As many as you like."

"One more," she repeated. "With you."

She let her forehead rest on his while she caught her breath for a minute. When Mark groaned from behind her, she turned to check on him. A wry grin twisted his lush mouth as he hunched with hands on thighs, looking as wobbly as a newborn deer.

"My new favorite dessert." He sank to his knees, sparking a wicked thought.

Lynn rolled in Sebastian's arms, coming to rest with her back nestled to his front. She wiggled until she sat up and could plant one foot on each of his thighs. He caught on quick, this man of hers. Before she could ask, he cupped her hips, supporting her, lifting her as she reached for his erection.

A whimper escaped when his longer, thicker hard-on stretched her engorged tissue. She'd always enjoyed the reverse cowgirl position, but this time somehow surpassed all others.

"Okay?" At least he didn't try to stop her this time.

"Perfect," she sighed when her ass met his abdomen, embedding him in her completely. His hands curled around her sides to wander up her belly to her chest, pinching her nipples then rubbing out the sting. His fingers roamed over her entire body, everywhere he could reach, waking up nerves she thought deadened by her prior orgasms.

Mark absorbed every touch with his rekindled stare from his spot in front of her.

She started fucking Sebastian with slow pumps of her hips, building the pleasure one final time. It might be another two years until she had sex again after this night. Her movements turned urgent when she considered her simple affair had only hours to go before it burned out. She would take what the men offered—drown herself in ecstasy so she never forgot what it had been like to shine in their arms.

She performed for Mark. He definitely got off on watching. From a foot away, he could see the minute details of her and Sebastian's joining. The flex of her pussy around her lover's cock, the flush of their skin as blood raced to their loins, the gradual scrunching of his best friend's scrotum as she picked up steam.

"Lick my clit, Mark." The man drifted closer to where she and Sebastian were joined at the edge of the table but stopped, in the double vee of their thighs, an inch short of her pussy and his best friend's cock. The heat of his breath washing over her as his chest bellowed drove her to beg, "Please."

He groaned then closed the gap, enfolding her tight bundle of nerves between his lips. After their intense fucking, she appreciated his gentle manipulation. Her eyes rolled in her skull when Sebastian countered with long, liquid glides of his hips that filled her with his cock.

Suddenly, the tender loving took her higher than all the rough fucking in the world. Between the fluttering swipes of Mark's tongue and the easy pressure of Sebastian's erection, she curled her toes in delight on Bastian's knees.

"Mark." She whimpered as she tried to hold on. She wasn't finished yet. Not without Sebastian and he needed something more than this delicate sway to get off.

The man between her legs angled his head until their gazes met and his attention focused on her.

"Put one of your fingers in his ass."

Sebastian went stiff beneath her. "What? I'm not gay, Lynn. Not bi either."

She lifted off him until the bare tip of his cock remained embedded then sank onto him bit by bit. "I'm not asking you to let him fuck you. You said I could have anything I wanted. You'll like this. Trust me as I've trusted you."

The urge to lead him somewhere he'd never gone before raged inside her. It was only fair after what he'd done to her — destroyed her for other men.

His hands tightened on her hips until she guaranteed she'd have bruises to show for it but the pressure ratcheted her arousal higher. He didn't object further. Mark stared at her in wonder but no hint of disgust dimmed the appetite she saw in his chocolate eyes.

"Go ahead, you know you want to," she dared him.

All three of them groaned together when Mark's finger slid beside the length of Sebastian's cock inside her, gathering her wetness. Then he retreated. The sight of his long finger poised to penetrate Sebastian had the beginnings of another orgasm looming near.

"Seb?" He hesitated.

"Fuck." The cock buried in her pussy swelled to epic proportions a second before her lover groaned, "Do it."

More of her lubrication trickled around Sebastian, onto his balls. She observed Mark's thick digit disappearing beneath them.

An extensive string of Italian poured from the man she rode as his best friend plundered his virgin ass. She laughed out loud when his cock bulged inside her. "I told you so."

"Yes!"

"Now finish what you started." She balanced on one hand, planted on Sebastian's chest behind her, and reached for Mark's hair with the other, but he came forward on his own. He turned sideways to make room for his mouth to latch on to her pussy while he continued to ream Sebastian in counterpoint to her escalating thrusts.

She ground against them both — Mark on each forward motion and Sebastian on the reverse. Her torso slithered like a snake as she maximized the contact with the pleasure-inducing bookends.

Her head tipped back, inviting Sebastian to strain upward to kiss her. Their tongues tangled. She stared into his eyes, hoping he could detect even a fraction of the joy he had gifted her. He smiled near her mouth then nipped her lip as he picked up the pace.

A tsunami of passion barreled down on her, so tall and strong she feared it might annihilate her. She tried to escape, but running from Mark's mouth impaled her on Sebastian, and going the other way wasn't any better. She couldn't avoid the impending destruction.

Lynn gasped, prepared to warn the men servicing her.

"What the..." Sebastian froze beneath her for a heartbeat then hammered her. The hitch in his stride shoved her closer to Mark's talented mouth, which now vibrated with his ragged moans. "He's coming. On my leg."

The idea of Mark's hot ejaculate splashing over Sebastian's furred shin sent her into orbit. Sebastian couldn't remain unaffected in the wake of their orgasms. His cock plumped inside her, the ridges of his veins amplifying the best climax of her life until she thought she might pass out.

She screamed, "Bastian!"

His arms banded around her, sheltering her while every muscle in her body seized and jerked. She crashed through dozens of spasms. The answering shouts, groans and grunts of the two men echoed around her until, at last, they melted into a tangle of arms, legs and shattered inhibitions.

They didn't stay that way long. She needed to see Sebastian instead of staring at the curved ceiling. Neither the table nor the floor ranked high on the most comfortable places to lie either.

Sebastian sat up, helping her to her feet. She whimpered when his soft cock slipped from her juicy pussy. Instead of slinking away from Mark, he extended his hand to help his friend up then grinned.

Thank God.

"Next time your chin comes anywhere near my balls, you're gonna have to shave first. Like fucking sandpaper, dude." Both Lynn and Mark laughed when Sebastian winced then rearranged his package.

"Didn't hear you complaining when her pussy practically squeezed your dick in half. Besides, it serves you right for cheating in our game, you bastard."

She stared at Mark, her jaw hanging open. "You knew? Then why...?"

"It's what I wanted too." He placed a sweet kiss on the corner of her mouth. "You were amazing tonight. The best."

Sebastian shuddered then took her hand. "Let's go. Shower time."

"Thank you," she whispered over her shoulder as Bastian led her toward the private cabin.

* * * * *

Soaking in a garden tub on a jet speeding through the sky didn't seem as odd as allowing Sebastian—a man she'd just met, a younger man, a man she cared too much about—to tend to the aches dotting her body. Still, she enjoyed the intimacy of the act. She'd watched him rinse his best friend's cum from his calf before drawing the steamy water for them to soak in.

Now she lounged between his legs, nestled against his slick chest as he dragged a soapy cloth over her torso. When his hand plunged below the water to wash her pussy, he swallowed so hard she heard it.

"It's okay, Bastian," she whispered. "I'm clean. And I've been on the Pill since I was twenty. I don't know if I could even have children anymore."

"I've never forgotten to wear a condom before."

She turned to face him. His heart pounded beneath her palm. "I've never failed to insist on it. So I guess we're even."

160

"Do you think I'm a poor excuse for a man because I don't want children? I hear other guys talk about passing on their legacy..." He shrugged.

The serious concern in his tone coupled with lines of strain she didn't like seeing at the corner of his luscious mouth. "If it does, then I'm in the same boat. Don't get me wrong, I like kids. But I can't see myself having them. I guess that's one of the reasons I never got married."

"I'm not stable enough. I travel all the time. No kid should have to have an absentee parent or be dragged across creation, away from all their friends. I don't see myself wanting to leave what I do. I love racing. Even when I can't drive anymore, I want to be a chief. Or maybe an owner someday."

"I respect you for knowing what you want, refusing to compromise and taking responsibility to ensure you don't impact anyone else. You're a good man, Sebastian. Never doubt that."

The kiss he shared with her overflowed with gratitude and relief.

Disaster averted, they soaked together while talking about nothing important in hushed whispers until the water had gone cold and their skin wrinkled.

Lynn yawned as he carried her to the thick mattress then deposited her on a pile of pillows covered in bedding as fluffy as a cloud. She burrowed into them then held out her arms, welcoming him beside her.

"I can't tell you how many times I'd have traded a year's worth of Belgian chocolate for a bed while trying to sleep sitting up on a flight across the Atlantic. Now I'd give anything to stay awake a little while longer." She fought the tears stinging her eyes. If she closed her lids, she knew she wouldn't be able to open them again. And, all too soon, they'd be going their separate ways.

"Isn't that the truth." Sebastian tucked her close then sighed. "We'll dream together, *tesoro*."

"Promise?"

"I do."

"Goodnight, Bastian."

"'Night, gorgeous."

Chapter Seven

℘

Lynn woke to unfiltered sunlight glinting from the cracks in the fancy shades covering the porthole-style windows. She rolled over, searching for Bastian with one hand. She found the warm depression where he'd rested but no man shared her bed.

So that was that.

She swung her legs over the side of the mattress, dragging the sheet with her like a toga. If he couldn't stand to wake up with her, she didn't want to flash her middle-aged imperfections in the harsh light of day for him to scrutinize.

Come on, what did you expect after a one-night stand? Just because she'd never done it before didn't mean she had no idea of the way people played the game.

A glance at her watch confirmed they had less than thirty minutes until they landed. He hadn't woken her for breakfast. Less awkward conversation that way, she supposed. She wrangled the spare set of clothes she'd stashed in her carry-on from the bag then consulted the bathroom mirror. It'd been a long while since she looked this alive. She'd take that.

Still, she had to plaster a fake smile across her face when she slipped into the main cabin. Mark occupied the same chair he had during takeoff, flipping through a motorsport magazine. Sebastian had gone missing.

"Good morning, *cara*. I was about to wake you. We need to strap in for landing."

"And Sebastian..." She hated that she'd asked but she had to know.

"Uh...he's taking care of some business in the crew quarters."

"I see." She dropped into the seat opposite him then feigned interest in the clouds coming closer with the passing miles. Not even the gorgeous formations could interest her this morning.

"Breakfast is on the table if you'd like a bagel, some eggs...yogurt?"

"I'm not hungry, thanks."

"At least let me get you some coffee—"

"Mark, stop." She winced at the bitterness in her command then whispered, "Please."

Lynn couldn't stand for the man to feel obligated to clean up his partner's mess. She had to keep it together long enough to make the world's longest walk of shame through the jet bridge and out of the airport.

"I'm here if you need anything, *cara*."

"Thank you."

And with that, he left her in peace for the remainder of the flight.

* * * * *

After landing, Mark helped her with her luggage then kept her company as they disembarked. What kind of fool did it make her that she still hoped Sebastian would show at the last moment? He'd checked every box on her wish list and then some in their oh-so-brief Cougar affair. She hoped they could part on favorable terms to keep the memories bright, untarnished.

Mark turned to her as they neared the exit to the cab lanes. People streamed by in all directions across Paris' congested airport. She planned to take the metro to her favorite hotel in the Etoile district, so she slowed to say goodbye when he peeled off.

"Are you going to recommend private jets in your guides?"

"Best in-flight service, hands down."

Mark threw back his head as he laughed. "Thank you, *cara*. For me too."

Lynn attempted a smile then angled her head so he wouldn't notice her sniffle.

"Ah, damn." He wrapped an arm around her shoulders. "I have no idea what *il bastardo* is thinking this morning..."

"Don't make excuses. He doesn't owe me anything." She accepted Mark's comforting hug. A few more seconds then she'd buck up and start off on her own.

"He's never pulled something like this before. You really got to him. Still, this is no way to treat a lady. I swear I'll kick his ass for you, okay?"

"How about a knee to the balls?"

"Deal." He kissed her cheek. "I don't suppose there's any chance you'd call *me* if I gave you my number, is there?"

Why couldn't exhilaration make her heart dance at the idea of a relationship with Mark the way it had for Sebastian? Sure, they'd had steaming-hot sex, but she'd conned herself into believing there'd been a spark, something greater than the physical, between her and the young driver.

"Oh *affunculo* no." Sebastian stepped between her and Mark, knocking the card from the navigator's fingers in the process.

"Look who decided to show up," Mark snarled, prepared to battle for her, but Sebastian ignored him.

"Shit. I'm sorry, *tesoro*." The endearment caused her to cringe. How could he mean it now? Had the whole thing been an act? "I was on the phone. Didn't realize they'd opened the doors. Thank God I caught you. We need to talk."

Lynn would rather wait in the absurd line outside the Louvre with all the suckers who didn't purchase advance tickets online on a Wednesday morning in July than listen to what Bastian had to say at that moment. Why couldn't he let her go with her dignity intact?

She'd already planned to stop by her favorite patisserie for a decadent fruit tart then wallow in her hotel for a few hours before burying the disappointment and savoring the wicked aches he'd inspired. But he refused to let her brush him off.

"Grab a taxi, Mark? I'll be out in a minute."

The other man looked to her for confirmation before nodding. "Safe travels, *cara.*"

He left with a wave.

Sebastian meshed their fingers together as though nothing odd had happened. "I have to head out. We're taking the TGV to Toulouse. But I have a surprise for you."

"You do?" *Why?* She racked her brain for some parting gift to give him in return. Like maybe her middle finger jammed into his gut.

"Yeah. I called my mom this morning and arranged for you to stay with her when you get to Erchie. It took some juggling to shift your reservation from Caprietto's but we worked it out. I can't wait for her to meet you. Then I figured you could swing by the circuit when we pass through Rome. I didn't plan for it to take so long but it's a bitch scheduling stuff this time of year. Tourists everywhere. But...all the tickets are here." He shoved an envelope at her. "You can write a whole book about Rome, right?"

She stared at him for a solid five seconds, trying to convince herself he was joking.

"You did *what?*" She scrubbed her hand over her cheeks. This couldn't be happening. "You didn't even stay this morning and now you're telling me you intended for there to be more?"

"Wait, you thought I was making a clean break?" He cursed under his breath in Italian. "It killed me to leave you

166

sleeping like an angel when all I wanted was to hold you. Or maybe slip in some morning loving. But I thought it more important to make sure we see each other again than to get my rocks off in another meaningless encounter."

"Last night was *meaningless* to you?" She sucked in a breath through her shattered chest. "Great. Maybe we better go our separate ways before this gets any worse. It's been...fun, Sebastian."

She spun, but his hand gripped her shoulder.

"No. Shit, Lynn, this is all coming out wrong."

"Why didn't you talk to me? Why didn't you let us decide together how things would go?" His manipulation betrayed her. "You know how I feel. I thought you understood how important it is for me to be independent...to decide my own fate."

"I do. But... There wasn't time. I didn't think. Don't you know how many girls have asked me for this privilege? I've never invited a woman to tour with me."

She recoiled as though he'd slapped her. "I'm supposed to be grateful for your interference? You arrogant — "

Mark leaned in the sliding door with an apologetic shrug before she could really pour on the steam. "Seb, we have to get a move on or we'll miss the train."

"One minute!"

The frustration radiating from him erased some of yesterday's bliss. She couldn't bear to have him obscure all the glory of the night before with this disastrous parting. "I can't do this, Sebastian. Please. Go. Good luck."

She reached up to kiss his cheek, frozen in shock, then gathered her luggage before spinning on her heel and darting between a baggage trolley and a tour group. By the time she'd crossed the busy lobby and turned, Sebastian had vanished.

* * * * *

LynnLuvs2Trvl: Younger men suck. Immature, cocky, bullheaded...

Rachel: You're starting to sound like my crotchety Aunt Imelda.

LynnLuvs2Trvl: Oh God. I am, aren't I? But it's been two weeks! Why the hell can't I forget about him?

Rachel: Maybe because he's emailed you every day, desperate for another chance?

LynnLuvs2Trvl: Thanks for giving him my address, by the way. I never would have thought you'd do that!

Rachel: He begged on the blog. He sounded so sincere. Despite what you think right now, there's something here, Lynn. I think you should answer him.

LynnLuvs2Trvl: I'd have to read his messages to answer them. I've deleted every one without opening it. For all we know, he's making sure he didn't knock me up.

Rachel: Lynn! You didn't!

LynnLuvs2Trvl: I did. I refuse to be tied to anyone. Especially not a controlling, infantile— Argh! You get the point. But now I'm screwed. I'm not with him and I can't stop thinking about him. I even went to the Rally Racing Museum today, like that's a top-five destination for a solo woman's travel guide. His picture was freaking everywhere. Do you have any idea how cute a man in a jumpsuit is?

Rachel: Holy crap, Lynn. This is getting out of hand. If you miss him this much, why not call him? Email, whatever.

LynnLuvs2Trvl: After what happened? No way. I can't stay with a man who wants to control me.

Rachel: If he's still dogging you, he's probably open to discussing your boundaries. You barely know each other. The way I figure, it'd have been easy for you both to write the night off but neither of you have.

LynnLuvs2Trvl: Worse, I leave for Erchie tonight. I tried everything. Including a bribe. But I couldn't get my original hotel back. There's no way he told his mom about us, right?

Rachel: That he fucked you in a limo an hour after meeting you then shared you with his best friend for a wild night that I am super envious of? Probably not. But I'm betting he raved about the gorgeous woman he met. You know, enough to make it uncomfortable.

LynnLuvs2Trvl: Damn it. That's what I thought too.

Rachel: Sorry, Lynn.

Lynn paused before exiting the deserted station to stretch her knotted muscles with a whimper. Nothing like hours on the regional train interspersed with mad dashes through terminals—traversing flights of stairs to platforms that never seemed close together with even the lightest luggage when attempting a quick connection—to tire a girl out.

On top of that, she'd gotten burned by notes she'd found online that cited the town's reliable tram system but had failed to mention it wouldn't be completed for another five years at least. If the dusty donation jar she'd spotted gave any indication, Erchie might never go high-tech. And that was part of its appeal.

She probably could have caught a straggling cab if she hadn't stopped to use the restroom. By the time she brushed her hair and popped a mint, in case Mrs. Fiori sized her up, the skeleton crew had departed. No one remained to listen to the buzz of the florescent lights but her.

These were exactly the hints she could capitalize on for her book. Though it didn't do *her* much good. She had a hard time imagining anything sinister lurking in the peaceful town when the *swoosh* of the ocean sang in the background. Still, survival instincts she'd honed over years of traveling alone had her dreading the walk through twilit streets to her accommodations.

Grabbing the last train into town had been a mistake.

Thank God she could cross the distance to the bed and breakfast in fifteen minutes at a brisk pace. She hauled her bag along the ramp, surprised to see a car running with its lights on at the curb.

Lynn had taken two giant strides along the sidewalk when the car inched forward. The window began to roll down. *Great.*

She picked up her pace, the wheels of her suitcase squeaking in protest.

"Buona sera, signorina."

Lynn debated ignoring the older gentleman but opted for a tiny wave as she continued along her way. Still, he persisted, the Peugeot creeping along to stay even with her.

"Scusami." The white-haired man flailed his hands in her peripheral vision.

Then he said two magical words. The only two that could have claimed her attention. "Sebastian Fiori."

She tripped over a crack in the sidewalk. At least she tried to convince herself something other than the instant rush of anticipation and longing caused her stumble.

Her stare whipped in the man's direction. Now that she really looked, she found countless similarities to the perfection she had memorized two weeks ago. The sappy part of her had feared she'd forget his face after such a short time together but the opposite had been true. Every night, visions of him had filled her imagination.

Almost as though they still dreamed together.

When she shook her head to clear the ridiculous thoughts, the man's eyebrow arched.

"Mrs. Fiori...hotel...ride..."

The man struggled with English but she understood. Sebastian came by his tendency to grab the reins naturally it seemed. She bit her lip as she considered accepting. To be honest, refusing the kind gesture would make her stupid *and* rude in this case.

She smiled. *"Grazie."*

Before she could lug her bag to the vehicle, the man had hopped out. He shooed her away while he took care of hoisting it into the hatchback. Then he turned to her, planting a double-cheeked air kiss on her. When they parted, he slapped his chest. "*Eduardo. Zio.*"

Ah, Sebastian's uncle. No wonder.

"Lynn."

The man nodded. Since they couldn't converse, Eduardo cranked up the zesty Italian folk music bouncing through the car's tinny speakers. She laughed in delight when he belted out the harmonies, encouraging her to clap along. His charisma was impossible to resist. Another trait that ran in the family, she supposed.

Just as Eduardo delivered the rousing finale, they swung into a narrow stone driveway.

The charming terracotta-tile-roofed villa nestled in a field of wild flowers and citrus trees. Perched on a low outcropping, it overlooked the warm waters of the Mediterranean, cerulean even at dusk. The hue of the waves washing the shore reminded her of Sebastian's eyes.

But before regret could overwhelm her, Eduardo cupped her elbow. He guided her toward the rear of the structure with a knowing smile. The crowd of laughing, drinking, joking locals gathered around an outdoor fire pit and a TV—plugged in via an enormous extension cord from the main house—surprised her.

Bright red and blue pennants adorned with Driven Wild and Sebastian's team logo strung across the lush yard, creating a ceiling over the gathered tables piled with pastries and wine. Eduardo whisked her suitcase inside before she could stop him. When she followed, a woman carrying a checked hand towel greeted her with a smile.

"You are Lynn Madison?"

"Mrs. Fiori?"

"*Si*, Maria." The woman welcomed her with open arms. In two seconds flat, she'd been smothered in a giant squeezy hug against Sebastian's mother's ample cleavage without so much as a hint of the appraising stare she'd dreaded. "Welcome to Erchie and to our home. You are just in time!"

"Thank you. Truly." Lynn tried to focus on Mrs. Fiori's easy acceptance despite the whispers spreading through the gathering like wildfire. More than one young woman shot her a glare sharp enough to sting across the patio. "Am I interrupting? I can go for a walk until your event is finished. Unless there's something I help with?"

"Not at all! You'll sit. Watch the race? Sebastian starts in five minutes." A hint of unease crept into the gracious host's eyes, which reminded her so much of the man who'd rocked her world.

"Tonight? I didn't realize…" God, flying along ridiculous courses in the dark! Why hadn't she considered the dangers inherent in his job? She reached out without thinking to pat Maria's hand where it wrung her apron. "I would like that very much."

They sank to a rustic bench together. Someone thrust a glass into her hand, the maroon wine sloshing onto her fingers as they passed by. What must it be like to have so many people rooting for you, supporting you? Sebastian had innumerable ties here yet still he seemed free to do as he pleased.

Could there be a difference between a bond and a restraint?

She took a slug of the cheap wine, savoring the burn as it slid through her system. The commentators finished their run-through of tonight's stage, the final section of this event. Lynn cringed when she studied the insane wiggles in the gravel course. Unease skittered along her spine, inciting a shiver.

"These are the worst for me to watch." Maria polished off her own drink then snagged a replacement. "He's leading by almost two minutes. He could play safe. But my son does not know how."

In the background, a flashy graphic plotted Sebastian's current time versus the world record. At this point, he edged out in front by several seconds. Never mind that he held the top five ranks, she knew he'd do his best to shatter his previous mark.

"How long will it last?" Her ignorance rankled. Why hadn't she paid closer attention to the facts at the museum instead of staring at his tight ass in all the pictures?

"This stage...twenty-seven kilometers." Maria nodded as she considered, "I bet he will finish in no more than ten minutes."

Some quick mental math had her eyebrows rising. "In these conditions?"

Maria didn't answer. Instead she made the sign of the cross then focused in on the television. People stood and cheered as three electronic beeps heralded the launch. Then, in a cloud of dust, Sebastian's car rocketed from the starting line. She could see two shadows inside the cabin of the car but couldn't make out either Sebastian or Mark's features behind the thick helmets they wore.

The cheers of the Fiori's friends, neighbors and relatives brought the night alive. Lynn couldn't believe how fast the bright car flew through twists and turns. The slides over treacherous lines left razor-thin margins of error. Each time Sebastian nailed a section, the gathering grew more rowdy until catcalls, whistles and yells drowned out the sound from the television not two feet in front of her.

Lynn took her focus from the screen for a millisecond to observe the outpouring of pure excitement for a man who had obviously touched many people in his lifetime. She didn't need to see the screen to know something had gone horribly wrong when the crowd hushed mid-cheer. A glass shattered in the background as it hit the pavers.

Her head whipped around to see Sebastian's car crash through the underbrush and clip the corner of a stone wall. It jolted to a stop, nose down in a ditch. The pain in her chest as her heart skipped a few beats alarmed her in the far recesses of her mind. She couldn't say who'd moved first but Maria clenched her hand so tight she thought her knuckles might crack, and Lynn returned the favor.

Though it seemed an eternity of uncertain terror passed, seconds later, a communal sigh of relief washed over her when the lights on Sebastian's car flicked three times in rapid succession.

"His sign to me." Maria explained between whispered prayers of thanks.

Lynn watched, numb, as Mark and Sebastian erupted from the vehicle then pushed it out of the rut, onto the course. Her eyes nearly bugged out of her skull when the crazy bastards piled into the deathtrap and took off along the route.

As though the world hadn't ground to a stop, cheers blanketed her again. But nothing could chase the chill from her bones. Both because she feared for Sebastian's safety in the remainder of the race and because she could no longer deny how deep he'd embedded himself in her heart during their *meaningless* night together.

She stayed long enough to watch him clamber onto the roof of his dented vehicle with Mark. The roar of the hometown crowd—not to mention the shower of champagne dousing them—making it clear they'd won yet another race.

Then she staggered to her feet. Maria rose with her, throwing an arm around Lynn's waist. She understood Lynn's sudden desire for solitude, guiding her through the cheerful citrus colored décor to Sebastian's room.

"I wish I could say the wrecks get easier but I can't." When Lynn didn't answer Maria's soothing rambling, the woman continued. "You've had a long day. I think some sleep would do you well."

The older woman flipped on the bare overhead light, casting the cozy space in a warm glow. Every inch of plaster had been covered by framed articles on her son's success. One corner held a rustic bookshelf buried in trophies. The bed had been turned down with fresh sheets, flowers spread over the pillow.

The idea of sleeping here, surrounded by the man she would never forget—but had already lost—had her aching and on edge. "Why are you doing this? Why let me stay here? I am nothing to him. To you."

"I've always wished one thing for my son. They say I spoil him but I want him to have everything he desires, no matter how big the dream. Sebastian says you're special to him."

"How can he know? We're almost strangers. And I'm so much older than him! Doesn't that bother you?"

"Hearts know nothing of time—not age or length of acquaintance. They know only what they need. The moment I met my husband, I knew. Here." Maria collected Lynn's hand, clasped it in her own as she touched it to the place over her heart. "My son has never said this to me before, please understand. You two are destined."

Lynn concentrated on preventing her eyes from rolling. A couple of wild fucks between strangers couldn't be written off as cosmic intervention. More like irrational, reckless and decadent decision making.

"You do not believe."

"In fate? No, I'm sorry."

"Then think of how you miss him. Call it whatever you like. I can see the truth in your eyes. Your fear for him is as deep as mine. I believe you are special and I would not have you hurt. That would cause my son pain."

Maria hugged her then turned to go. "Sleep well, Lynn. Sebastian says he dreams with you still."

Lynn sagged onto the comforting flannel sheets. She sighed as she burrowed into Sebastian's bed, deluding herself into thinking she caught the scent of him on the pillow.

That must have been why visions of him surrounded her all night long.

Chapter Eight

ഇ

Lynn tipped her chin to catch rays of the mid-afternoon sun on her face. With her eyes closed, she savored the breeze fluffing her hair, making her gauzy sarong dance around her legs. She curled her toes in the damp sand, at peace for the first time in many months.

She'd decided.

Today she would read Sebastian's emails—she hadn't yet emptied her recycle bin—with an open mind before sending him a note in return. Maybe she'd get his number from Maria so she could hear his voice again. Just for a minute.

She could admit to herself that she'd overreacted now. Yes, he'd gone too far but she'd worried so much about her precious freedom that she'd overlooked the difference between a leash and an invitation.

Regret had her sighing as she considered the time she'd wasted. Unwilling to exacerbate her mistake, she pivoted, heading for the netbook she'd stowed in her room. Sebastian's room.

Her foot froze mid-step when she caught sight of the man ambling toward her.

He hesitated, as though unsure of his welcome, but she couldn't deny the thrill that raced through her at the sight of him. His unbuttoned shirt rippled in the gentle wind, revealing the perfection of his sculpted torso above low-slung cargo shorts. Olive skin shone, making her fingers tingle with the need to explore.

But his piercing blue eyes, shadowed with uncertainty, had her bolting across the distance between them until she molded to his solid chest.

He wrapped her in a bear hug then whispered in her hair, "*Come, mi sei mancata!*"

"Did you just call me pasta?" She separated the scant inch necessary to peek up at him.

"Definitely not," he laughed. "Though you look good enough to eat. *Dio*, I missed you."

"Same here," she sighed. Before she could think better of it, her fingertips traced the gash on his bold cheekbone. "You scared me half to death last night."

"Sorry 'bout that, *tesoro*." His head dipped, his lips nearing hers. "But I'm glad to hear you still care. I thought I might have ruined everything. Ruined this..."

Lynn's breath caught in her lungs when Sebastian kissed her. Their lips brushed then melded as they both took and received in turn. The sparks she'd thought she'd amplified in her memory flared between them, setting her on fire.

Sebastian scooped her into his arms, her ass resting in his broad palms as she wrapped her legs around his trim waist. She practically climbed him in her desperation to get closer. He walked them to the water's edge, slipping behind an outcropping of rock, shielding them from anyone who might be watching from inside.

He laid her in the soft sand, following her down. "Lynn, wait—"

"Talk later." She yanked the hem of his shirt over his head, stripping the well-worn fabric off his shoulders. "Please, Bastian, show me you still feel it too. Nothing else matters."

For long minutes they lost themselves in the simple pleasure of kissing—tasting, nipping and licking—until the bliss overwhelmed reason. She had to have him again, had to fuse them until separation became impossible.

"Wait, *tesoro*." Sebastian groaned as he lifted off her. "I need you to know this is not meaningless to me. Far from it."

"Shh." Lynn gathered him close once more, peppering his face, neck and shoulders with kisses. "Not for me either."

"Thank God." Waves lapped at their toes where their legs tangled on the beach. He bracketed her face with gentle hands then sipped from her lips as he nudged her thighs apart to make room for his frame in the cradle of her hips.

His hard cock branded her through the khaki shorts separating their heat. She plunged her hands beneath the waistband then grabbed his bare ass under the fabric.

"Ever make love on the beach before, Bastian?"

"I've never had sex like this. Not in the daylight, out of the water, where anyone could see if they walk by or pass in a boat." He tossed a glance over his shoulder to be sure no one lurked in the background. His sudden modesty amused her, tempting her to push him until he murmured, "And I've never made love to a woman in my life. But I'd like to try it with you."

"Same here." She rolled, tucking him beneath her as she straddled his hips. While he licked his lips, she reached behind her to loosen the tie on her bikini top.

Bastian's hands glided over the sides and back of her thighs, allowing her to reveal herself to his hungry stare. When she'd tugged the laces free from their bow, she dropped her hands to her waist and allowed the fabric to flutter from her breasts.

"So gorgeous," he growled as he gripped her shoulder then tipped her forward until he could surround the tip of one mound with his lips. He flicked his tongue across the puckered surface of her nipple, causing a moan to escape from her parted mouth.

While he drove her insane with his sensual assault, she loosened the strings at her hips then peeled the scrap of her bathing suit from between her legs. The crotch of the fabric glistened in the sunlight, drenched with her arousal.

"You smell delicious." He shimmied lower, his hands bracing her waist until she hovered over his face. "Come to me. Let me taste you."

Her spine arched—hands bracing behind her on his raised knees—when his talented tongue traced the furrows of her pussy. He sipped the slick honey from her with aching delicateness that had her heart blossoming in her chest.

Tender swipes of his lips on her clit primed her for something deeper, stronger. She squirmed in his hold, dragging the soaked folds of her pussy over his chin when her instincts took control. Her hands fisted in the material of his shorts in a weak attempt at divesting him of the damn things before she came without him.

A frustrated whimper clued him in to her plight. He rolled, tugging her to the sand next to him. In two seconds flat, he'd lifted his hips and slid the shorts off, kicking them to the side. He cuddled her into his arms so they lay on their right sides, her back plastered to his chest.

The thick length of his hard-on pressed between her legs, stroking her soaked slit. Sebastian buried one arm in the sand beneath her then draped the other over her waist, giving him complete access to touch her breasts, her belly and her clit. She tilted her head to the left, meeting his seeking lips for another scorching kiss.

He rocked into her in time to his tongue, thrusting against the palate of her mouth. The plump head of his cock stroked her pussy, nudging her closer and closer to ecstasy.

"I want you inside me." She gasped when he angled his hips, probing a bit deeper on the next pass. "Please, Bastian."

He reached around her hip, using two fingers on the underside of his cock to feed it into her waiting clutches. The initial penetration left her trembling. The sweet pressure of him working inside her drove her mad with desire.

When he wedged in the swollen depths of her channel, he slid his hand from his cock to the inside of her knee. He lifted her leg, spreading her until she feared she might split open from the decadent force of his invasion.

"So tight," he groaned near her ear. "*Molto dolce.*"

The flex and release of his toned abdomen stroked his shaft over her sensitive flesh. Slow, deep and controlled, he massaged her from within. Curls of flame licked her abdomen, making it difficult to breathe without calling out her satisfaction. When the fingers of his spread hand strayed from her belly to circle her clit, she cried his name over and over.

The dual sensations primed her body while his affectionate ministrations had her heart clenching in her chest. As they strained together, his cock flared inside her. The defined ridges of his veins teased her inflamed nerve endings. She panted, trying to smother the urge to shatter. She didn't want their passion to end so soon.

But resistance didn't get her far. The harder she fought, the more he focused. He tapped the bump of her clit in time to his thrusts. She stiffened, her pussy clamping on his shaft. She screamed as she came apart in his arms, trusting him to drive her orgasm.

Through the hurricane of desire, he maintained his pace, gritting his teeth above her. When she could process thought beyond the overwhelming ecstasy drowning her, she sighed. He hadn't come with her. Without his pleasure, hers seemed pale and incomplete.

Lynn rolled to her stomach, offering herself for his use. She wanted nothing more than to provide him the means for satisfaction, for half the joy he'd gifted her. She spread her legs then raised her hips, her face pillowed in the sand.

Sebastian couldn't refuse her offer. He pumped into her from behind, driving her into the warm earth. She absorbed his powerful thrusts. His fingers laced with hers as he pinned one wrist to either side of her head.

All vestiges of his gentleness vanished as he staked his claim. She welcomed him, rocking back to meet his thrusts. His chin landed on her shoulder when he dropped lower, covering her back. Without thinking, she angled her head, exposing her neck. He shouted something in Italian then fit deeper within her.

A sense of power washed over her. She could give this to her man and, in doing so, set them both free. The knowledge fanned the embers of her passion, renewing the spasms of her pussy around him in an endless orgasm.

Bastian attacked the vulnerable skin without hesitation. His teeth sank into the crook of her neck and shoulder as he pummeled her. A roar of primal completion echoed around them as he claimed her. The hot splash of his cum pouring deep inside her followed.

Instead of panic, a sense of rightness descended over Lynn. She allowed herself simply to react to the magic their coupling generated. The rush of her climax peaked as the last of Sebastian's seed jetted inside her womb.

Together they collapsed onto the beach, too exhausted to sort through what had happened. She closed her eyes as she snuggled into his chest, content to drift off for a few minutes before dealing with reality.

When Lynn jostled awake, she found herself cradled in Sebastian's lap in the shade of the rock outcropping. He'd gathered her sarong and used it to cover most of her skin.

"Sorry, *tesoro*." He beamed down at her. "I was afraid you'd burn. You're so…white."

She laughed. "I know. I can't tan at all. I go from pink to red."

"You're gorgeous the way you are."

Their gazes met and held for a solid thirty seconds. Then they both spoke at once. "Where—"

"What—"

Sebastian gestured for her to finish but she shook her head. "No, go ahead. What were you going to say?"

He took a deep breath then nodded before asking, "Where will you be next Monday? My races end on Sunday. I have a two-week hiatus after that."

"Florence, I think. It depends...on how my research goes. I could try — "

He cut her off with a finger on her lips before she could offer a compromise she might come to regret. "Do what you have to do. I'll always find you. Wherever you are is where I want to go...if I'm welcome there."

Tears blurred his perfect, if sand-covered, features. Could it be possible?

"And if someday you decide you want to come with me — see the world and do your research from my circuit stops, I'd be honored."

"Can we take things one step at a time?" If she thought that far ahead, she'd get too scared of losing everything and she'd screw it all up.

"Absolutely. Let me begin the journey with you and it'll all work out, *amore mio*."

"Promise?"

"I do."

"Then we'd better go tell your mother the good news." Lynn tied her bikini before waiting for him to tug on his shorts. His grin lit up his entire face as he scrambled to his feet.

She tore up the beach toward the sanctuary of his house, Sebastian two steps behind. Not a shred of doubt remained that he'd follow. When they reached the wooden stairs, her sole caught a jagged edge. Without checking over her shoulder, she flung herself backward before it could splinter her foot. Arms open, she let Bastian catch her in his strong embrace.

"Careful, *tesoro*." He whirled her around in the fresh sea breeze before setting her on her own once he made sure she could stand steady.

Tears filled her eyes as she stared into his determined expression. Though it seemed ridiculous, she knew he'd be there to catch her if she needed him but would always set her free when she craved her independence.

She swore to do the same for him, supporting his career and their relationship in whatever shape it took on. The forces of nature that had driven them together would permit nothing less.

Epilogue
Six months later

ଚଡ

LynnLuvs2Trvl: Hello, ladies! I have some great news. Sebastian won his fourth world championship! Yes, that's right, we're off to celebrate with a three-month trip to Asia. Bali, here we come. I'm not sure how great the internet connection will be at the beach but don't worry, Bastian will be taking good care of me. ☺

I think this will be a great chance for us to see how things would work out if I decide to accept his proposal. I miss him so much when we're apart. I'm starting to forget why I thought it was a good idea in the first place.

So, anyone feel like visiting me in Europe next year? I think I'm going to need someone to hold my hand during the circuit events. Watching them live is scarier than on TV.

Besides… I know another hot young guy who could use a sexy Cougar.

Okay, Bastian's giving me that look. Yeah, you know the one. Gotta run, I'll write when I can!

NOTHING BUT SEX

Fran Lee

ഞ

Dedication

℘

To all the wonderful people who have extended a helping hand on this long journey, from family and friends to authors and editors with the patience of Job, I dedicate this book.

Trademarks Acknowledgement

℘

The author acknowledges the trademarked status and trademark owners of the following wordmarks mentioned in this work of fiction:

Ellora's Cave: Ellora's Cave Publishing, Inc.

Golden Globe: Hollywood Foreign Press Association Corp.

NASCAR: National Association for Stock Car Auto Racing, Inc.

Ripley: Ripley Entertainment, Inc.

Stetson: John B. Stetson Company Corp.

Victoria's Secret: Victoria's Secret Stores Brand Management, Inc.

Chapter One

છ

"I can't believe you just said that!" Lee Blackhorse yelled after her ex as he climbed into his big 4x4 and slammed the door, glancing back at her from the rolled down window. "You lousy bastard! You know absolutely nothing about how I feel. Nothing about how I function. How dare you..." Her voice dwindled away as he peeled out of her graveled driveway and swung the gleaming black truck south. All she could do was stare after him, helpless rage boiling over inside her.

Again.

It never failed. No matter how many times she told herself she would never let him take advantage of her again, she continuously found herself falling back into that old trap. After ten years of supporting the asshole, she should know better than to take anything the man said at face value. Oh! She stomped one booted foot into the gravel that comprised her house driveway and swore at her own stupidity. She should have seen it coming.

She had been online, checking out her favorite websites, buying a few erotic romances from Ellora's Cave again and lurking once more on the Tempt the Cougar Blog. Reading the posts and wishing she had the guts to accept what they all called The Cougar Challenge.

The seven women who had started the blog were a lot like her. Supposedly over the sexual hill. Except that they had all taken a challenge tossed out by one of them after they had all attended the RomantiCon readers and authors convention a few months back. So easy...or so it sounded. But for someone like Lee, nothing was ever as easy as it sounded.

Monica Allen was the one who challenged the others to find a hot younger man. Then, one by one, the women took up the challenge. And then one day, Lee had scraped up the courage to post a comment on one of the posts.

Oh, seeing you gals do this gives me courage to go out and try, at least. I will go to Victoria's Secret, by damn! Lee B.

Or should she say Victoria's Secret's latest online catalog?

Of course she had never found the courage to post again. She wasn't Cougar caliber. Cougars were emotionally strong, smart and had the guts to go after what they wanted. Not Lee Blackhorse. She still had a soft spot deep inside for the handsome, engaging man she'd once been married to. But the things he'd done and the way he'd treated her should have squeezed that damn soft spot into a tiny kernel and buried it so far down it would never reappear. Instead, she would end up letting him "borrow" money again and again, never to see a dime of it come back.

Howard had started gambling again over at the Tribe-owned casino. His new wife's daddy had closed the vault doors when he found out how much money Howard had blown gambling. So who could he turn to when the bill collectors threatened to take his precious truck because he couldn't make the payments? His soft touch ex-wife. After all, hadn't she supported him well during their ten-year marriage? The typical sap-headed *wasichu* blonde. Funny how she had become the epitome of all known blonde jokes in her own thoughts. And it must be true that her blue eyes meant her head was filled with air. Only a total airhead would let Howard finagle another hundred bucks out of her. Damn it all! Those Cougar women wouldn't have allowed that to happen.

Her mother had warned her not to marry the hot, sexy Native American movie star. "Nothing good will come of marrying that man." But Lee had been swept away by the man's image. His hot eyes. His delicious good looks. He had played to her love of NA culture and he had pretended to be the kind of man she admired. After all, Howard Blackhorse was an actor, right? But in the end, his clay moccasins had shown up, and he had fallen off that tall, bright pedestal she'd put him on.

Children? She'd wanted them. He hadn't. He'd won.

She'd found out that he had cheated almost all through their marriage, usually with groupies who followed the handsome, swaggering man who had won a Golden Globe Award for his portrayal of Crazy Horse in his one and only big bucks film, back in 1989. The fact that he hadn't made a dime in the film industry since didn't matter. Women flocked after him like bees after a honey pot. And she could see why.

Howard wore his waist-length black hair loose with a leather tie over one ear with a fake eagle feather dangling from it, all part of the persona he'd evolved. Oh, he had tried for more important roles after that big one was released, but by the mid-nineties the NA film craze had died down and there were hundreds of hot, good-looking NA actors all fighting for scraps. And Howard, in his late thirties, was unable to compete with the young bucks, scrambling for bit parts and leads in whatever movies came along. He'd gotten a dozen small parts, but nothing much, money-wise. By the mid to late nineties, there were a large number of handsome, well-educated, theatrically trained NA actors to compete with, and that had put Howard out of the running.

So he had taken the remaining royalties from his one hit film and had bought himself a place just south of the Rosebud res, bought a couple of new cars, and had set up a "back to nature" spa ranch of sorts. That was about the time Lee had met him.

Lee had been working for the Rosebud School when the handsome actor had visited as part of a school-sponsored NA awareness festival. Like all the other women around him, she had been swept off her feet, but he had asked her to marry him. And despite her mother's worried pronouncements of impending doom, she had allowed him to sweep her up and carry her home.

As she thought back, she couldn't figure for beans what had attracted him to her…a plain, mousy Anglo woman. It had just been so flattering that he chose her over dozens of pretty women, that she'd fallen head over heels. But her mother had told her that he just wanted a woman with a good-paying job.

Thanks, Mom. Real flattering.

The polish had started to wear off the apple when Howard had started gambling. They had been married five months. The money hadn't been a lot at first, and of course he had promised that it was just an off the wall thing…would never happen again. Etcetera. She hadn't found out about his philandering until she'd heard some intentionally loud gossip at the feed mercantile that had made her go home and confront him about what she'd heard. He'd had the gall to laugh in her face. It had hurt desperately.

After ten years of paying for his trucks, his cars, his clothes, feed for his horses and taxes on the ranch when the profits turned into the red, the innumerable affairs he admitted to having had with girls young enough to be his daughters and his unquenchable thirst for more of everything had galvanized her to take a final stand. And when she had demanded that he stop his philandering and take his marriage seriously, he had chosen to run off with his current nineteen-year-old flame, and Lee had divorced him.

The words he'd just thrown at her when she'd told him she didn't want him coming to borrow from her anymore were definitely the final straw. Still shaking with indignation and rage, she did her best to swallow the pain his words had caused, as she sank onto the white-painted wooden porch, burying her face in her hands. And the tears slid down her face unheeded as sobs racked her body. His words reverberated through her.

I only married you in the first place because you would do anything I asked. You were pathetic. You really believe I wanted you for any other reason when I could have any woman I looked at? You're nothing, Lee. You are less than nothing. You couldn't even satisfy me in bed, you dried-up bitch! If you felt anything for me back then, you sure never showed it where it counted...in the sack.

Michael Running Elk slammed on his brakes as the familiar gleaming black 4x4 blew the stop sign in the center of town and swung wide, nearly hitting the front of his beloved old green pickup. Pretty boy Blackhorse was on the rampage again. Made him wonder what had happened this time. Usually it was his father-in-law telling him his funds were cut off because he'd blown a month's allowance in one night of gambling. But the direction he was coming from made it seem more likely that his ex had told him to fuck off. And it wasn't often that Lee Blackhorse, as sweet-tempered and good-natured as she was, told anyone to fuck off.

Mike drew a deep breath and frowned after the speeding 4x4. It was barely past ten in the morning and if he was any judge, the man was drunk already, driving wild and crazy. If he wasn't careful, he'd pile that bright shiny truck into the ravine someday. Might serve him right, at that. The bastard had worked his way through half the women on the res in the past couple of years.

The thought of Lee Blackhorse made him swing the wheel left and head down the highway toward her place a couple of miles down the road. It was too early to do the chores yet, but she probably needed a shoulder to cry on about now. Maybe she would cry on his shoulder.

Nope. More likely she would just have him clean the stalls. As for the crying on his broad shoulder, he wished she would. At times he wanted to just grab and shake her and haul her upstairs to her bedroom. But he respected her too much for that. God knew he had thought about that woman more than was decent, her being the highlight of a great many of his very graphic, favorite wet dreams. God, but he wanted to make a move. Problem was, he was scared shitless of having her laugh at him. He was not some hot stud like her ex, and he worked hard. He worked with his back and his hands. No. She was all class and grace—not for the likes of him. No education to speak of. You didn't need a four-year college degree to know good horseflesh. And his dad had taught him all about running his own place. The two years he'd spent learning to do books and how to stitch up and treat animals had given him the rest of what he'd needed. But it hadn't given him the polish and pretty manners that Lee deserved in a man.

But somehow his truck ended up stopped and idling on the shoulder of the road a couple hundred feet from her driveway as he watched her sitting on her porch, hunched over and...crying? He swore under his breath, and they weren't pretty words. The self-important prick must have been out here asking for more money. From the looks of it, things hadn't gone well. He clenched his fists around the steering wheel, debating on what he should do. What he wanted to do was walk up to her and kiss her silly. But what she would accept was probably something quite different, so he simply pulled into her driveway and climbed out of the old truck, slamming the door to let her know she had company.

Lee heard the truck and hurriedly swiped at her tears, not wanting Mike to see her crying. Mike Running Elk was a good kid, one of the most polite and helpful in town. He came by every Saturday like clockwork to clean out her barn, mow her wild and woolly lawn and fix whatever needed fixing around the house. She paid him the pittance of fifty dollars a week to help out around the place for a few hours, but she knew he would have done it all for free. He didn't need the money. He earned a decent living running his own horse ranch. He probably made as much in one hour training horses for others as she could afford to pay him for his help, but he good-naturedly accepted her small payment and her thanks, as well as a sandwich and soda. And Lee enjoyed his company.

Bless him, she didn't want to let him see her tears.

He'd been helping her around the place since way before she and Howard had split. Back then, he had needed the cash to help pay off his dad's funeral bill and help support his mother and brothers. He had been helping out for over twelve years. It seemed he understood how much she welcomed the help. And she certainly did. Working a full-time job with the school district left little time for the chores that Howard once did, before he'd started drinking so much he slept all day.

She sniffed and made certain there were no tears still on her face when she turned and smiled up at him. "Hi, Mike. Look, I'm a little short today. I'm sorry that you made the trip out here for nothing. I would have called but..." She shrugged. *But* the reason she was short on cash was driving back to the bar to spend the "truck payment" he'd just borrowed. Of course, Mike didn't need to know that. She fished a ten out of her pocket and said, "Here's money for the gas you spent coming over today. Take this Saturday off."

Mike stared down at her slim hand and the wrinkled ten dollar bill. He calmed the sudden need to follow the man who'd made her cry like this and ram a few fists down his throat. Instead of cursing viciously, he lifted his hat and ran a lean hand through his dark hair before settling the battered Stetson back onto his head. "No problem, ma'am."

He winced. He had planned to call her "Lee", but he'd blown it again. How the hell was she ever going to realize he wasn't the kid she always thought him to be if he kept calling her "ma'am"? He swallowed hard, hesitated for a few moments, hoping she would change her mind. But she avoided his gaze and pretended to find something on the step beside her completely riveting. *Come on, idiot...say something.*

"No need for gas money. I was driving this way anyway." Still she didn't lift her face to look at him. "Look, I have nothing to do today but kick my heels. The hands have the ranch taken care of. I'm goin' around to the barn and you can pay me later. Or better yet, you can cook me up some of that great stew you make. We'll figure something out…" He left the innuendo hanging, but she didn't seem to pick up on it.

When she simply shrugged, he sighed and headed around the side of the old house to start the usual simple chores he had been doing for her since he was eighteen. He swore under his breath. The chore he wanted so desperately to do for her was out of the question. She would have a damn cow if he did what he so eagerly wanted to do, and dragged the woman into her house to fuck her until they both fell in a heap, unable to move or think.

He glanced down at his hands and clenched them into fists. She would be horrified if he put those calloused hands on her — *in* her — the way he wanted to. He pulled his work gloves out of his rear jeans pocket and tugged them on. But even if she didn't mind his calluses and his rough skin, what the hell would she want with a guy who was about as polished and gentlemanly as a horned toad? That slime ball she had married was the kind of guy she wanted. Slick, smooth and able to talk a woman into about anything. Shit! She still wanted the bastard, or she wouldn't let him keep coming back.

With a snarl of frustration, he grabbed a pitchfork and stabbed the nearest open bale and started slinging hay over into the feed bins to the waiting yearling heifers.

Chapter Two
ରେ

Was she going totally crazy here? Dear God! What the hell was happening to her? Had she just had a wild sexual reaction to a kid twelve years her junior? Lee shook her head and swallowed the tightness in her throat. She was forty-two freaking years old, for Pete's sake! Michael Running Elk was what? Maybe twenty-nine? Thirty? Dear Lord, but she was so freaking horny just hearing the kid's voice and staring at those long, lean legs in those well-worn jeans, she could barely control her thoughts.

What the hell? Sure, she'd always found Mike sexy and attractive, but it had never hit her this hard before. She had always managed to shake it off and get back to reality. What was she? Some sort of impressionable nitwit? Lee rose from her seat on the step and climbed to the porch again, dusting off her jeans and chewing her lip. Had she really just had a vision of Mike Running Elk poised stark naked over her...nudging her thighs apart and fitting his cock into her wet pussy? *Oh my God.* She desperately needed a glass of ice water.

She hurried into the house and through to the kitchen and poured herself a chilled glass of water from the fridge, adding ice. Could fighting with your ex cause you to daydream about humping the hot kid who did your barn chores? She stared out the kitchen window at the man who was forking hay into the feed lot for the cattle. Her eyes strayed over the lean, tight ass inside those worn jeans. The wide back that rippled with hard muscle. And then he jabbed the pitchfork into a bale and stripped his t-shirt off over his head with one movement and she damn near swallowed her tongue. Holy shit! Long black hair was plastered to his sweat-damp skin as he draped the shirt over the feed lot fence poles and resumed his work.

Something hot and needy curled deep in her belly and a shot of white-hot lust zinged straight to her pussy.

Whirling away from the window, she almost ran into the den where her laptop computer sat, open and waiting, and she sank onto the chair, her insides a puddle of hot mush. Taking a deep swallow of the ice water, she set down the glass and logged in, immediately typing the URL for Tempt the Cougar.

As the Tempt the Cougar blog flashed to life on her screen, she drew a deep breath. This blog had opened her eyes. Had made her seriously think about getting back to some sort of normalcy. And the thought of having a younger man hot for her? God, that had sounded so good back then. It had made her begin to look at things differently.

Before reading the blog and comments, she had genuinely thought that older women who went after younger men were slightly perverted. After reading, she'd wondered why anyone would think that having sex with a man younger than yourself was perverted, when there were millions of men out there — like her ex — who quite happily fucked the brains out of younger women all the time. And still she had simply lurked, reading their posts, laughing at their jokes and wishing to hell that she had the courage to make a move back out into the male-female world. Of course, she had never thought she would get all hot and bothered over some kid half her age — okay, so he wasn't half her age — and start getting ideas about seducing the poor guy.

As she sat there, reading the most recent posts, she decided that it was time to start asking questions. Was she so far out of it that she couldn't attract some guy like Mike? Was she crazy to even dream about trying to get him into her bed? The answers were yes, and yes. But she still wanted to ask. The "challenge" was making her question her own rationale.

She scrolled down to the comments, and began typing.

Lee B: I am a divorced woman age forty-two and I just had the most shocking daydream of myself having sex with a kid of thirty. Help!

There. It was out. She had said it. It felt weird, but somehow it had liberated her. She felt as if a hundred-pound weight had been lifted from her shoulders.

Then she realized that she had just admitted that she had the hots for Mike and she blushed furiously. Thank God these blog posts were anonymous.

She sighed and checked her email to see if her mother had sent her the recipe for chocolate chip walnut cookies she'd asked for. It was there. She smiled and printed it and was about to close the email program when an incoming email popped up. Her eyes widened, and her face grew red. It was an email response to the post she had just left on the Tempt the Cougar blog.

Lee B,
You think thirty is a "kid"? Come on, girl! Get real. He's over eighteen. He's old enough to have sex with. It isn't the age difference that's the issue here…it's your fear of being thought of as a cradle-robber. Right? There is no cradle. The guy is a full-grown man. So what's the hold up? Take the Challenge.
Cam

Her throat tightened. How the hell had Cam gotten her email addy? Oh, duh! What on earth had given her the idea that no one would know who left the post? She'd signed in. She wriggled her fingers over the keyboard. Should she reply? She wanted help here.

Hi, Cam,

I was shocked that I could think of this guy in the light of a sex partner. I've known him since he was like sixteen. To me, he's a kid. Shit! He does my chores for me. And here I am, lusting over him. Just not right.

Lee

The screen remained still for about two minutes before another email popped up.

Lee,

We all got past that idea. It was part of the Challenge. If you are afraid to take the leap, you will never get out of the rut. Hell, all of us had to take that leap, girl. Just don't give up on yourself. Challenge yourself.

Cam

She didn't know how long she sat there, but the sound of a loud knock on her back door brought her out of her trance and she shook her head to clear away the amazingly erotic thoughts that were flitting through her head. She rose and hurried into the kitchen to see Mike standing inside the back porch, his hand dripping blood.

"Oh my God! What happened?" she cried, jerking the inner screen door open and dragging him bodily into the kitchen as she grabbed a clean tea towel and slapped it over the dripping cut.

He shook his head and said, "No big deal. I was moving that coil of barbed wire and caught myself. Do you have some alcohol and a bandage?"

Her gaze shifted from his bloodied hand to his naked torso and every nerve in her body started screaming for her to touch that coppery, smooth skin. Dragging her eyes away from his chest, she swallowed hard and said jerkily, "Come on upstairs. There's a first-aid kit in the bathroom. That looks like it might need a stitch or two."

Mike swore foully as he caught his glove on one of the murderously long barbs on the roll of wire fencing that he was trying to move and he tugged his leather work glove off to find that the barb had made it through to his palm. He shook his head and shoved his hair back from his face with his other hand before he tugged his unused handkerchief from his back pocket and wrapped it around his hand, which did very little to stanch the flow of blood. Swearing at his own clumsiness, he headed across the wide work yard to the back porch and stepped inside, knocking on the inside screen door.

She appeared from the archway to the living room, her face pink and her lower lip caught between her teeth as she caught sight of him and he realized that he hadn't bothered to pull his damn shirt back on. He saw the way her eyes darkened as they slid over his body and he felt a shot of anticipation run from his gut to his cock. Her lips were full. Her eyes were smoky blue. A small vein throbbed in her throat. And it struck him forcibly that she most certainly was as aware of him as he was of her.

But before he could wrap his mind around her reaction to him, she was hurrying up the stairs to the bathroom and he was following, his appreciative eyes on the lush swell of her generous, gorgeous ass as he held the tea towel tightly to his bleeding hand. Sweet Jesus, but he loved her ass. He had loved it ever since he'd first seen her, when he was just eighteen, and he had asked her if he could do some odd jobs around the place to make some cash every week. Right after his dad had died. Watching her walk around in tight jeans had made him forget a lot of the pain in his life back then.

She filled a pair of jeans like they'd been poured onto her. His mouth watered and his cock grew impossibly harder. Even the stinging pain in his hand couldn't distract his attention from that ass.

As she entered the bathroom and stretched up to the shelf above the toilet to lift down the first-aid kit, he almost whimpered. Was she trying to kill him? If she didn't stop wiggling around, he was gonna blow.

"I can handle it from here," he grated as she opened the box and started to take the soaked tea towel out of his grip. But she shoved his free hand away and gently placed his hand in the sink, rinsing it with icy-cold tap water that nearly made him yell at the pain. He stared down at her bent head as she probed and cleaned the wound and each time her body brushed his, he almost lost it.

He lost track of what was happening with his hand as every drop of blood in his body raged into his groin, threatening to explode. Maybe that was a good thing, because his hand might stop bleeding.

"I still think we need to get you to the clinic and get this stitched. It's way too jagged to heal right, and it's still bleeding."

Her words were lost in the hot muddle of his emotions and body. But when she looked up into his face, he forced himself to pay attention. "Hold this clean towel in your palm. Press it tight. I'll get my car keys."

And as she left the bathroom, he sank down onto the closed toilet and gasped for breath. If he didn't get his cock to calm down, he would throw her down on the damn bathroom floor and fuck her blind. And somehow, he didn't think she would respond well to that technique.

Chapter Three

❧

As she entered her bedroom and grabbed her purse and a clean t-shirt that had once been Howard's, she found herself wondering what the hell she was going to do about the way she was reacting to Mike Running Elk. She was going to make a complete fool of herself if she didn't get control...and fast. This was getting way out of hand. She could barely breathe when she was next to his hot, hard body. And if she didn't get a shirt on him before she took him to the clinic, she was going to orgasm just looking. Good grief. The kid was *ripped*. And the way his package had bulged against his stressed zipper had made her tongue feel like it wouldn't go back into her mouth right.

She dashed back to the bathroom and found him trying to take a leak and keep his injured palm under pressure at the same time. It wasn't working. He glanced sideways at her, and growled, "Can you hold this damn towel on my hand while I take care of business here?" At the look on her face, he amended, "Unless you'd rather help me take a leak. Either way is fine with me."

Blushing wildly, she averted her eyes from his open zipper and grabbed the towel wrapped around his hand, applying a bit too much pressure that made him give a grunt of pain. "Sorry," she whispered, her cheeks hot enough to fry eggs on.

What the hell was she so damn embarrassed about? She'd seen Howard take a leak thousands of times. And this kid certainly didn't have anything she hadn't seen before. Yet she felt like a dirty old lady ogling him. Cam's words came back to her.

You think thirty is a "kid"? Challenge yourself.

Of course he was no child. He was a full-grown man and she was an adult woman. It was simply a matter of perspective. And as she tried not to sneak a peek at his cock as he managed his business a bit clumsily with his left hand and tucked himself back into his jeans, she still felt totally naughty even considering looking. He swore softly and said tersely, "Can you get the zipper for me? I'm not so damn good one-handed."

She allowed him to replace her hand with his on the bloody towel and she reached to pull his zipper up. He hissed in through his teeth and jerked as her fingertips grazed his swollen cock, and she said tersely, "If you jerk like that, I'll end up zipping *you* into the zipper. Stop moving."

"Yes ma'am…Lee." His voice sounded strangled.

The sound of her name on his lips almost made her jerk and zip his cock into the fly of his tightly stretched jeans. She managed to complete the task without killing him, and then she gently dragged the fresh shirt down over his head, helping him to get the towel-wrapped hand through the sleeve. When he was decent, she grabbed her purse again and said jerkily, "Let's get you to the damn clinic."

Mike almost blew his wad when her fingertips slid over his aching cock as she tried to zip him up. He was so damn swollen, she was having trouble, even using both her hands. He was breathing raggedly as she ordered him out to her car, and he even tried mentally reciting the Psalms to keep his mind off saying to hell with his bleeding hand and dragging her into her bedroom. Nothing worked. He remained hard as a fucking rock.

He slid into her car and folded his long legs under the glove box. When she noticed that he was sitting like a jockey, she pressed a button and his seat slid back. He breathed a quiet thank you and accepted her help with his seat belt without comment, gritting his teeth as her breast brushed his arm and her sweet-smelling hair brushed his nose. Sweet Jesus. Did she think he was made of wood?

She peeled out of the driveway like a race driver and he tried not to wince as she took the turn onto the secondary road leading to the clinic on two wheels. He was damn surprised that Lee Blackhorse had the guts to drive like this. He wouldn't have believed it if he hadn't seen it with his own eyes.

The twenty-minute drive to the clinic was managed in a little less than ten minutes and as they climbed out of the car, he glanced down at her and grinned wickedly. "I didn't know you went in for NASCAR, Lee."

Her blue gaze snapped to his face and she frowned. "You think Sam would ticket me for speeding if he saw that hand?"

In answer, Sam Rainfeather's voice came from the driveway behind them. "You know you were going eighty-five back there, Lee?" She glanced at the big man who was climbing out of his patrol car.

"Mike's hand got ripped up and he's bleeding. You can ticket me after we get him taken care of, Sam."

Mike drew a deep breath, taking in the scent of her floral shampoo and the scent of woman and he almost tripped over his own damn feet. The clinic nurse grabbed a wheelchair and Sam eased him down onto the seat before he could explain that his dizziness didn't come from loss of blood. But he decided to keep his trap shut and let her baby him some more.

Her hand on his arm was enough to keep the blood rushing to his groin and he desperately wanted that hand to ease downward to see what she was doing to him. Man, he was pathetic. He almost whimpered when she removed her hand to let the nurse wheel him into the surgery to see about getting him stitched up. As the door closed behind him, he gave a deep groan and bent forward to ease the pressure on his fucking fly. The nurse thought he was gonna puke and jammed a basin under his nose. If only it was that easy.

Lee sank onto the chair in the little waiting room and gratefully accepted the cup of coffee that Sam handed her. She glanced up into his face and gave him a wry grimace. "Still going to ticket me, Sam?"

"I ought to, Lee. You were flying low in that damn seventies-comet of yours. I don't know how the hell you got that thing to go eighty-five without it falling to pieces. But I'll cut you a break, since you were playing kamikaze ambulance driver." His deep voice rumbled as she sipped the hot, reviving liquid. "Next time, call me. I'm never more than five miles from your place and can get there in two minutes."

She flushed warmly at the proprietary tone. Sam was one of her many married admirers…hanging around the divorcée hoping for a bit of sack time. At least Sam had never actually come out and asked. He just hinted. She should be grateful for that, at least. She really liked Ramona Rainfeather and she would rather cut her thumb off than make that poor woman's life any lousier than it was, being married to the good-looking and philandering town Chief of Police.

She sighed and took another sip. Sam's hand came to rest on her shoulder and it took all her willpower to not shrug it off. "You call me next time you need anything, Lee. Okay?"

She glanced up into his face and smiled tightly. "Sure, Sam. Thanks."

He rubbed her shoulder suggestively, then he grinned at her. "You take care."

She watched him exit the clinic and slide back under the wheel of his patrol car before she gave a shudder of revulsion. Lord! Did she have a sign on her forehead that said "Hard Up and Easy"?

With a sigh of resignation, she finished the black coffee and tossed the cup into the trash basket beside the reception desk. So far, in this tiny town of a hundred-sixty-seven souls, she'd been propositioned by roughly thirty-six married men since her divorce. Oh…and one unmarried man of eighty-six…old Gabriel Whitecloud. She shook her head and gave an unamused bark of laughter. No damn wonder she was lusting after her weekend help. At least he was under seventy and unmarried. And hot. And succulent.

The sound of boots on the pristine tile floor brought her up short in her mental molestation of the man and she glanced up to see Mike stepping out of the surgery door, gently flexing the new bandage that bound his right hand. Dr. Harris was walking out behind him and she caught the last half of the conversation.

"I'll expect that you will be off work for the next five days. I don't want you tearing those stitches. I want you back in three days to check the wound. Jackie will give you a brace so you won't bend that hand like you're doing. If you shower, keep that hand dry. No driving unless you have a car with no stick shift. And Jackie will give you that tetanus booster before you leave."

Lee chewed the corner of her lower lip as Mike nodded and allowed the little Lakota nurse to shove his sleeve up over the bulging muscle on his upper arm to administer the shot. Jackie fitted a metal brace that was padded with foam and leather onto his wrist and palm and strapped his hand in snugly. And when the pretty Lakota woman smiled up into Mike's dark eyes and said, "Anything else you need, you just call." Lee almost blurted out something stupid like "He's mine! Keep your freakin' hands off!"

She noted the proprietary way the woman's hand rested on Mike's bulging biceps, and she cleared her throat, bringing his dark eyes up to her face. And for just one breathless moment, she thought she saw a flicker of raw need in those eyes. Raw need that was quickly masked as he grinned down at her and the girl's hand slipped off his arm. A quick glance at Jackie's face brought hot red to her cheeks as she realized that the younger woman was staring at her as if she'd just stolen a juicy apple out from under her pretty nose.

A sense of elation filled her. Pretty little Jackie was jealous! Jealous of frumpy, forty-two-year-old Lee Blackhorse. And Mike Running Elk had looked at her as if he wanted to take a big bite out of her. Dear God…she knew that it would only take ten minutes for the gossip mill to start churning out lurid stories about the woman who had once been married to Howard now turning her sights on Mike Running Elk. She had already heard it all…*an Anglo woman carrying off the res prize. Why couldn't white women leave the res men for res girls?* She shook her head slightly and realized that Mike was smiling down into her hot face with a quizzical expression.

"Um—sorry! I'll take you back to your place and I'll have someone bring your truck out. And I'll pay for this treatment, since it was all my fault."

Mike wanted to pick her up and carry her into an exam room and tell her the bill was settled, but he managed to say almost calmly, "Are you gonna drive the speed limit this time?"

The small jibe broke her embarrassment and she laughed jerkily as he used his body to herd her away from the nurse who was glaring at her and out the front door of the clinic.

"Now that you aren't bleeding to death, sure." Her voice sounded sexy and breathless and he couldn't wait to get her alone in the little car again.

He knew that Jackie Red Cloud was gonna spread the word that Mike Running Elk had fallen into the *wasichu* woman's trap, just like Howard Blackhorse had. He had heard all the sour grapes that had rolled through the little town when their famous and good-looking hero of the Hollywood screen had married a white woman instead of one of the hopeful res girls. Not a woman within a hundred miles had not had her say on that matter. Including his own mother.

"I wish these Anglo women would stick to their own men and leave our young men for our girls!"

Jackie and all the girls in town had eventually had their own fling with the lecherous star of stage and screen, so what were they bitching about? It had been Lee who had taken the humiliation and pain of watching her husband fuck everything in skirts and flaunt his "marriage" as some sort of status symbol. Mike had wanted to kick the shit out of the bastard more times than he could count.

He had damn near cleaned Howard's clock the time the bastard had made a comment about "keeping his eyes off his woman" when he had caught Mike staring at Lee while she was working around the garden in a halter-top and brief shorts that had given him one hell of a hard-on.

The older man had been very drunk and had taken out his ire on his wife instead of the guy who had looked. Howard had shouted at her and humiliated her about wearing clothes that only a whore would wear...and when Lee had raced into the house in tears, Mike had taken it upon himself to plant a fist in Howard's handsome face, knocking him—and a tooth—out. Luckily, Lee hadn't seen it and Howard had never mentioned it, probably too humiliated to admit a twenty-year-old kid had taken him down.

Mike had simply kicked a pile of leaves and dirt over his inert body and had gone back to finishing up in the barn.

As he edged her out the door, using his body to nudge her along, he recalled that day and the way she had looked and his cock decided right at that moment to salute. He felt her stiffen and inhale sharply as that part of his anatomy pressed firmly against her rounded ass, and she moved more quickly, not even hesitating to climb into the driver's seat as he went around to the passenger door and slid in.

He noted her high color and saw her hands trembling on the steering wheel as she started the little car. "You gonna help me with my belt?" he asked softly, and saw her pink tongue flick out to moisten her lips.

"Um—sure—sorry…" she said shakily, leaning across his body to grab the belt and haul it across his chest and lap.

When her hand grazed his stiff fly, she lost hold of the belt and had to reach again, and Mike said raggedly, "I think I just died and went to Heaven…"

She was unnerved by the feel of his hard, eager body shoving her out the clinic door and toward the car, but when she felt his cock ram between her butt cheeks, she almost gave a yelp of shock. Heat flashed through her as she fumbled to climb into the car and when he asked for help with his seat belt, she tried to hide her hot face from him. Dear Lord! The scent of him nearly made her lose control of her hands. He smelled like a dark pine forest—and like man. Probably from using pine cleaner on the concrete floor of the tack room, and working hard. The combined scents did not repel her. They made her damn mouth water.

But when her knuckles grazed his cock through his jeans and she heard his intake of breath, she lost hold of the buckle and had to fish it back over his lean frame. She clicked the buckle into the latch and sank back into her own seat as he breathed what sounded sort of like "Heaven". And then she managed to pull her thoughts back together enough to start the car and pull out of the gravel parking area and back onto the highway.

"I'll get you back to the ranch and bring Shorty or Jack back to take your truck."

"Take me to your place."

She jammed on the brakes and jerked her head around to stare at him. "My place? Why? It'll be easier to just take you home, so you can be comfortable."

His dark eyes were in shadow, but she could feel them on her face as she hesitated in the entrance to the clinic parking area. "I want to be with you."

His quiet statement nearly put her into cardiac arrest. It took a few moments to compose her thoughts to reply.

"With me?"

"Just turn left and drive. Please."

She found herself turning toward her place and she drove slowly, terrified that her agitation would show in her speed. Not another word passed between them until she pulled into her own rutted driveway and cut the engine. As she unfastened the buckle of his belt, then her own, she murmured softly, "If you're hungry, I have some leftover stew…"

Before the words were out, his left hand slid into her hair and caught the back of her head and she was pulled halfway over the small console between the seats as his mouth covered hers in a hot, sensuous command. The hand swathed in metal, leather, and tape was cupped over her left cheek and as she opened her lips to ask what he was doing, his tongue slid in to stop her protest cold. O.M.G. No one had ever kissed her like this. Her belly was doing a hot tango and her breasts ached to be touched. Her pussy clenched and warm cream flooded her panties as she gave a throaty groan of surrender and let him plunder her mouth.

The sound of the deep, visceral growl that rolled from the wide chest beneath her flattened palms almost made her orgasm on the spot. Thoughts of a shifter romance she had recently read tore through her and she moaned as he eased the kiss and nibbled her full lower lip gently, while his injured hand slid down her throat and over her collarbone to cup her supersensitive, aching breast. The unexpected and very embarrassing orgasm that rolled from her pussy to her nipples and back brought her off the seat with a mewling sound of pleasure and white-hot sparkles of lust threaded their way through her body, bouncing around joyfully.

He slowly squeezed her throbbing breast through her shirt and lifted his head to stare down into her glazed eyes. His lips curved wickedly into a grin and his voice whispered huskily, "Damn, I must be good."

She choked back a gurgle of embarrassed laughter as she struggled to right herself on the driver's seat. "Or I'm just a horny old woman."

Hearing her own words brought a groan to her lips as she closed her eyes and wished she could just slither through the nearest crack in the floor. What must he think of her now? After this display, she was gonna have to hide from him for the rest of her life. Or would she? Had she just taken up the challenge?

Chapter Four

✌

Mike knew that he was taking a damn risky step, but he seemed to lose control totally when she reached over and unbuckled his belt. When his hand slid into the soft strands of her sweet-scented hair, he went on autopilot. He cupped the back of her head and swiveled in his seat to catch her mouth like a starving man finding an unattended gourmet meal. His injured hand moved to catch her face before she could jerk back and chastise him for his brashness, and when she opened her mouth to tell him off, he buried his tongue in her sweet heat and his fucking cock almost scalped itself on his zipper as it burst through the open fly of his boxers and headed for what it desperately needed.

And then he had cupped her delicious breast and she had orgasmed so readily. He had damn near blasted cum into his jeans as he smelled the moist sweetness of her hot cream and heard the little mewling sound of her climax. And then when she replied to his jocular comment the way she had, he knew for damn sure that she was as eager and interested as he was.

He calmed his body and thoughts and savored the taste of her on his lips as she struggled to scoot from her seat and run to the safety of her porch. *Oh, no, sweetheart, you aren't getting away from me that easily...not after waiting forever to know you want me, too...*

He was out his door and on top of her before she got five steps and his good arm dragged her lush curves back against his raging body, his face buried in the curve of her neck and her sweet silken hair. "Whoa...what are you scared of, Lee?"

211

She shivered as his hand cupped her belly and slid down to caress her where the seam of her tight jeans pressed against her clit. He felt the shudder of reaction go through her.

"I shouldn't have let that happen," she whispered huskily.

"Let what happen? Me jumping you, or the orgasm?"

She shoved at his wrist as he continued to press the seam of her jeans just under her zipper. "I'm way too old to be doing stuff like this! For God's sake, Mike. I'm almost old enough to be your damn mother!"

He kept his hand right where it was and slid his injured hand around to cup and squeeze her right breast. "My mother? Send that one in to Ripley. Old? Shit, Lee. You aren't too old to want to be touched. You sure as a hell aren't too old to want a man inside you again. And I'm sure as hell old enough to give you what you need…and to take what I need." Jesus, was he desperate or what?

Lee's heart hammered hard against her chest walls as he toyed firmly with her mons and clit and when his injured hand cupped and teased her breast and erect nipple, she exhaled explosively and leaned her head back against his shoulder, her eyes closed as he spoke in a rumbling growl against her neck. Dear God. How many years had she waited to hear a man tell her these things? Howard would have given her a pity fuck, if she'd have flipped out a hundred dollar bill. But here was a man who was young, hot and very obviously horny, if that cock jabbing into her ass was any clue. And he wanted *her*. She could have bitten her damn tongue off when she blurted out that she was "too old" to be doing this. He was right…she was trying to run from what she desperately wanted.

His lips nuzzled past her hair and he sucked lightly on the soft skin of her neck, his teeth nipping gently as even more hot cream filled her panties. "Please, Lee? You have no idea how much I want to strip that hot body and nibble every inch of skin. How much I want to bury my face in your pussy and eat you until you scream. I'm about to explode here, baby. Please say yes and put me out of my fucking misery."

Her entire body trembled at the sound of his voice asking her for something she wanted desperately to give. So what if tomorrow morning he woke up and found himself in bed with a woman twelve years his senior, with a soft belly and love handles and breasts that were slowly answering the call of gravity? *Sweet Jesus.* He was hers for the asking tonight and he was beyond caring if she was his dream girl. And she wanted nothing more than to give him exactly what he wanted.

"If we stand here on the porch much longer, Sam will come asking if I'm abusing you." Her own voice sounded choked.

His soft, deep chuckle vibrated against her back. "More likely, he'll be asking if he can join the fun."

"Let me get my keys…"

Once inside the door, she was dragged around to face him and her soft sweater was whisked off over her head. Howard's old t-shirt was gone and her feverish palms rested against smooth, solid, rippling muscle. "You'll tear your stitches." She gasped as he hefted her and pulled her legs around his lean hips, using his injured hand as well as the uninjured one. The feel of the closed door against her back and the feel of his hot mouth covering her erect nipple through the satin and lace of her bra made her forget what she was saying. All she could feel was the hard ridge of his denim-covered cock rocking hard against the seam of her tight jeans as he tugged her bra cup down and took her bare nipple in his lips, sucking hard.

"Oh, my God!" she wailed as another throbbing climax engulfed her and Mike's soft chuckle brought more hot color to her cheeks. She clung to his shoulders as she rode the waves of pleasure while his cock continued to press and ease against her clit. Had the man just dry fucked her to oblivion? She sobbed into the long hair that fell forward over his naked shoulder and he murmured soft words to calm her in his

213

native tongue, kissing her throat and breast gently as she came back to earth from one of the most intense orgasms she'd ever experienced. She almost laughed to think that being dry fucked through two pair of jeans had just given her the most sexual pleasure she had ever felt.

As he lowered her feet to the floor and leaned in to kiss her lips sweetly, she reached to loosen his ornate silver belt buckle and he put his uninjured hand over hers, shaking his head slowly.

"Why not?" she whispered huskily against his mouth.

"I don't carry condoms on me. And I reckon you never had to stock them, not being one to have men guests."

Her cheeks burned as she stared into his dark eyes. "How do you know I don't have men over?"

"You aren't the type to have one-night stands, Lee."

Her eyes narrowed. "You saying that nobody would want me?"

He stopped her angry words with a kiss that set every nerve in her body aflame, and she bit his lip sharply. "What was that for?" he panted as he rested his forehead against hers.

"Because you didn't answer me. You didn't tell me why you were sure I didn't have one-nighters."

She waited breathlessly for him to speak. "Because I would drive by most nights to check to see that there were no cars parked in your driveway."

"You…what?"

"You heard me. I stalked your sweet ass to make sure you were alone. And when you came with me just touching you, I realized you probably haven't been with a man since you dumped Howard."

She didn't know whether to be elated that he liked that idea, or horrified and offended that he had spied on her. Elated won as his thumb and finger rolled her nipple and he whispered hoarsely, "God, I want to fuck you...without the jeans between us..."

Her hands returned to his belt buckle and his heart almost stopped beating for a moment as her fingers dragged his zipper down and reached in to circle his cock. Her voice was husky as she whispered against his lips, "I have never done this before, so you might have to coach me." He almost lost reality totally as she sank down the front of his body and took his aching cock into her sweet, hot mouth, sucking the head and gently stroking him from base to crown with her hands as he leaned into the wall and gave a groan of pure pleasure.

"Is this right?" she asked, looking up. His fingers tangled into her tousled hair and he stared down at her as she licked the vein that ran from his root to his swollen crown.

"Sweet Lord, woman...anything you do is right." His voice was thick as he watched her smile and slurp his hard-as-nails cock back into her mouth and he fought to keep from thrusting his hips forward and gagging her with his full length. Then her gently probing hands found his tight balls and he gave a shout and bit his lip hard.

"Am I hurting you?" she asked, glancing up with a sweet smile.

"You're killing me," he growled and dragged her from her knees into his arms.

He swung her from her feet and carried her up the stairs to her room. He knew where it was. He'd seen her light come on often enough when he was spying. "As much as I love what you were doing, I really want to get you naked, Lee—and I want to bury myself in you. If you don't have a condom, I'll have to figure something else out."

She was shocked that he was carrying her one-hundred-fifty-pound frame up the stairs like she weighed ounces. His words made her pussy clench and her nipples harden. Oh,

Christ. He wanted to see her naked? Big mistake. There went the confidence she'd just gained This ripped, stacked, gorgeous man wanted to take her clothes off her and look at her forty-two-year-old body. Oh, shit!

When he unerringly headed for her bedroom door and kicked it open, she prayed he would decide not to turn on the lights, but he did exactly that. He carried her to her bed and tossed her onto it and then began to strip his own clothes off. She watched, mesmerized, as he bared that marvelous young body and then gave his deliciously erect cock a slow stroke, inhaling deeply as his dark eyes turned to her where she sat like a frozen statue in the middle of her bed.

She swallowed hard and whispered shakily, "You really don't want to see me totally naked, Mike. Trust me…"

His eyes slipped over her lacy bra and down over her rounded tummy. He shook his head slowly. "I've seen you totally naked hundreds of times, baby." He tapped his head with one finger and his lips curved into a wicked grin.

"Imagination is fabulous…you don't want to spoil that image by asking me to strip. I look absolutely nothing like you probably imagined, and I certainly don't want to scare the hell out of the first unmarried man who's asked me for sex in seven years." She chewed the corner of her lip as he moved to the edge of the bed and reached out to pull her up to her knees.

"Let me be the judge of that, sweetheart."

Hot color flooded her face as his fingertips gently slipped her bra straps off her shoulders and his large uninjured palm cupped her right breast, while his other hand gently slid the bra down to her waist. The look in his eyes was enough to shake her world and when he murmured something in Lakota and slowly sucked her nipple deep into his mouth, she almost fainted dead away from the pleasure.

"Oh, God, that feels so good," she moaned as he gave delicious attention to her other nipple, and before she realized it, her jeans were unfastened and pooled around her knees. His thumbs hooked her panties and shoved them slowly down. He licked the bottom of one breast as he tweaked the nipple of the other and she clutched at his head to keep from falling over.

Her self-consciousness faded as he laid her back on the pillows and stripped her boots, socks and her jeans and panties away. He ran his uninjured palm over her body, from her breast to her hip, and on down her thigh, before it circled back up to rest on the mound of her belly. "You are beautiful." His breath was ragged and for a moment, she believed him.

In the light of her overhead bulb, his body was shadowed and hard. He ran the fingers of his good hand through the soft hair of her mound and sought the wet lips of her pussy, his eyes darkening. "I want to eat you. I want to taste this. And then I want to know what you feel like deep inside."

She couldn't speak. She just nodded. And when he slid down and spread her thighs, propping them up over his wide shoulders, she arched and gasped. As his tongue replaced his lean fingers and he growled against her pussy, she felt his tongue drag from her anal rosette to her clit and she came up off the bed with a cry of need. He pulled her back down, positioning her to his liking, and then he opened his mouth over her pussy and began a hot, deep, methodical seduction that was designed to destroy all resistance and give maximum pleasure. She grabbed the long hair on the crown of his head and clung, bucking and crying out and coming apart with orgasm after orgasm as he fucked her with fingers and tongue. She barely noticed when he gently slipped a finger into her anal rosette...and when he probed her with two, she was so aroused she didn't give a damn. The third finger startled her, but the ongoing pleasure of his assault on her clit and pussy eased away the burning pressure and full feel of him fucking her ass with the fingers that were wet from her pussy.

"You think you can take me there?" he whispered huskily against her ear.

"I don't know…you're pretty big, and hard as hell." She moaned as he lifted her and rolled her onto her belly, lifting her ass by placing her pillows under her belly.

"If it hurts too much, I'll stop. Just tell me." He breathed softly against her neck as she felt him rubbing the tip of his thick cock over her wet pussy. "I'm gonna get it wet. Just relax."

She moaned as his cock slid slowly into her pussy, stretching and filling her to perfection. He moved gently and slowly, and then he withdrew and pressed the bulbous head into her anal rosette. Dark pleasure slid through her body as he slipped slowly past her tight muscle, and as she relaxed, he pressed deeper until his cock was fully sheathed in her tight ass.

"Oh, God, Mike…it actually feels good," she groaned. She closed her eyes and fought to breathe, feeling totally filled.

"Use your fingers on your clit," he urged as he slowly began to pump his hips, pulling gently out and then sliding carefully back in.

She obeyed, and his words teased as he whispered, "Pinch your nipples."

The thick shaft that stretched her ass pressed deep and she moaned as her own fingertips tantalized her erect little knob of nerves. And then he bit the back of her neck gently, as his hand came down with a smart slap on her butt cheek, causing her to cry out in shock. "Ride it, baby…feel it, love," he rasped as he smacked her other ass cheek.

"What are you…" she gasped as he reached between her legs and pinched her clit between the thumb and forefinger of his injured hand. "Oh! God!" she screamed into the quilt on her bed as the orgasm that struck rippled through her like a tsunami. She bucked against his hips as he pounded into her tight ass, and she felt his seed spurting deep inside her as he gave a shout and stiffened against her, then fell over her back and rasped raggedly, "Did I hurt you?"

Unable to reply, she panted into the quilt, savoring the feel of his cock still buried deep in her ass. When she was able to speak, she rolled her head and said shakily, "No, but my ass cheeks are burning."

His soft laugh rumbled in his chest and he rolled onto his side, taking her with him. "I'll make sure to stock up on condoms. I love your tight little ass, but I really want to be inside that pretty pussy next time I come."

He was amazed, and still so fucking horny he couldn't breathe right. She had let him come in her sweet ass. Not very many women enjoyed that. He had made her come with him, but he was pretty sure she would prefer him to be inside her pussy next time. He calmed his body as she fell asleep in his embrace, so weary she couldn't hold her eyes open. How many nights had he dreamed of having her like this? How many nights had he envisioned her naked in his arms? His body ached to take her again, but he didn't want to scare the shit out of her and make her think he was after nothing but sex. No, he wanted far more than hot sex, but it was gonna take some time to convince her he was old enough to handle her needs. And he fully intended to prove he was the man to make her completely forget Howard Blackhorse.

Chapter Five

ဢ

She awoke to the sound of someone in her shower, and as she started to roll over to look toward the bathroom door, she gave a little groan of surprise at how damn sore she felt. Memory flooded back in like the dam had just burst and she planted her palm over her face with a moan of embarrassment. Oh, God. Had she really just fucked Mike Running Elk? Had she truly let that hot young stud see her in all her naked glory? Biting her lower lip, she sat up and realized with some trepidation that she most certainly had. She was stark naked, and when she was fully upright, she realized with a sense of surreality that the evidence of their orgy was soaking into her rumpled sheet.

"Noooo…" She shook her head and grabbed a handful of facial tissues to clean up with. She blushed beet red as she realized what she had allowed to happen and she glanced at the clock. Was it truly 5:45 a.m.? Was he in her shower? Oh, Lord…his hand. He would soak the stitches and end up back in the clinic.

Scooting out of bed, she tiptoed to the partially open door and peeped around, and almost burst into laughter. The injured hand was sticking up above the top of the shower enclosure and the minute he heard her laugh, his voice rumbled, "Don't laugh. Get the hell in here and help an injured man with his one-handed shower."

"You're naked…" she trailed off with a swallow of mortification. Duh! He was truly going to think her brain dead with her scintillating conversational skills.

"You've seen me naked before, and I can't get this fucking washcloth soaped up one-handed."

Feeling decidedly adolescent in her embarrassment, she slid the shower door open far enough to step in behind his broad back and then shove it shut. "Give me that." She took the washcloth and picked up the soap from the shower floor, pausing as her nose almost brushed his marvelously muscled ass cheek.

"If you plan to lick or bite, at least let me turn around," he growled, and she straightened quickly, her face hot.

"Shut up. You want me to scrub your back first?" Her voice sounded thready even to her. In response to her question, he turned in the stall and his cock nosed up against her belly as he grinned down into her red face.

"It's my front I want clean. Especially that."

She bit her lip hard to keep from whimpering as she soaped the cloth and stroked his chest and abs and then circled the soapy terrycloth around his rigid cock and gently cleaned the shaft and head. When he gave a growl of pleasure, she peeped up to see his head pressed back against the tile beside the shower head, his chest pumping for air.

"Like that?" she murmured as she stroked him with just her soapy palm and felt the shudder go through him.

"Christ, yes," he groaned and she pressed a soapy kiss over his copper nipple, enjoying the power she held over his body at the moment.

"Then maybe you'll like this even better," she whispered, sliding slowly down his trembling body, her wet and now soapy breasts dragging over his body as she sank to her knees and gently rinsed the soap from his cock before taking him all the way into her mouth until he touched the back of her palate.

"*Oh, God,*" he almost shouted as she massaged his tightening balls and stroked his shaft with each deep suck on his cock's dark red crown.

He couldn't believe her. She was too fucking good to be true. So eager to investigate and so damn responsive to his unspoken needs. He held his injured hand in the air above the shower, but his good hand instantly threaded itself into her wet, silken hair and he gasped throatily, "I'm gonna come...you need to stop now."

She didn't seem to hear him and her mouth slid all the way over his cock until he felt the back of her throat. Unable to pull out of her mouth because she was gripping the root of his cock with her fist, he came totally unglued, spurting hard into her sweet mouth and apologizing profusely as he shuddered with pleasure and closed his eyes.

"Sweet Jesus, baby...I think I'm gonna die here...." He groaned, and when she had milked every drop of cum from him, she rose to her tiptoes and dragged his head down to give him a good taste of himself. He opened his mouth over hers and accepted the salty sweet taste of his own orgasm, unable to believe what she had just given him—willingly—without him asking. And he wanted desperately to taste the heady juices that slid down her inner thighs as she straddled his thigh muscle and began to slowly hump it.

"You don't have to do that, baby," he whispered into her mouth. "Let me take care of you."

"It feels so good," she whispered shakily against his lips and he groaned as he felt her sweet pussy open to rub over his skin. He felt the turgid little nub of her clit as she gave a whimper of pleasure and ground her pussy on his muscle.

"I can make it feel a lot better," he growled and reached to shut off the water. Once the water was no longer a danger to his bandage, he sank to his knees in front of her and hoisted her thigh up over his wide shoulders, pressing her back into the corner of the shower stall. He smiled when she reached to pull her glistening wet labia apart to bare her lush pussy and clit, and he took the invitation instantly. His mouth and tongue claimed her, sucked her clit, buried his strong tongue in her creamy opening, and thrilled to her arching, screaming orgasm as she humped his face and begged him not to stop. Shit! As if he ever would.

He was ready for another go, but she gently shoved his mouth from her after a few more minutes and she whispered huskily, "I think I'm going to die of pleasure, Mike. Please, I can't take any more."

He kissed her pussy lovingly, inhaling her delicious scent, before he slipped her thigh off his shoulder and supported her as he rose to his feet again. "I have to get over to the ranch early. I made an appointment to show a horse to a special customer. I wouldn't go if I had anyone else I trusted enough to handle the sale." He ran his mouth along her jaw and licked her throat slowly, enjoying the shiver of pleasure that rolled over her skin.

He met her eyes and saw what he was afraid he would see...resignation. She obviously didn't expect to see him again. "Will you come with me?"

Her eyes widened and she blinked up into his face. "You want me to come with you?"

He couldn't stop the wicked grin. "My shower is bigger. So is my bed. But if you prefer to stay here and fix brunch, I'll more than happily come back after I clinch the sale."

She stared into those dark, glittering eyes, unable to believe that he wanted to see her later. But then, what red-blooded man would pass up a sure thing? Hell, she was so damn horny, he wouldn't be able to walk when she finished with him.

"Your hand is getting wet." She breathed numbly as he cupped her wet face with his brace.

"Which is it to be?" He ignored her worry, holding her eyes with his gaze. "Because I'm not walking away and giving you the chance to rethink what happened here last night and this morning. I can see that delicious mind of yours worrying this into the dirt. You either come with me, or expect me back here in a few hours. Your choice."

She swallowed hard and brushed her fingertips over his massive chest and leaned in to lick his nipple. "Don't forget to bring condoms."

His mouth swooped to take hers, hard, desperate…hot. Then his mouth switched to her dripping nipples, sucking them deep one at a time as he planted his uninjured palm firmly over her mons and slipped his long middle finger into her wet heat, bringing her up onto her toes as she whimpered.

"I'll be back before noon. Don't bother to get dressed. I'll just have to strip you naked again." He slipped another finger deep into her pussy as he returned to her breasts, and when a third finger pressed inside and they curved up to gently massage her G-spot, Lee came apart with a violent scream that she muffled against his hair, riding his hand helplessly until it subsided. He slowly pulled them from her, lifting them to his lips to taste, his dark eyes burning into hers.

"Please, condoms," she rasped.

"How many packages will we need?" His lips curved.

"As many as you think you will need. You're the only one who knows that."

"Hope they have a shelf full," he growled.

Sitting once again at her computer, she logged into the Tempt the Cougar website, and had to smile as she saw even more encouragement posted to her comment.

Monica: Dreams reveal our most secret desires. Or not so secret. Helllllooooo Internet!! But, seriously, the only help you need is figuring out how to let the "kid" know you're interested. You were joking about that, right?

I mean, did YOU feel like a kid at thirty? I know I didn't. How much do you want to bet he doesn't either? I bet he just doesn't look like a full-grown man, he acts like one, too. Mmmmm. I like it when they do that. And he's several years older than my man, btw.

Lori: Wow, daydreams huh? , for one, love to hear about those. Tell all, Lee, and then go get him! What are you waiting for?

She felt a bit too embarrassed to share last night with the whole group. Maybe next time... She bit her lip and checked the IM to see who was online at the moment. Cam's avatar showed. Oh please, God, let her be at her computer.

Lee B: Cam...are you there? I sure hope so, because I need advice!

She sat in front of the laptop, biting her lip. She hit send, and waited. She read some email. She checked a couple of blogs. Then when the response came, she wondered if she were crazy to be telling anyone what she'd done.

Cam: What's up?

Lee B: Dear God. You won't believe what happened last night...and again this morning.

Cam: Well, spill, girl!

Lee B: I took your challenge. The kid...the one who isn't a kid. O.M.G. I can't believe I did all those things...I mean...holy shit! And he wants to see me this afternoon. What should I do?

Cam: Did you enjoy what you did?

Lee B: Hell, yes!

Cam: Then why not? Enjoy him while you have him. If he wants more than one hot night, that's good.

Lee B: But, what on earth will people think? I have a "history" in this town. I was literally the scourge of the earth when I married a NA guy. The women hated me because I took one of "their" men. Now they'll probably want to string me up for doing it again.

Cam: They're jealous. But it's not your fault that "their" men find you attractive, girl. Whatever you have, just offer to bottle and sell it to them. LOL!

Lee B: But is he thinking that I'm just a hard-up fuck? I really have to live in this little town, and I hate the thought of being a laughingstock.

Cam: You have a point, dear, but if he wants to see you again after he had you once, he has to be more than just thinking of you as a handy fuck. I'd say roll with it. Let the chips fall where they may, and all that cliché shit. Just enjoy the hell out of the man. Be the Cougar you were meant to be. ☺

She shut the laptop down and closed it slowly. Glancing at the wall clock in the hallway, she swallowed her nerves and rose. It was nearly noon. He hadn't called to say he'd changed his mind, but she was a nervous wreck. She had made some Belgian waffles and had whipped some raspberry jelly into a pint of heavy cream. As an afterthought, she had opened a jar of maraschino cherries.

A plate of chicken canapés was in the fridge and a bottle of Riesling was chilling in a bucket of ice chips. Every sound nearly gave her a heart attack. She listened for the sound of his newer SUV, the one that had an automatic tranny. He had promised he wouldn't drive the old green pickup once he arrived at the ranch, until his hand healed.

At 12:15, she heard a truck, but it wasn't his. She cringed as the heavy booted steps crossed her porch. Why the hell did Howard have to pick today to restart their fight?

She opened the door and glared up at him. He was obviously drunk already.

"You aren't gonna invite me in? What is it? You expecting your cowboy?"

"Go away, Howard. I'm not in the mood to fight with you again." She started to close the door, but his hand stopped it and she gasped as he pushed his way through her door into her living room. "Get out! Now. Or I'll call Sam." Her panic was visible as Howard circled her in the middle of the floor like a tiger sniffing at raw meat.

"You fucking whore. You think I'd just let any man fuck my wife?" he snarled as she tried to bolt for the kitchen. His arm snaked out to catch her, throwing her backward onto the sofa.

"I haven't been your wife for seven years, Howard. Let me go!" She struggled as he shoved a knee between her legs and pinned her wrists above her head. Panic welled in her chest as his dark eyes slid slowly down her tiny tank that showed way too much of what he had forsaken long ago. "I'll scream!" She gulped as he reached for her belt buckle.

"I'll bet you will, like you did when the cowboy fucked you? I got what you want, bitch. I got what you need. Scream for me." His voice was a deep snarl that reminded her of the time he had come home drunk and had shouted at her for telling him he had to stop drinking and screwing around. The night before she called her lawyer and told him she wanted to file for divorce.

She inhaled a deep lungful of air and let out a shriek that should have broken all the glass in the place, but before she could scream a second time, his big calloused hand closed over her mouth and his teeth sank painfully into the top of her shoulder as his free hand tore her belt from the buckle and fumbled with her zipper. He lifted his mouth from her welted skin and hissed, "You should have fought a little harder when you were married to me, Lee. I might have enjoyed it more."

His hand reached inside her open jeans and he grabbed the lace that peeked through the opening, ripping it so hard it cut into her skin. He caught her hand as she tried to claw his face and he laughed as he wrenched her arm behind her back. She managed to get to his perfect face with her other hand, though, and he roared in rage as she dug her short but strong nails into his left cheek, and screamed again as his hand left her mouth to grab her wrist.

"Fucking whore," he roared as he planted a knee against her chest and hauled back to punch her in the face. She closed her eyes and lowered her face to lessen the danger of a broken jaw or neck, because Howard had a punch like a jackhammer. But the sharp blow she expected never came. She felt his weight lift from her and she heard something heavy hit the floor. Her coffee table flew, broken into three pieces.

She screamed again as hands closed over her shoulders and was ready to struggle, but she was hauled up off the sofa and into strong arms, her head cradled against a solid shoulder as Mike's shaking voice said against her temple, "Easy, it's me. He can't hurt you."

Without conscious thought, her hands flew from behind her back and grabbed the solid body in front of her, wrapping him in a death grip as she broke into tears and her legs gave out. "Shhhh, you're safe," he murmured against her ear as the siren of Sam's patrol car made her jump.

"Jesus H. Christ, Mike! What the hell are you calling me out here for?" Sam's angry voice stopped as Howard groaned and rolled over to try to get to his feet. Lee opened her eyes to the tableau and felt like she wanted to die of mortification.

"I got here just as Howard was about to beat the shit out of Lee. Seems he didn't want to take 'go to hell' as an answer, and I evened the odds a little."

Sam had drawn his service piece and was settling it back into his holster, his dark eyes shifting from Howard's bleeding face, to her open jeans and then to Mike's proprietary hold on her shaking body. She felt like she could just slither through a crack and be happy. Howard staggered to his feet and cursed foully, pointing at Mike.

"I was just trying to talk to my wife and this snot-nosed son of a bitch barged in and started swinging! I want the fucker arrested!"

It was at that point that Lee decided to take a stand, regardless of the consequences. "Howard showed up drunk, Sam. I told him to leave, but he forced his way in and started to force himself on me. I tried to get away but he caught me and he threw me down. I clawed his face to get him off me. He was about to pound my face in when Mike stopped him. I want a restraining order, Sam. I don't want this bastard within a mile of me ever again." She leaned her face into Mike's solid chest and Sam inhaled deeply, looking at Howard's bleeding face and the broken nose he was sporting. His gaze slid over the fresh, livid bruises on her upper arms and bare abs. He winced as he glanced at the teeth marks on her shoulder.

"I'm going to need statements from all three of you. Better get a jacket on, Lee, and come on down to the station house."

"In case you didn't notice, Sam, Lee is bruised and badly shaken up. I would suggest that you take that piece of shit down to the station and book him for attempted sexual assault and battery, and get that injunction in to Judge Wyatt. Send Sadie and Doc Harris out to get her statement. I'll be right here until they show up."

Howard wiped the blood from his face with the back of one hand and sneered. "She's my fucking wife. You gonna leave this bastard here and haul my ass off to jail, Sam? She's been fucking him, for Chrissake! He's gonna lie to keep his own ass out of trouble, and she'll lie to protect him!"

Lee stiffened. "I am not your wife, Howard. You don't own me. And I can fuck any man I choose in my own home. I have no need to lie about you. Everybody in town knows you are a liar, a cheat, a drunk and a philanderer, Howard Blackhorse. You hit me before, and I divorced you. You hit me today and you got what you deserved. You ever hit me again, and I promise you I'll blow your sorry ass to hell!"

Still in a high rage, Howard almost screamed, "I want this son of a bitch arrested for breaking in when I was trying to talk to my...Lee! He had no right barging in here and attacking me. This isn't his property," Howard snarled.

Chapter Six

** හ**

The look on Sam's face and the way Howard was puffing up like he was going to explode made his decision for him. Not that he hadn't decided earlier, but if ever there was a moment when he needed to protect his woman, it was now. Mike pulled her tightly into his chest to calm her trembling body and he met Sam's gaze.

"A man has the right to protect what's his, Sam. And Lee is mine to protect. She agreed to be my wife. That gives me the right to kick the living shit out of any man who tries to harm her. So unless you are planning to get any deeper into this matter by questioning that right, I'd suggest you get this prick out of my sight before I beat his ass some more."

He ignored the startled jerk of the body clinging so tightly to his and he stared Sam in the eye. He gently squeezed her hip and stroked his hand slowly down her stiff spine to gentle her. He felt her hot breath on his neck as she calmed her breathing. He just hoped she wouldn't make a damn liar out of him in front of the Chief of Police and her prick of an ex.

Sam cleared his throat. "Um...that right, Lee? Is Mike Running Elk your fiancé?"

Mike silently urged her to say yes as she turned her face to the man. He pressed his lips against her temple and hoped she wouldn't leave Howard an opening to have him arrested for assault.

What the hell was he doing? Her shocked gasp was muffled against his throat and she felt his strong hand gently cup and squeeze her hip, then slide over her back caressingly. She swallowed hard, recognizing the gift even as she turned her face to stare stonily at Sam. He was giving her a way to prevent gossip, to prevent her from becoming a laughingstock, to prevent Howard from continuing his constant barrage of insults and unwanted visits. He was putting himself on the line to protect her.

"That's right, Sam. He's my fiancé. But I still want that injunction. If Howard so much as turns into the lane in front of my place, I want him arrested. I don't expect Mike to have to beat him shitless every time he shows up. I want the *law* to do something to protect me from this. I want to feel safe in my own home when Mike isn't here. Howard needs to learn the hard way what *no* means."

She turned her face up to Mike, and said softly, "I don't mind going to the station house and clinic to give a statement and let them gather evidence against him, Mike. It'll be my pleasure."

* * * * *

Howard cursed and shouted and threatened, but Sam locked him into the cell and told him he could call his lawyer as soon as he got the paperwork done. It had taken over an hour for Sam to finish the paperwork for the restraining order before they had taken Lee to the damn clinic. She refused to go until she saw the order in the envelope and on its way to Judge Barclay. She was a very stubborn woman, but he couldn't blame her. At the clinic, he was told to wait in the outer area. His last look at her was when she glanced over her shoulder and shot him a tear-filled look. He had almost forced his way in there to be with her.

He sat there flexing his abused hand—the one he'd planted squarely into Howard's pretty face. The one with the metal and leather brace, which had worked damn well to break that finely-hewn nose with. He would have to thank the doc for it later. He'd always thought Howard was too damn vain about his perfect Lakota nose.

He tossed the crumpled coffee cup into the waste bin on top of several others he'd worked his way through during the long wait. He glanced at his watch again. What the hell was taking so damn long? A scraping sound came to him, and he came to his feet instantly as the inner door opened.

After three excruciatingly long hours, Lee emerged from the clinic exam room with a borrowed blanket wrapped around her shoulders, and he simply opened his arms and she walked into them. He sensed her humiliation and pain, and he thanked the deputy and Doc and swung her from her feet and into his arms. She lay in his embrace like a weary newborn foal, too tired to even move. He carried her out to his SUV and carefully fastened the seatbelt around her, before moving to the driver's side and sliding in. She was silent as the grave as he started the engine. They got out of the parking lot and he swung back toward her place in total silence. But about halfway there the dam burst and she began to sob uncontrollably, huddling like a frightened child in the bucket seat as he pulled to the side of the road and shut off the engine.

The res deputy Sadie was quiet and professional as the doc examined Lee and photographed her bruises, especially the livid bite marks on her neck and shoulder. She felt the humiliation and the pain of the last hours like a vise clamped around her stomach. She saw the strained look on the woman's face as the doctor cleaned one cut and took two stitches in it. Sadie obviously had some words she wanted to say, but was holding them back. The gossip mill would tell the world what kind of asshole Howard Blackhorse was.

She felt numb to the core as she slipped off the exam table and tugged her jeans back on, leaving her torn lace thong with the deputy as "physical evidence". Her body ached. Her heart ached. And she wanted nothing more than to go home and fall into her bed and just die of the humiliation that Howard had put her through...again.

They gave her a blanket to wrap around herself when she mentioned the chill, and as she left the exam room she expected to find Sam waiting to drive her home. She wasn't eager to deal with him after all that had happened. Tears stung her lids and she swallowed convulsively.

The sight of Mike standing there, his eyes dark and worried, made her want to run and hide. But when he simply opened his arms, she felt as if her legs were on autopilot as she walked straight across the waiting room to feel them closing around her gently.

She lost the ability to hold herself erect and as she sank into his arms, he bent and swept her legs out from under her, cradling her against his chest as he murmured thanks to the deputy and Doc and simply carried her from the clinic like she was a small child instead of a grown woman.

He said nothing. She bit her lip to keep back the tears. She knew that he was hoping she would consider his earlier words for exactly what they were — an offer of temporary protection. She was as embarrassed to be in this ignominious position as he was, and despite her attempts to remain strong, she lost it totally.

She curled into a small ball on the seat and buried her face in her hands and let the tears flow. Let the pain and fear and anger wash through and over her as she stopped fighting the emotions that swamped her. The car slowed and stopped. Great. Now she was making a total ass of herself and he would certainly be thrilled to see her out of his car and out of his sight.

She felt his hands unbuckling the belt and she swiped her face with both hands, struggling to sit up and make her apology. "I...I'm so sorry." She sniffed as he turned her on the seat and pulled her legs around his hips. The feel of his hard, thick cock pressed against his zipper and nudging her pussy through their combined jeans once again made her look up into his face as the late afternoon sunlight lit his features. The light caught the dark gleam in his eyes and she sucked in a shaky breath as he caged her face between his hands and whispered, "You have nothing to be sorry for. You didn't ask to be brutalized. And you didn't ask for him to try to rape you. And you didn't have to ask me for what I planned to give in the first place."

A hiccup and a sniff made him smile slowly as his mouth swooped down and caught her lips in a sweet, gentle caress. Her heart began to beat a tattoo in her chest as he rocked against her slowly, sending hot splinters of pure lust through her body.

"I want you so much," she whispered against his mouth.

"Nowhere near as much as I want you, sweetheart." He kissed her nose and gave her one more firm thrust of his pelvis before he abruptly swung her legs back inside the SUV, refastened her belt and moved back to the driver's side door.

No more words passed his lips until they were parked in her driveway and he shut off the engine again. When he spoke, he didn't look at her. "If I carry you in there, I'll be there 'til morning. If you don't want that, you better get out of the car and get inside. I won't leave until you have the door locked."

One last pity fuck for the abused ex-wife. One last night of untrammeled sex. Could she handle that, after all that she'd been through today? Her aching body grew hot at the memory of his gentleness and his power. It didn't matter if it would never happen again. She wanted it to happen tonight. To be able to carry the memory of this delicious man with her for the rest of her days.

"My legs won't work..." she lied huskily. "I can't walk without help."

He sat there waiting for her to make her decision. He was giving her an out. And praying she wouldn't take it. His hands clenched the wheel, while his body throbbed with need. He knew she had been shocked, most likely embarrassed all to hell by his claiming her as his fiancé. The way she had stiffened, he realized instantly that she didn't feel the same way about him that he felt about her. But he still wanted her. Even if all she had to offer him was nothing but sex. He would take it. He would take it as long as she was willing to have him.

When she spoke, the fist that was squeezing his heart relaxed and the blood that had almost stopped moving began to pound through his veins once again. He slid out of the seat and almost bounded over the hood of the SUV to jerk her door open and drag her into his arms. He carried her up the steps to the porch, and after she unlocked the door, he carried her into the darkened house. She struggled to get her feet on the floor and he watched numbly as she closed the door, flicked the lock again and pulled the shades in the living room windows. When her eyes turned back to his, he drew in a deep breath and held it. "What?"

"I made us lunch, but we never got to eat it. And I'm starving."

His breath whooshed out as she dropped the blanket and stripped her tiny tank off over her head, to reveal that she was braless.

"Aren't you hungry?" she whispered as she ran her palm down his shirt front. He ripped it off over his head without a word and let her hands caress his skin slowly, setting fire to his body when her nails gently dragged seductively over his nipples.

"Starving," he growled as she reached for his belt buckle. He unbuckled hers as she opened his fly and gently fisted his cock as she shoved his jeans over his hips.

"Mmmm...commando?" Her lips trailed over his collarbone and her hot tongue flicked his nipple. He pulled back as he saw the stitches, and his face tightened.

"That fucking bastard," he hissed.

"Forget Howard." Her voice was a shaky rasp as she drew his gaze back to hers.

He growled as he bared her body and let her jeans pool at her ankles. Her thong had been torn off and the resulting bruises and scrapes on her thighs and soft belly where he had planted his knee enraged him. He sank to his knees on her Navajo rug and ran his mouth over her bruises. Her thighs were trembling. He slipped her feet out of her sandals and helped her lose the jeans. And as he rose back up her body, his tongue trailed slowly over her thigh, mons and belly, then swirled around her nipple.

"Oh, God!" She clasped his head to her breast and buried her lips in his thick black hair. "Oh, Mike. Oh, Lord!"

He dragged her throbbing peak deep into his hot mouth as he kicked his own jeans off, after toeing off his boots. His palms then slid up her ribs to gently lift and cup her breasts and he felt her widen her stance as his eager cock prodded her belly.

"What was for lunch?" he murmured around her nipple.

"Belgian waffles with whipped raspberry cream and maraschino cherries, and chicken canapés. In the fridge. But the Riesling is likely warm by now..."

"I always wanted to eat food off a naked woman. Like they do in Japan." He switched to her other breast and she gasped and almost orgasmed. "Think you could let me have one little fantasy?"

He slipped his fingers over her erect little clit and she whimpered and shuddered. "Maybe nibble a dollop of raspberry whipped cream off this little thing here?"

His finger slicked deeper into her swollen pussy. "Maybe lick up a spoonful of cream from inside this?"

"Oh, God," was her only response. He nipped her nipple.

"Or how about me wrapping a canapé around this and nibbling it off bit by bit?"

His words drove her wild to let him have his fantasy. She managed to find her voice. "Only if you let me eat off yours first."

"Anything you want, baby, anything at all," he growled around her nipple, and she shoved him away a bit to catch her breath.

"The shades are up in the kitchen."

"I'll pull them while you get the food out."

He allowed her to feast on him with mixed feelings. He felt like an idiot to be spread-eagle on her table, but after a few minutes, that feeling was replaced with sheer, white-hot lust. He could get real used to this.

It was amazing how it made her hot all over as she placed bits of food on strategic parts of his anatomy, watching his muscles flex when she touched something ultra sensitive. He was sprawled in the center of her kitchen table, stark naked and she gave a moan of enjoyment as she bent over him to lick a bit of spiced chicken and red pepper from his right nipple, chewing slowly as she sucked on the erect bump. Her teeth scraped his nipple a couple of times and he inhaled sharply, making the square of waffle topple off his cock.

She loved the way he trembled and shuddered each time she nibbled a morsel from his abs, his thigh, his throat. She picked each morsel at random, but left the waffle and cream that decorated his stiff shaft until last.

When she slid between his thighs, he gave a groan of anticipation, and when she took the bit of waffle off his shaft, he lifted his ass from the table.

"Please, you're killing me." His voice was thick with need.

"Patience," she whispered and licked the line of raspberry cream off the heavy vein that ran the length of his cock from base to swollen crown. As her mouth closed over the cherry at the tip of his aching cock, he caught the back of her head and pressed his cock deeper into her mouth. "Sweet Jesus, Lee. Yes."

He arched and she took him in until the cherry went down her throat with a slow swallow. The taste of pre-cum was salty and sharp as she began to devour him in earnest, sucking and stroking as he begged her to take him deeper. He trembled like a leaf as she gently squeezed his balls, and when he burst in her mouth, he gave an exultant cry of pleasure as he cupped her face with his trembling hands and stared down into her eyes as she took every drop he had to give her. When his body had ceased shaking, he dragged her up to kiss her, and whispered hoarsely against her lips, "My turn..."

She lay on the table, arms and legs splayed wide as he prepared her for his own feast. He covered each turgid nipple with curry sauce and balanced a canapé on top. He gently painted a line of whipped cream over her anus and labia and placed a dollop of cream with a cherry over her clit. But when he pressed a chilled spoonful of cream into her pussy, she almost came right there. Food was placed strategically on her ribs, her newly shaved mons and her throat, and when he was ready, he said roughly, "I am really going to love eating you."

His mouth and tongue teased and tantalized as he nibbled each morsel. He started with the canapés on her mons and navel and shifted to the ones on her throat. Her body shivered and trembled with each gentle nip, with each swirl of his tongue. Her nipples ached to be touched as he nibbled the savory chicken off the top of each little pile of curry sauce, and then his mouth closed over the first nipple and she almost lost it. He spent a great deal of time devouring the delicacies on each breast, and she was almost a mental and physical wreck by the time he cleaned the last of the sauce from her throbbing nipples.

He moved between her legs and whispered huskily, "Time for dessert."

His tongue snaked over the cream that he had decorated her inner thighs with. Her hips kept lifting from the table and he kept pressing her back down as he murmured, "Patience..."

He licked the line of dripping raspberry cream from her anal rosette and swollen labia, and then spread her gently with his thumbs as he settled onto his knees and hooked her legs over his shoulders. "Ready for this?" he growled against her pussy, and then he was slowly dipping his tongue inside to taste the delicious combination of raspberry and woman, his tongue probing to reclaim the delicious sweetness that he had buried inside her.

"Oh my God," she cried as his tongue dragged over her raspberry-flavored labia and he found the cherry over her clit, sucking it up and settling in to suck the tight little bud of nerves, his fingers invading her pussy to massage and tease her vaginal walls as he devoured her clit with little growls of pleasure.

The orgasm began deep in her belly and radiated outward to every nerve in her shuddering body, bringing her hips up and her back into an arch as she bit the back of her wrist to keep her screams of ecstasy from echoing all the way to the police station. The last thing she wanted or needed was to have Sam rush into the house to see who was murdering her.

He fed her orgasm to a fever pitch and gently kept up just enough pressure and suction to keep her peaking for several delicious minutes before he gave her a final heated lick and rose over her prostrate form to stare down into her glazed eyes. "I want to finish this right. You game?"

He was standing in a direct line with her sweetly wet, still clenching pussy and he stroked his stiff cock and rubbed the head gently back and forth over her wet clit before he grabbed the condom packet he had placed on the table next to her hip, tearing it open and rolling it slowly over his swollen, wet crown to settle it firmly over his thick shaft.

Her words freed his spirit as she whispered huskily, "Oh, please. I want you inside me, Mike."

It was as if the air in the room had gone as he entered her and pressed slowly into the cradle of her tight sheath until his rough nest of pubic hair was pressed hard against her bare mound. His hands closed gently over her plump breasts, his brace abandoned so that he could feel her soft globes in both palms. He stared down into her half-closed eyes and rocked his hips gently to fully enjoy her tight channel. Her mouth parted on a shaky sigh as he slowly drew back until only the head of his cock remained inside her, before returning to her wet warmth with a guttural cry of joy. He watched her face as she closed her eyes and threw her head back in ecstasy. His woman. Whether she knew it or not. She was his woman.

The friction was perfect. The head of his cock caught her G-spot with each well-aimed thrust and after seven long years of celibacy, her body rose in a crescendo of orgasmic response that went on and on and on. Her drawn-out sobs of perfect pleasure urged him on until her pussy clamped him so damn tight that the sound of his muffled shout of exultation told her that he shared her ecstatic joy.

As he lifted her gently from the table, his lips caught hers in a breathlessly erotic caress and held for a long, satisfying time as he wrapped her thighs around his hips and carried her slowly up the stairs. Words were totally unnecessary as he stepped into the bathroom and pulled open the shower before setting her on her feet and withdrawing to dispose of the condom. She stood under the spray as he soaped the residue of their feasts from their bodies with sure, slow strokes of his big hands, and then rinsed them both off. He gently pressed her thighs apart and used the soapy washcloth to clean the raspberry cream from her, and as he dried her off with a thick towel after he shut off the spray, she felt as if she could sleep for days.

He seemed to understand her weariness, as he carried her into her bedroom and used the fluffy towel to dry her hair. He took her soft bristle brush to her mop to untangle it before he swept back the covers on the bed and eased her into the warm nest, bending to kiss her lips gently and murmur, "Sleep."

He leaned against the doorjamb and watched her sleep for nearly an hour before he swung away and went downstairs to find his boots, jeans and shirt. As he tugged his clothes on, he set about cleaning up the signs of their orchestrated feast. In the living room, he cleared away the mangled coffee table and swept up the broken ceramics that had suffered at Howard's hands. Once the little house was set to rights once more, he fished his car keys out of his pocket and glanced at his watch. He figured she would sleep awhile. He had some arrangements to make, and he definitely needed clean skivvies. He slipped out of the house, taking her keys with him so he could get back in without disturbing her.

Chapter Seven

∞

She awoke to the sound of his SUV starting and tires crunching on her driveway. She rolled her head to stare blearily at her bedside clock's LED readout. Three a.m. The ball was over and Prince Charming was riding off into the dawn. She chewed her lip as she thought of the mixed metaphors she was spouting, and she gave a sad little moan of loss. He was gone. She was alone again. And she was sore and aching in places she hadn't known existed. Her eyes drifted shut for a moment and then she buried her face in the pillow and let her self-pity out in a torrent of tears.

God, but she wanted him. She ached for him. But she was too damn old for him, and she knew it. The blush would be off the apple soon. When he noticed her crow's feet and the cellulite, he would realize his error and quietly wish he hadn't allowed this to happen. She had to let him go now, before she came to desperately need him.

Her alarm went off at five thirty as it always did. She reached out lethargically and slapped her hand over the shutoff button. Fuck the alarm. Shutting it off told her how stiff and sore her body felt. Her damn eyes were puffy and nearly swollen shut from crying. She had the cattle and hens to feed. The little American pony she boarded for a teenager whose mom didn't have a place to keep him would be kicking his stall down if he didn't get fed, and soon.

All she wanted was another friggin' hour...

Habit dragged her ass out of bed and into her bathroom, where her savior must have cleaned up the wet towels and the mess, because the bathroom was sparkling and neat. She stared at the horrible black bruises on her belly, ribs, and arms and she shivered again at the sight of the bite marks on her shoulder. No damn wonder she felt like a bull had run over her at full gallop. And speaking of bulls... Her hand cupped her bruised belly and she felt her pussy tighten and tremble at the memory of him inside her, hard and thick, yet gentle and slow to allow her the thrill of his lovemaking without the pain of his considerable size.

"Oh, Mike," she sighed softly as she closed her eyes and leaned against the porcelain sink. Memories of his hands, his mouth and his marvelous cock left her trembling with a need that would never be fulfilled quite so deliciously ever again. Even her ten-inch "Mr. Mann" would never look quite as enticing again.

She stood there for a while, until the call of nature brought her back to reality. After using the toilet and brushing her teeth and splashing her swollen face with cold water, she padded back into her bedroom and pulled out underwear and a fresh pair of jeans, then tugged a clean tank on, eschewing a bra. The bruises on her ribs wouldn't take well to the pressure.

She tugged on socks and her boots and went downstairs to make her ritual pot of strong black coffee. As it began to drip fragrantly into the glass carafe, she turned and stared at the neatly cleaned table, her cheeks growing hot just thinking of the things they'd done on its painted surface last night. She would never be able to sit at it again without seeing his hard, muscular body stretched out across it, his eyes burning into hers as she arranged bits of savory food on his coppery, smooth skin.

"Hoo boy." She exhaled sharply as she turned away to reach into the fridge for milk to pour over her cereal. Her hands were shaking. Well...she'd wanted memories, right? As she set the milk back in the fridge, she saw the remains of the raspberry whipped cream and she dipped a finger into it and brought it to her lips.

The rich, fruity scent and flavor twined around her senses once again and she almost orgasmed standing in front of her open refrigerator. She would never be able to look at a jar of raspberry jelly or a carton of heavy cream again without her belly flip-flopping. She could just imagine her future shopping trips — avoiding the jelly aisle and feeling her way past the dairy case with her eyes closed.

The cereal tasted like cardboard, but she forced it down, glancing at her wall clock. Heaving a sigh, she walked into the living room and blinked. He had cleared away the chaotic mess and her clothes had been picked up. She turned to look for her keys. She remembered tossing them onto the lamp table just after she locked the door and hot color flooded her cheeks as she recalled exactly what she had done after tossing them there. Her keys were gone? Damn. He must have accidentally picked up hers along with his. She supposed he would drop them off later.

Dawn was breaking when she stepped out the back porch door and headed for the barn and feed lots. Cattle lifted their heads and then moved laconically toward the troughs. The chickens came racing out of the hen house and almost tripped her in their eager pursuit of the grain she flung to them as she walked. She dumped the rest of the small feed bucket on their heads as they tried to peck some corn from her boots. She flung a broken bale of meadow hay over the feed lot fence into the trough and spread it out so the six young heifers could get to their own share more easily, before heading into the corral and across to the barn where the hooves of the appaloosa pony rang against the door of his stall.

"Hold your horses, Chickapee. Yours is coming." She grinned at the perfectly proportioned head that popped out over the door of the box stall. She opened the door of the big loose box at the far end of the barn and forked a pat of meadow hay into the feedbox and dumped a quart of mashed oats into the smaller feed cup on the wall, before filling the trough bucket with fresh water. When she snapped the lead onto his halter and swung the door open, Chickapee tried to bolt past her and she laughed and shoved him back, making him behave. "Be a gentleman, please. You won't starve."

But she recalled that she hadn't fed him yesterday afternoon, having spent time with the doc and the police. And with Mike. She rubbed his forehead and kissed his muzzle. "Sorry. Forgot you *are* starving, you poor boy."

She unclipped the lead as he entered the loose box and she closed the gate, watching him dig hungrily into his oats first, then the hay.

It had been years since she'd had a horse in here, until Lilly Santiago had asked her to board Chickapee for Suzi, her teenaged daughter. Now the pleasure she derived from caring for the beautiful little championship jumper helped her feel less cheated by life. Suzi came over after school and groomed and rode him, while Lee was busy grading homework from her students. It worked out perfectly.

Knowing how Lee had loved to ride before she'd had to sell the horses, Suzi had offered to let her ride the classy little POA, but she had declined, thinking of her one-hundred-fifty-pound weight on the almost delicate-looking little show-jumper, despite Suzi's assurances that a POA could carry her easily. Last thing she wanted to do was cause damage to those dainty, fine legs.

She leaned on the unpainted top rail of the loose-box and was dreamily admiring the coloring of the animal when the sound of a heavy truck coming into the barn's side-drive made her heart clench, and she almost panicked, wondering if Howard had managed to finagle his way out of jail somehow.

Instinctively reaching for the hay fork, she turned and walked to the barn door and stopped dead at the sight of the big horse van that was just rolling to a halt in the open space between the house and the barn corrals. The gleaming blue and silver fifth-wheel trailer matched the big 4x4 that hauled it, and she stared at the symbol on the side of the 4x4 numbly.

The depiction of a bull elk leaping over a crossed pair of lightning bolts made her mouth go dry. O.M.G.

She had known that Mike owned a horse ranch, but she had no idea it paid well enough to allow for equipment like this. She leaned the pitchfork against the barn wall and walked slowly around to the driver's door just as it opened and the object of her fantasies slid out and hopped to the packed dirt yard, and the long, lean, hard look of him nearly made her knees give out.

She became instantly aware of her tiny tank that her generous breasts filled to capacity as his eyes dropped from her bruised neck and shoulder down to her boots and back. "Hi." Her breathless greeting was barely audible as she shoved her hands into the pockets of her jeans to keep them from shaking.

He nodded to her and shook back his thick, long hair. Her eyes widened as she realized that it was down, and worn with a leather and porcupine quill ornament that secured a real eagle feather and a strand of glass beads in many colors. He cleared his throat self-consciously and said quietly, "I wanted to do this right for you."

"Um...do what right for me?" She swallowed the knot in her throat and watched him as he walked to the back of the big horse van and unhooked the latch on the tailgate. A moment later, a long ramp slid out and the end planted into the hard-packed earth. Her heart snagged in her throat as she heard him murmuring soft words, and moments later, she stared in mute shock as he emerged from the van, followed by a stunningly beautiful black Quarter horse, and another stunningly beautiful palomino, and another equally glossy and gorgeous pinto, and finally, a solid white appaloosa with a blanket of chocolate leopard spots over his rump.

As the beautiful animals stood patiently, nudging his shoulders and back like very large dogs awaiting praise, his eyes turned to hers and he said quietly, "Normally I would have given these to your father and if he accepted them, I would have asked for his daughter. My great grandfather brought an entire herd of ponies to my great grandmother's father. So if you want more, I have another hundred just like these, but they wouldn't fit in the van."

The realization of what he was trying to tell her struck her in the gut like a fist and she almost sank onto the dirt. She barely managed to remain on her feet. Her lips were trembling too hard to reply.

"There are other gifts, too. It was customary to present the woman's family with hides, meat, knives, rifles, buffalo robes and blankets. But I figured maybe this would work until we got around to picking out the rest."

She stared at him as he shoved a hand into his pocket and fished out something small and stepped across the space that separated them. He opened the small velvet box and the blinding glitter of a stunning diamond caught the rays of the early morning sun, making her blink. "I think this will be easier to wear than a buffalo robe, and I didn't want to leave out any Anglo customs you might expect as part of the bargain."

He stood waiting, his heart pounding hard against his ribs. Her shocked face seemed to go white, and his hopes sank. Had he been too eager? Had he misread her? The appaloosa came up behind him and gave him a solid head-butt between the shoulder blades and he slammed into her, his arms catching her as she staggered back. The ring flew. After about half a second of shocked silence, Lee screamed and fought free of his arms and he wanted to die of humiliation. Until he realized that she was on her hands and knees in the dirt, sobbing and hunting for the lost ring.

"Oooohhhh! Noooo! A man gives me my first frigging diamond, and right off the bat, it gets lost." She was muttering to herself as she ran her fingers through the dirt beside the empty ring box. His lips twitched and his heart flew. He bent down and dragged her up out of the dust and as she opened her mouth to speak, he bent and covered her sweet lips with his hungry mouth, stopping her protests, and dragging her sweet pussy hard up against his raging cock with both palms on her delicious, round ass cheeks.

"The ring will still be here. It's not going anywhere. Sweet Jesus, woman, put me out of my fucking misery and just say yes."

His words stopped her frantic struggle and she stared up into those night-dark eyes, her heart going into hyperdrive. Her brain kicked in after a brief struggle with reality, and she found her voice.

"You—I—we..." she croaked.

His eyes glittered. A wicked smile curved those lush lips and he said roughly, "Yes. And you aren't getting rid of me even if you don't accept the damn horses. I have lots more. You have to give in sooner or later."

She swallowed convulsively and touched his lips with her fingertips, then laughed as she left a trail of rich dark dirt over them. "I just put war paint on you."

His eyes darkened and his jaw flexed. His breathing deepened and he placed his un-bandaged palm over her heart and whispered huskily, "*Le mayak'u kte.*"

Her belly did a little flip and she turned his palm and pressed her lips against it. "Whatever you just said, the answer is yes."

He gave what sounded remarkably like a war whoop as he picked her up from the ground and swung her around in a circle before pressing her back into the side of the gleaming van and kissing her into oblivion. The sound of the horses snorting and stamping and a nudge from the appaloosa's satiny nose made him growl raggedly against her mouth, "Need to corral them and get them fed before they tear the place apart. Give me two minutes?"

As he backed away from her, his face ruddy and his eyes glittering, she swallowed hard. Dear God, he really…truly wanted her? She managed to move away from the van and she walked over to where the ring box lay on its side in the dust. She picked it up and scanned the packed dirt around it. There wasn't a sign of the ring. Her heart ached just a little. No one had ever given her a diamond before. Not even Howard. It must have hit the ground and bounced. Later, she would borrow Lilly's metal detector and find it. She had to find it.

Her thoughts were interrupted by the feel of his large body pressed against her back and his hands turning her to face him.

He was there, his hands slipping over her ribs and ass, his lips caressing her full breasts. The horses were happily munching on hay in the main corral. He pressed her gently back against the side of the van and tugged her tank down to find her swollen nipples, and then he gave a short laugh and burrowed his lips between her heavy globes.

When he lifted his smiling face, she realized that he was holding her brand new diamond ring in his teeth. "That's a damn convenient item of clothing you're wearing, woman. It holds the most beautiful breasts I've ever seen, and it's a handy catch-all."

He removed the ring from his mouth and picked up her left hand, biting his lip. The ring slid easily over her ring finger and he let out his breath. "It fits."

She stared at the stunning diamond, then she stared up into his flushed face. "When did you get this?"

"About a year after you dumped Howard's sorry ass."

Her eyes widened and her mouth flopped open. "You bought this ring six years ago? For who?"

He kissed her nose lightly. "For whom…"

"Okay…for whom?"

"For you. I found the ring you lost in the barn and checked the size before I told you I'd found it." His throat moved as he swallowed hard.

"You…bought…" She felt lightheaded.

He stopped her words with a light kiss and whispered huskily, "Let's take this conversation inside where I can convince you to shut up and fuck my brains out again."

Once inside the kitchen door, her tank was gone, then her boots and jeans. He tossed his own shirt and then toed off his boots before stripping off his own jeans. He kissed her deeply and then turned to wash the corral dust from his hands in her kitchen sink. She stared at his fine ass and his powerful, rippling back as he dried his hands and turned to stare at her across the kitchen.

"You are beautiful," she whispered softly as he stalked slowly across the tiled floor to pick her up and set her on the countertop, level with his stiffly solid cock.

"Glad you think so," he whispered against her throat as he gently kissed the black bruises from Howard's teeth softly and licked the vein that throbbed on the side of her neck. "Since we are now officially engaged, would it be proper to believe you wouldn't say no to me not using a condom?"

Her throat clenched. Her pussy clenched. "I could get pregnant…"

"Fine by me, woman, an added bonus, but I really want to feel your hot pussy wrapped around me without anything to keep me from feeling everything inside you."

He waited only for her little moan of need and her little twitching movement as she offered him her bare, slick folds. He gently leaned her back against the upper cabinets and dragged her hips forward to greet the tip of his cock, and as it slipped into the wet, ready sheath of her pussy, he hissed in a deep breath and let it out in a whoosh. As her cunt clenched tight around his shaft, he whispered hoarsely next to her ear,

"Ride me, woman, and when you've come a dozen times, I'll spread you wide on the table and enjoy my dessert."

Her body shuddered as he slowly lowered his head and caught her lips and began a decadent rhythm that insured that he would keep his promise to her.

If she didn't die of pleasure first...

Epilogue

❧

Cougars...

I know it's been a while since I asked for help, but things just happened so fast, I haven't really thought about it since you offered me all that marvelous encouragement. I'm the one who had suddenly developed the hots for my Saturday helper...remember?

I want to thank you all for this wonderful blog. If I hadn't had you there to vent to, I think I would have made the biggest mistake in my life. I would have ignored my feelings one more time, and I would have missed finding the man meant for me.

I wish I could return the wonderful gift you gave me. Here's a photo of my hubby...does he pass muster?

Hugs,

Lee R.E.

She sighed and clicked the "post comment" button. She sank against the chair back and felt his wet arms slip down around her body as his lips caressed her damp hair just above her temple.

"I still think posing for your little impromptu photo shoot with nothing on but my wet towel was a bit risqué." His whispered words sent a shiver of anticipation down her spine. "But a deal's a deal."

"Oh, yeah. A deal's a deal." She gasped as he slipped to his knees and pulled the chair around to face him. And as his hot, strong tongue ran from her naked breast to her navel and he pressed her thighs apart, Lee Running Elk ran her fingers through his shower-wet hair and prepared to be deeply satisfied...again.

The blinking of her screen made her laugh as the reply popped up.

Cam: O.M.G.
Momma Mia!
Enjoy that man, girl! And welcome to the ranks!
Cam

Also by Regina Carlysle

∞

eBooks:

Breath of Magic
Cougar Challenge: Drilled
Edge of Nowhere
Ellora's Cavemen: Flavors of Ecstasy IV *(anthology)*
Elven Magic *with Desiree Holt & Cindy Spencer Pape*
Feral Moon
Highland Beast
Jaguar Hunger
Killer Curves
Lone Star Lycan
Ringo's Ride
Spanish Topaz
Tempting Tess
Texas Passions: Eagle's Refuge
Trouble in a Stetson

Print Books:

Aged to Perfection *(anthology)*
Ellora's Cavemen: Flavors of Ecstasy IV *(anthology)*
Lone Star Beasts
Mistletoe Magic *(anthology)*
Riding the Edge
Tempting Turquoise *(anthology)*
Torrid Topaz *(anthology)*

About the Author

ഔ

Regina Carlysle is an award winning, multi-published author. She likes writing that is hot, edgy, and often humorous, and puts this trademark stamp on all of her stories. Regina lives in west Texas with her husband of 25 years and counting and is a doting, fawning, and over-indulgent mother to her two kids. When she's not penning steamy erotic tales or hot contemporary stories, she's indulging in long chats with friends who help her stay sane and keep her laughing.

Also by Jayne Rylon

&

ebooks:
Driven
Phoenix Incantation
Picture Perfect
Shifting Gears
Through My Window

About the Author

ॐ

Jayne Rylon's stories usually begin as a daydream in an endless business meeting. Her writing acts as a creative counterpoint to her straightlaced corporate existence. She lives in Ohio with two cats and her husband, who both inspires her fantasies and supports her careers. When she can escape her office, she loves to travel the world, avoid speeding tickets in her beloved Sky and, of course, read.

Jayne is a member of the Romance Writers of America (RWA), the Central Ohio Fiction Writers (COFW), International Heat and Passionate Ink.

Also by Fran Lee

ഇ

eBooks:
Double Your Pleasure
Hallie's Cats
Her Own Set of Rules
Jillian's Job
Nothing But Sex
Out of Her Dreams
Woman on Fire

Print Books:
Out of Her Dreams

About the Author

ℬℬ

Fran Lee began writing romance novels at the age of 14. Life intruded on a budding writing career–namely, paying the bills, raising a family, and the usual run-of-the-mill things that leave a writer no time to pursue a career as frivolous as authoring romance books. Or so everyone told her. But she never gave up on her childhood dreams of writing.

Other things caught her fancy over the years—horses, eBay, martial arts–not necessarily in that order. Her childish dreams were set on the back burner over and over again. But the things that caught her fancy blossomed into self confidence–she achieved her black belt in her chosen martial art, spent a fortune on eBay, and had the great pleasure of owning a number of wonderful equine friends.

Now she concentrates on her various fancies by collecting horse statues and figurines, teaching karate to kids, and spending time dragging out those old romance novels and bringing them up to snuff for the 21st century. The dream has come true–and it was well worth the wait.

The authors welcome comments from readers. You can find their websites and email addresses on their author bio pages at www.ellorascave.com.

Tell Us What You Think

We appreciate hearing reader opinions about our books. You can email us at Comments@EllorasCave.com.

Why an electronic book?

We live in the Information Age—an exciting time in the history of human civilization, in which technology rules supreme and continues to progress in leaps and bounds every minute of every day. For a multitude of reasons, more and more avid literary fans are opting to purchase e-books instead of paper books. The question from those not yet initiated into the world of electronic reading is simply: *Why?*

1. *Price.* An electronic title at Ellora's Cave Publishing and Cerridwen Press runs anywhere from 40% to 75% less than the cover price of the exact same title in paperback format. Why? Basic mathematics and cost. It is less expensive to publish an e-book (no paper and printing, no warehousing and shipping) than it is to publish a paperback, so the savings are passed along to the consumer.

2. *Space.* Running out of room in your house for your books? That is one worry you will never have with electronic books. For a low one-time cost, you can purchase a handheld device specifically designed for e-reading. Many e-readers have large, convenient screens for viewing. Better yet, hundreds of titles can be stored within your new library—on a single microchip. There are a variety of e-readers from different manufacturers. You can also read e-books on your PC or laptop computer. (Please note that Ellora's Cave does not endorse any specific brands.

You can check our websites at www.ellorascave.com or www.cerridwenpress.com for information we make available to new consumers.)

3. *Mobility.* Because your new e-library consists of only a microchip within a small, easily transportable e-reader, your entire cache of books can be taken with you wherever you go.

4. *Personal Viewing Preferences.* Are the words you are currently reading too small? Too large? Too... ANNOYING? Paperback books cannot be modified according to personal preferences, but e-books can.

5. *Instant Gratification.* Is it the middle of the night and all the bookstores near you are closed? Are you tired of waiting days, sometimes weeks, for bookstores to ship the novels you bought? Ellora's Cave Publishing sells instantaneous downloads twenty-four hours a day, seven days a week, every day of the year. Our webstore is never closed. Our e-book delivery system is 100% automated, meaning your order is filled as soon as you pay for it.

Those are a few of the top reasons why electronic books are replacing paperbacks for many avid readers.

As always, Ellora's Cave and Cerridwen Press welcome your questions and comments. We invite you to email us at Comments@ellorascave.com or write to us directly at Ellora's Cave Publishing Inc., 1056 Home Avenue, Akron, OH 44310-3502.

COMING TO A BOOKSTORE NEAR YOU!

ELLORA'S CAVE

Bestselling Authors Tour

UPDATES AVAILABLE AT

www.EllorasCave.com

ELLORA'S CAVE

Romanticon

Annual convention
for women who
refuse to behave

CPSIA information can be obtained at www.ICGtesting.com
Printed in the USA
268961BV00001B/39/P